Promised to Me

Promised to Me

Robin Lee Hatcher

Book 4

ZONDERVAN™

GRAND RAPIDS, MICHIGAN 49530 USA

This book is a work of fiction. The characters, incidents, and dialogues are products of the author's imagination and are not to be construed as real. Any resemblance to actual events or persons, living or dead, is entirely coincidental.

ZONDERVAN™

Promised to Me
Copyright © 2003 by Robin Lee Hatcher

Requests for information should be addressed to:
Zondervan, *Grand Rapids, Michigan 49530*

ISBN 0-7394-3396-2

Scripture quotations are taken from *The Holy Bible,* the King James Version, and the *New Living Translation,* © 1996. Used by permission of Tyndale House Publishers, Inc., Wheaton, Illnois 60189. All rights reserved.

Interior design by Tracey Moran

Printed in the United States of America

To the Neu family
With love

Acknowledgments

Special thanks to Sue Brower and Dave Lambert at Zondervan. It was your enthusiasm for the Coming to America series that brought about this book.

Thanks to Karen Ball. You made me look better than I am—and you did it painlessly, no less!

Also, thanks to the wonderful authors of ChiLibris. You are a constant source of enlightenment and encouragement to me. I feel blessed to know each one of you.

Prologue

April 1897

*I*t was good that God made Jakob Hirsch the son of a farmer, for he could never have been a sailor. Seasickness had plagued him from the beginning of this voyage.

But at the moment he wasn't feeling so bad. The steamship was making its way into New York harbor. Today he would feel the good, solid land of America beneath his feet.

Laughter reached his ears, and he glanced across the deck toward three young women standing near the ship's railing. The unlikely group of friends—as different from one another in appearance as night is from day—had first captured his attention soon after the RMS *Teutonic* left Southampton, England. Something about their nervous excitement, their sense of adventure, their unspoken hopes and dreams for the future—obvious to anyone who looked at them—defined this trip for Jakob.

The English girl, an elegantly dressed, auburn-haired lady of means, was pretty and shapely. The blonde from Sweden was plain, unusually tall, and much too thin for Jakob's taste. The Irish girl with the wild mane of black hair—the one with the wedding ring and slightly rounded belly—had an earthy beauty and a spark in her eyes that must spell trouble for her husband, poor fellow.

Not that Jakob had met the woman or her friends. Nor did he want to make their acquaintance. Jakob had a girl of his own back in Germany. Still, watching those three young women had helped dispel some of the boredom of the shipboard journey.

A gust of wind caught Jakob's cap and nearly swept it away. Just as he caught it, he heard someone exclaim, "There it is!" He surged to his feet and rushed to join the others at the rail as the Statue of Liberty came into view.

He'd made it. He was here. America! Here he would make his way, buy his own land, have a freedom and a hope that a poor farmer, the youngest of five sons, couldn't have in his homeland. Here he would find his future.

"*Amerika,*" he whispered. "I have made it, Karola, *mein Liebling*. Soon you will come, too. I promise."

Chapter One

*M*iss Breit?" The inspector looked at her, bored indifference in his gaze. "Are you traveling alone?"

"*Ja,*" Karola replied.

"And who will be meeting you?"

This time, Karola answered in English. "I will not be met. I am going by train to Idaho. I am to be married when I arrive there to Mr. Jakob Hirsch. He is a farmer."

"Do you have proof of those arrangements?"

"*Ja.*" She removed Jakob's telegram and the train fare—in American dollars—from her satchel, just as she'd been told she would have to do.

The inspector looked at them, grunted, then marked something on a paper and sent her to the next line.

Helga Wehler was already there. Like Karola, Helga was traveling alone, coming to America to be married. Unlike Karola, Helga was only seventeen and afraid of her own shadow. The girl had attached herself to Karola soon after they'd met in the crowded women's quarters below deck.

Helga turned around, her eyes wide. "Are you afraid, Fräulein Breit?"

Helga was referring to the next inspection, one every immigrant dreaded above all others. Using a buttonhook, a doctor turned up both eyelids, looking for trachoma. If the disease of the eye was detected, the immigrant would be detained on Ellis Island, then sent back to Europe on the next available ship.

"*Nein,*" Karola answered. How could she be afraid now that she was finally in America, now that she was finally about to be married to Jakob Hirsch?

Eleven years. Eleven years since she'd promised to marry Jakob. Eleven long years of waiting and wondering and doubting and despairing. She had lost hope, of course, with the passing of time, but now she was here. She was to be Jakob's wife at last.

After leaving for America, Jakob had written to Karola regularly until the spring of 1901. Then the letters had stopped. Never a reply, no matter how often she'd written to him. By the end of the following year, believing that something terrible must have happened to him—he had to be dead—she'd stopped waiting to hear from him. Only pride had kept her from allowing others to see her broken heart and shattered dreams.

Then, last December, a letter had arrived from America. A letter from Jakob.

She remembered standing in the parlor of her parents' home above her father's bakery, holding that letter, her heart racing, her emotions swinging wildly between hope and bitterness, anger and joy, love and hate.

He owned a farm in a place called Idaho, Jakob had written. The soil was rich, and there was a fine house and outbuildings. If she was unmarried, would she consider coming to America to be his wife?

As she'd read his letter, she'd pictured herself seated with her parents in their small church each Sunday or working with her father in the bakery every day. She'd felt the pitying stares of the young married women of her village. *Poor Karola. No one wants her now.* Others, she'd known, laughed behind her back. *Serves her right for thinking she's better than everyone else. Going to America. Ha!*

Oh, she'd known what they whispered when she was out of hearing.

In those first years after Jakob left, she had bragged to everyone about how rich they were going to be in America, about how much Jakob loved her, about how perfect their new lives would be once they were together again. When other men had tried to court her, she'd rejected them, firmly and plainly—even at times, she supposed, cruelly.

Then Jakob's letters had stopped arriving, and by the time she'd stopped hoping, most of the suitable young men of Steigerhausen had either married or moved away. The few who remained wanted nothing to do with the baker's daughter. Who wanted a wife with a head full of impossible dreams and a heart that still longed to see the world beyond the borders of their small village? No one, it had seemed. Not until Helmutt Schmidt. The very idea of being married to him made her shudder.

And so, as Karola had read Jakob's letter, asking if she would come to America, she had made a quick decision: *Ja,* she would. She would do anything to get away from the life she'd been leading. Anything.

The first steps of her journey had begun four months later . . .

All of Karola's worldly goods were packed in a battered old trunk and two suitcases. Tomorrow morning, she and her father would begin the journey to Hamburg, where she would board a ship and sail to America. She was certain she wouldn't sleep a wink all night.

Her mother sat in the chair beside the bed, her Bible open on her lap. "It is not too late to change your mind."

"*I do not want to change my mind, Mother. This is what I've dreamed of.*"

"*Oh, Karola, Karola. You always have your head in the clouds. I fear the pain it will bring you. What do you know of America? What do you know of Jakob Hirsch? He is no longer the boy who went away. He cannot be. Remember that marriage is forever. If you make a mistake because you are rash—*"

"*Would you have me stay and marry Herr Schmidt?*" Karola pictured the cobbler, a man older than her father, with skin as tanned and rough as the leather shoes he mended. He'd asked her father for her hand in marriage last year.

"*Nein, but I would not have you act in haste either.*"

"*Haste! Mother, I have waited eleven years. Every day since Jakob went away, I have worked in the bakery and shared this apartment with my parents, as if I were still a child. Every day, I have known others whisper about me because I want more than what I can find here. They think I am haughty and proud. Maybe I am. But Jakob understood me. Jakob is like me. And now he owns his own farm in America. He owns it, Mother. He is not a tenant. No man tells him what to do. He made his dreams come true. I want to do the same.*"

Her mother shook her head as she lowered her eyes to the open book in her lap. Softly, she asked, "*Have you asked God what he wants you to do?*" She didn't wait for an answer. "*Karola, mein Tochter, you will never be truly happy until you choose God's way instead of your own. I will pray that he will have mercy as you learn this truth for yourself.*"

Jakob sat on the front porch, enjoying the cool of evening after a day spent in the fields. His muscles ached, but in a good way. The way of a man who works hard on his own land.

He glanced down at the letter in his hand, one he had read numerous times. If all had gone according to schedule, Karola

Breit arrived in New York earlier today. Even now, she should be on a train, headed west. Headed toward him.

Memories of his own arrival in America flooded his thoughts. He remembered the elation and fear as clearly as if he'd come through the immigration depot yesterday. Only it hadn't been yesterday. It had been more than a decade ago. He'd been a young man of twenty with a head full of unrealistic expectations, but he'd had courage to spare. America was the land of opportunity, overflowing with milk and honey. Nothing, he'd believed with the arrogance of youth, could stop him from having anything and everything he wanted.

Life had a way of cutting an arrogant man down to size.

Jakob closed his eyes as he recalled the moment he'd seen the Statue of Liberty, the first thing every immigrant watched for at the end of a long and torturous journey.

Give me your tired, the lady proclaimed, *your poor, your huddled masses yearning to breathe free, the wretched refuse of your teeming shore. Send these, the homeless, tempest-tossed, to me. I lift my lamp beside the golden door!*

He opened his eyes again.

Lady Liberty hadn't lied. America had welcomed Jakob Hirsch. She had allowed him to breathe free. Although nothing had come easily and he'd suffered much, he now owned this farm, free and clear. Three hundred and twenty acres of good land, land he'd earned by the sweat of his brow. He wasn't rich, but neither was he poor. He'd put down roots, deep ones, and he'd made a home here. He was an American citizen. He'd managed to remove all traces of a foreign accent from his speech. He thought and talked and acted like those who'd been born in these parts. There was little about him of the youth who'd left Germany so long ago.

His thoughts returned to Karola, imagining her as she moved from one line to another in the immigration depot. He hoped the experience hadn't been too difficult.

Would he still recognize her? Had the years changed her as much as they'd changed him? Had life been kind to her? She'd been a girl of seventeen when they'd said their good-byes. What was she like today?

Jakob had carried Karola's likeness with him in his pocket watch when he left for America. But the watch had been stolen, and without the photograph, added to the relentless passing of time, her image had faded, becoming misty and unclear in his mind.

When he'd sent his letter to Germany last winter—a rash act, he acknowledged—he'd never expected a reply, let alone one of agreement. At best, he'd thought she would have forgotten him. At worst, he'd expected to be despised.

Jakob rose from the rocking chair and stepped toward the railing that framed the porch. The setting sun had stained the horizon blood red, and shadows stretched across the ground to the east. The evening air was crisp and smelled of freshly turned soil—ambrosia for a farmer's soul.

He was thankful Karola had agreed to come to America. He needed a wife. He'd known it for some time. Of course, there were several unmarried women in this valley between the ages of eighteen and thirty-five, but he hadn't been able to imagine himself married to any of them.

Then one night last fall he'd dreamed of the old country and of his father, now dead; of his brothers, now living in Berlin; of Gottfried and Freida Breit, the baker and his wife, and of their only child, Karola. The dream itself had made little sense, but for some reason, Jakob hadn't been able to shake Karola, the sweetheart of his youth, from his thoughts.

And so he'd written his letter.

Now he wondered what had happened to her since they'd parted all those years ago. He wondered if she'd never married or if she'd been widowed. She hadn't told him any of that in the few letters they'd exchanged these past months. Nor had she commented upon the circumstances of his life after he'd detailed them for her in his second letter. Perhaps she thought he'd said everything there was to say.

Well, he supposed none of that mattered. He would be able to ask her anything he wanted soon enough. If all went according to plan, she would arrive in Idaho in less than a week.

Chapter Two

*A*merican Falls, next stop," the conductor announced from the rear of the coach.

Karola looked out the window, wondering when the station would come into view. After several days of train travel, she was weary, dusty, and rumpled—not unlike when she'd arrived in America on the steamship the week before—but this time her arrival meant the end of her journey. In a short while, she would see Jakob. By tomorrow, she would be Mrs. Jakob Hirsch, and she would live in a fine house and have all the things she'd wanted. No one would ever again have the right to whisper and titter about her.

She tried to picture Jakob but failed. She remembered thinking him the most handsome of all the young men in Steigerhausen. She'd known the other girls in their village had been green with jealousy because he'd chosen her. If she concentrated, she could almost hear his laughter, a sound that she remembered had risen from deep in his chest.

Was he still as handsome? Did he have that same laugh? What was he like now? Would she recognize him when she saw him? And, the most persistent questions of all: Why had he stopped writing to her? And why, after so many years, had he written to her again?

Her mother had told her to ask him those things and more before she accepted his offer, but Karola hadn't listened. She'd wanted out, and Jakob's letter had provided the way. As far as she could tell, there was no good reason to refuse his proposal of marriage. Jakob had always adored her. He wouldn't have sent for her if he didn't adore her still. Whatever the cause for his long silence, it was in the past now. He would love her, she would forgive him for abandoning her, and all would be well.

"Miss Breit?"

Karola gave a start, pulled from her thoughts.

"We're almost there," her elderly seatmate, Mrs. Rankin, said. "You must be excited to see your fiancé."

Excited? She supposed so. Or was it trepidation that caused Karola's pulse to race?

"My goodness," Mrs. Rankin continued, "I can only imagine how overwhelming this must all seem to you. Did I tell you I came west over the Oregon Trail when I was a bride of twenty?"

Ja, she had. The woman had rarely stopped talking since she'd boarded the train in Chicago and taken the seat beside Karola.

"My, what a wilderness it was back then. The wide-open prairies and the Indians and the forests and the rivers. No trains, you know. Not like it is today. It was wild, I tell you. The Wild West, just like that Buffalo Bill's show called it. Well, maybe not exactly the same, but near enough."

Karola looked out the window. What would she do if she saw a wild Indian?

"Perhaps I mentioned this already, but my niece lived in Shadow Creek for a time. She said it was a nice town, although much too small for her liking. Quite the little organizer, that girl. All involved in the suffrage movement."

Karola turned to the older woman, unable to translate the word *suffrage* from English to German.

Mrs. Rankin seemed to understand the question in her eyes. "*Suffrage.* A woman's right to vote. That's why my niece moved to Oregon. Idaho women have had the right to vote for quite a spell, but Oregon hasn't seen the light yet." She laughed. "Land sake, I can see that's buffaloed you. Young woman, the West is chock-full of opportunities if you aren't afraid to try."

The train began to slow, drawing Karola's gaze once more to the window. Her heart pounded hard as she wiped the palms of her hands against her skirt. This was it. The time had come. Her journey was about over.

Amid hisses and creaks—sounds she had heard countless times as she crossed America—the train rolled to a stop.

"American Falls," the conductor called.

Karola stood and reached for her two battered suitcases.

"I've enjoyed talking with you, my dear," Mrs. Rankin said. "I wish you and your intended every happiness."

"*Danke,*" Karola replied. Then with a suitcase clutched in each hand and her satchel pressed against her ribs beneath her right arm, she made her way toward the exit.

She paused before stepping from the train, scanning the platform. And there he was. She would have recognized him even if he hadn't been the only person waiting for passengers to disembark. He was, indeed, as handsome as ever. Not that he hadn't changed. He had. A little heavier, perhaps even taller, and he had grown a beard, something she hadn't expected. It made him look . . . older. She realized she hadn't expected that either.

Their gazes met. She forced a tight smile; he nodded in recognition. The conductor placed a hand beneath her elbow and assisted her down to the platform.

Karola swallowed hard, then said, "*Guten Tag,* Jakob." Her greeting sounded more like the croak of a frog.

Jakob moved toward her. "Karola, you look well."

When they were young, he'd told her she was beautiful.

"As do you," she answered.

Now that he was closer, she could see tiny lines around his mouth and at the outer corners of his hazel eyes, eyes that used to sparkle with excitement but now seemed humorless. His neatly trimmed beard had a reddish tint, unlike the light brown color of his hair.

Jakob's hand brushed against hers as he took one of her bags. It was the touch of a stranger.

Her mother's words rang in her ears: *"He is no longer the boy who went away. He cannot be."*

Sudden panic urged her to get back on the train, to flee as quickly as possible.

"All aboard!" the conductor shouted, even though there were no departing passengers in sight.

I will not be afraid. I will not run away. I will not go back. I will not. I will not. I will not.

Jakob took her other suitcase. "It'll take us a few hours to reach the farm. We'd better begin. Do you have more than these?" He didn't sound like Jakob; he sounded like an American.

"Ja." She glanced behind her and saw the large trunk that had accompanied her from halfway around the world now resting on a cart near the caboose. "There it is. That is mine."

The train hissed and jerked into motion.

Jakob raised his voice to be heard above the noise. "The wagon's over there. I'll put your suitcases in it, then come back for the trunk."

All will be well. This is what I have wanted and waited for all these years. We will marry and be happy. All will be well. It will. It will. It will.

Jakob turned and walked across the platform. Clutching her satchel, Karola took a deep breath, then followed.

The ground at the bottom of the platform steps was uneven with deep ruts carved over time by wagon wheels. Karola held up her skirt with her free hand and hoped she wouldn't trip and fall on her face. She kept her gaze fixed a few strides in front of her.

"Maeve," Jakob said in a stern tone. "Bernard. What did I tell you?"

Karola glanced up.

"Karola," he said, "these are my children."

The earth seemed to tilt beneath her feet as she looked from Jakob toward the wagon. Three children, one barely old enough to walk, stood near the rear wheel, holding hands, the smallest between the two older ones.

Jakob carried her bags to the back of the wagon and tossed them onto the bed. Then he turned to face her. "This is Maeve," he said, motioning toward the child farthest from him. "She's going on six." He touched the boy's shoulder. "This is my son, Bernard. He'll be five soon." He stooped and lifted the toddler into his arms. "This is my daughter Aislinn. She turned a year old last week."

Karola's mouth was dry as cotton. There was a whirring noise in her ears.

His children.

"Say hello to Miss Breit," Jakob commanded.

"Hello," the two older children responded obediently.

He had children. He'd been married. All these years, and he'd been married. She'd feared him dead while he'd been siring children. He'd had a life while she'd been left behind, unwanted, in Germany.

Again she heard her mother's voice: *"Oh, Karola, Karola. You always have your head in the clouds. I fear the pain it will bring you."*

Jakob set the toddler into the wagon beside Karola's bags. Then he picked up the other two children, one in each arm, and deposited them beside their little sister. "Sit down," he told them. Turning to Karola, he motioned to the bag in her hand. "Want that in the back, too?" He reached for her satchel.

"You did not tell me, Jakob." She took a step back from him, clutching her bag close to her bosom. "Why did you not tell me you were married? Why did you not tell me you have children?"

A look of surprise crossed his face. "But I *did* tell you. I wrote you all about them."

She shook her head.

"Karola, it's true. I swear to you." He rubbed his forehead with the fingers of one hand, as if trying to rub away a problem. "As soon as you replied to my first letter, I sent another that told you everything about my marriage and my children. I said if it made a difference to you that I'd understand." His gaze pleaded for her to believe him. "I said you didn't have to feel obligated to come."

"I never got that letter." How she spoke around the tightness in her throat she didn't know. "I never got it."

When Karola first appeared on the passenger car's steps, Jakob had felt a surge of confidence. For the first time, his decision to bring her to America to be his wife had seemed right.

But now the doubts returned.

She hadn't known about his wife and children. She hadn't received his letter.

Karola stared at him, her blue eyes swirling with emotion. She looked both confused and frightened.

What was he supposed to do? He didn't have the money to send her home. Not now. Maybe come harvesttime, if the weather stayed good and there were no calamities or setbacks. But not now. Not today. He'd spent all he could afford to pay her passage here.

"I'm sorry," he said. "I didn't deceive you. I assumed you got my letter."

"You needed a mother for your children. That's why you asked me to marry you." It wasn't a question, just a statement of fact. A lengthy silence ensued before she asked, "What was your wife's name?"

"Siobhan." Saying her name conjured images of the fiery-tempered Irish girl who'd loved him, wed him, borne his children, and left him too soon. "Siobhan Gaffney."

"Tell me how it happened, Jakob."

"She died in childbirth."

"Nein." There were tears in her eyes now. "Tell me why you married her instead of sending for me."

He heard the words Karola had not spoken: *As you promised.* He knew he owed her an explanation. It had been easier writing it in a letter than it would be saying it to her face.

"I waited for you," Karola whispered. "I waited. I trusted you. And then, when your letters stopped coming, I thought you were dead."

"I'm sorry." The words rang false, even in his own ears.

"Tell me what happened."

He sighed softly, knowing he must do as she asked. He owed her that much. "I will, but we need to get started for the farm. Otherwise, we'll be on the road after dark."

He saw that she wrestled with her decision, even understood the resigned look that finally entered her eyes, a look that said, *What choice do I have?*

At last, without a word, she stepped to the side of the wagon and allowed him to assist her to the seat.

"I'll get your trunk," he said and strode away.

Chapter Three

*K*arola didn't immediately insist upon Jakob's explanation once they were on their way, and he was more than willing to wait until she did so. But after an hour of silence—even the children seemed to know not to speak—she said, "Tell me what happened, Jakob."

His thoughts drifted across time, back to Germany and that snowy February day in 1897. He remembered kissing Karola good-bye, promising he would send for her soon, declaring his undying devotion. He'd been young and filled with dreams, certain that only good fortune lay before him. Nothing was impossible for him then. He remembered his farewells to his four older brothers and to his father, a stooped and beaten man, wearied by life, worn down by hardship and poverty. He remembered the arduous journey—most of it made on foot—from his remote village to Hamburg. He remembered his surprise when he'd discovered himself feeling homesick.

"When I first got to America," he began at last, "I found work in a factory in New York City. I hated it. I only stayed until I had enough money saved to strike out for the West."

"*Ja,* I remember. You wrote to me about it."

What he hadn't told her in his letters was how near impossible it was to save anything from the meager wages he'd earned, how often he'd gone to bed hungry in that miserable room he'd rented, how more than once he'd wondered if he'd traveled all that way for nothing.

"After I left New York, I found work on a farm in Pennsylvania, then I moved on to another farm in Ohio, and after that, I went to work in Minnesota."

"You liked it in Minnesota best of all."

He nodded, remembering the many nights he'd sat at that rickety table in the farmhand's quarters, a candle flickering nearby, penning his letters to Karola. *I'll send for you soon,* he'd written. He'd never meant for it to be a lie.

"I worked hard, Karola, and I saved almost every dollar I earned so I could buy land, so I could have a farm of my own, be my own man, make my own way. I planned to stay in Minnesota. There were many German immigrants there. But then I met a man who told me about California. It sounded like heaven on earth, so I decided to see for myself."

This part was more difficult to tell. How he set out for the West in the spring of 1901, traveling by rail and on foot. How he was robbed of all his money and possessions, including the pocket watch that had been his grandfather's, the one with her photograph inside. How the thieves had beaten him afterward and left him for dead.

"Sweeney Gaffney and his daughter, Siobhan, found me lying on the side of the road."

Siobhan. Different from any woman Jakob had ever known. She'd been as strong as a man of equal size, and her Irish temper had been *twice* that of any man, large or small. Siobhan, with her red hair to match her fiery temper and a passion for life that burned bright and hot.

Siobhan had been there to nurse him back to health. She'd been there to listen as he poured out his loneliness and despair. His dreams for a farm of his own seemed to have vanished forever, and with those dreams went his hope. He had failed. He would never have the things he'd once wanted.

But Siobhan had lifted his spirits again, encouraged him, made him laugh, made him forget. The old country—as well as his old promises—had seemed distant, unreal, dreamlike. As had Karola. Siobhan, her good-natured father, and a hardscrabble farm in Wyoming—those were what were real.

Jakob had been twenty-four and lusty; Siobhan had been twenty-two and willing. They'd got on well enough, and so they'd wed.

Looking at him for the first time since they'd left American Falls, Karola asked, "Did you love Siobhan?" Her voice was barely audible above the creak of the wagon wheels.

He hesitated only a moment before giving his answer. "Yes. Maybe at first I married her for other reasons, but I grew to love her."

Karola nodded, then looked away again.

Jakob continued with the story, thinking it best to get it over and done with. "Maeve came along nine months after we married. Bernard ten months after that. Siobhan lost the next two."

His wife had mourned those babies with the same fervor with which she loved their two surviving children. Jakob had mourned them, too, in a private corner of his heart. The same year as the second miscarriage, things worsened for the family when the bank took possession of Sweeney Gaffney's farm. They had been forced to pick up stakes and move to Shadow Creek, Idaho, where Sweeney's brother, Tulley Gaffney, lived. Not long after they got to Idaho, Sweeney had died.

Loss heaped upon loss heaped upon loss.

"I borrowed money from Siobhan's uncle to buy our farm. The soil is rich, and the crops were good those first two years. We paid off the loan the same day Siobhan discovered she was expecting another baby."

He hadn't been happy at the news. He'd told Siobhan they were just getting their heads above water. For the first time in a long while, Jakob had felt real hope for the future. It hadn't been a good time for their family to grow. Not right then.

"Sure, and what would you have me do about it, I'm wonderin'," she'd said, her eyes sparking in defiance. *"'Tis a bit late for you t'be wishin' for no more wee bairns."*

Jakob swallowed the hot lump in his throat. "Aislinn came a month early. It happened fast. There was no chance to send for the doctor. This birth wasn't like the others." He swallowed again. "Siobhan died the next morning."

Loss heaped upon loss heaped upon loss.

Karola wanted to scream, to rage, and to weep. She wanted to hate Jakob for what he'd done and to rail at herself for her own stupidity. She was sorry his wife had died. She was sorry for his troubles. But she had plenty of troubles of her own.

What do I do now?

She had little money left, a few dollars tucked in a pouch inside her corset. She knew no one in America other than Jakob. Her parents wouldn't be able to afford the cost of passage home, and even if they could, she couldn't bear the thought of going back, of knowing people would be laughing at her.

She stiffened her spine. "There must be women here who were willing to marry. Why send to Germany for me?"

Jakob glanced over his shoulder into the wagon bed. Karola followed his gaze. The children slept, draped across one another like newborn puppies in a basket.

"I couldn't trust their keeping to just anyone, Karola. I remembered how loving you were with the children in our village. You'd said you wanted a large family. I remembered that, too. I thought I could trust you to care for them, no matter what you felt about me." He pulled on the reins, drawing the team of horses to a halt. "Karola?"

She looked at him.

"I'll find some way to pay for your return to Germany if you choose not to stay and marry me. I won't hold you against your will."

She thought again what would await her if she returned to her parents.

"Nein," she whispered. "I will stay, Jakob. I will marry you."

Jakob's farm—land that gently rolled and dipped—lay in the shadow of mountains. The house had two stories and a slate roof. A wide porch stretched across the front of the house, and there was a second, smaller side porch off the kitchen at the rear.

Jakob jumped down from the wagon seat, then came around to help Karola to the ground. As her feet met earth, he said, "We'll let you rest tonight, then go into Shadow Creek to see Pastor Joki in the morning. He's expecting us."

She nodded.

He glanced into the back of the wagon. "They're still asleep. Come on." He grabbed her suitcases. "I'll show you the house."

Again she nodded before following him up the path to the front door.

The ground floor of the Hirsch home held a spacious parlor, a dining room, and a kitchen with a large pantry. A stairway near the front entrance led down to the basement and up to the second floor where the bedrooms were, three in all, plus a bathroom. Karola was amazed by this last luxury but didn't comment upon it, not wanting to appear ignorant. For all she knew, every home in America had indoor plumbing and bathrooms.

Jakob showed her through the house hastily, not giving her time to linger in any one room. Even so, Karola noticed the many touches that only a woman brought to a home. She suspected he hadn't changed anything, that he'd left it all as it had been on the day his wife died. Looking at Siobhan's things, Karola felt like an intruder. She'd come here, expecting to be loved, and instead she was to be a stand-in for the woman Jakob had loved and lost.

"You'll sleep in Bernard's room tonight," Jakob announced as he opened that bedroom door. "Would you like a bath? I can heat some water for you."

"Ja." Anything so she could have time to herself to think.

Jakob seemed just as anxious to leave her alone. He excused himself and hurried away.

The instant the door closed, Karola sank onto the bed near the window. Giving in to her vacillating emotions, she lay on her side, hid her face in the pillow, and wept.

"How long's she going to stay, Da?" Maeve asked as she walked beside Jakob.

"How long's she gonna stay?" Bernard liked to repeat whatever his sister said.

"She's staying for good," Jakob answered. "I told you that before."

Maeve frowned. "The others didn't stay."

"They didn't stay," Bernard parroted.

"This is different. After tomorrow, Karola's going to be my wife and your mother. That means she'll stay here for good."

"But our ma's in heaven. Uncle Tulley says so."

"Yeah, Ma's in heaven."

Jakob pictured Siobhan, riotous hair swirling around her as she spun in a field ablaze with red and orange wildflowers. He could almost hear her laughter floating on the clouds. Oh, she must be setting heaven on its ear.

"But, Da, what if she—"

"Maeve." Jakob stopped on the front porch and looked down at his elder daughter. He understood her uncertainty. There'd been little permanence in her life this past year. "I know it isn't easy to understand. Just trust me. This time it's different."

Bernard gave his sister a little shove. "Yeah, it's different, Maeve."

She shoved him back, then the two raced inside ahead of their father.

Jakob carried the still sleeping Aislinn into the parlor where he laid her on the sofa. Before straightening, he caressed the child's soft cheek, feeling the swell of love in his chest as he did so. When he looked at her . . .

He swallowed the lump in his throat.

He would not—could not—regret asking Karola to come to America. It had been the right thing to do because he was certain she would care for his children no matter how she felt about him.

The rest would have to work itself out over time.

Chapter Four

*K*arola didn't get a bath her first night in Jakob's home, for she fell asleep as she wept, still dressed in her traveling clothes.

Awakening as the sun rose, she sat up and glanced about the child's bedroom, feeling grumpy and out of sorts. She was hungry, too, but she was certain she would be sick if she tried to eat a single bite.

Today was her wedding day.

Mother was right. What a fool I have been.

From the moment she'd received Jakob's letter, asking if she would come to America and marry him, she'd purposefully deceived herself. She'd wanted so badly to believe he'd asked because he still loved her that she hadn't considered any other reason. She'd created a fantasy in her mind that suited her rather than the truth. But Jakob had loved his wife. He'd wanted Karola only because he trusted her to be a good mother to his children.

Karola knew what Jakob was asking of her happened to women around the world every day. Second wives were frequently taken out of necessity to raise the children of the first, and third wives were taken to raise the children of both the first and second. It was a common occurrence, and there wasn't any shame in it.

Would I have been better off married to the cobbler? Karola shuddered at the thought. *Nein.*

She closed her eyes. If she was going to be totally honest with herself, she must admit that her reasons for agreeing to marry Jakob had no more to do with love than his had. She'd wanted to leave Germany, to see America. She'd wanted her dreams to come true. Most of all, she'd wanted to prove the gossips in her village wrong. She'd wanted them to know she wasn't an old maid. She hadn't been forgotten.

A soft rap sounded at her door.

"Karola," Jakob said softly from the hall.

She stood, touching her mussed hair with one hand. She must look a sight.

"Karola?" Another rap.

"Ja." She moved to stand by the door but didn't open it. "I am awake, Jakob."

"We'll want to leave for the church in a couple of hours. Would you like something to eat? I've got ham and eggs frying in the skillet."

Her stomach fluttered. *"Nein,* but I would like a bath, if it wouldn't be too much trouble."

"No trouble." He cleared his throat, then added, "I'll heat the water for you now."

"Danke, Jakob."

Karola's mother had labored long hours on a wedding gown of ivory mousseline de soie. Laced, ruffled, and embroidered, the dress had been made with love for a daughter who was traveling far, far away.

The wedding gown remained in the trunk. Karola didn't want to wear it. It seemed all wrong to her now.

After a bath, she donned a cream-colored blouse with a high collar and billowy sleeves and a pleated skirt of a soft dove-gray fabric. Over the blouse, she wore a sleeveless bolero with a buttoned front closure. It was a pretty outfit, but ordinary enough.

She didn't bother to fuss with her hair either. Without so much as a glance in the mirror, she twisted it into a knot at the nape and secured it with hairpins, then placed a wide-brimmed straw hat on her head. Finally, she grabbed her gloves and her handbag from atop the chest of drawers and left the bedroom.

The Hirsch family awaited her in the parlor. The children were wearing what she guessed was their Sunday best, their faces shining. Jakob wore a striped wool suit, dark gray in color, and his leather shoes had been shined to a bright finish. In his right hand, he held a black bowler; in his left he gripped a bouquet of wildflowers.

"Maeve picked these for you."

Karola took them, then looked at the young girl. *"Danke."*

The child cast an uncertain look at her father.

Jakob placed the bowler on his head. *"Danke* means thanks."

"Danke." Maeve pondered the word for a moment, then grinned. "You're welcome."

Pleasure warmed Karola's heart, and her nerves quieted.

"Karola," Jakob said, "are you sure you don't want to eat something before we go?"

The nervous flutter in her belly resumed. *"Ja,* I am sure."

"Then I guess we're ready." He lifted Aislinn into his arms. "Let's go."

Jakob led the way out of the house, off the porch, and to the carriage that awaited them. The two older children scampered up onto the backseat while Jakob assisted Karola to the front one. After a questioning glance, he handed Aislinn to her.

For one panicked moment, Karola thought the toddler would burst into tears. But then her father appeared on the seat beside them, and Aislinn smiled.

It is clear he is a good man. His children love him. He is a hard worker or he would not own a farm or house such as this. Perhaps that will be enough for happiness.

If only it felt like enough.

Jakob gave the horse its head, allowing the animal to set its own unhurried pace. It took over a quarter of an hour to reach the main road.

As the carriage turned south toward Shadow Creek, Jakob cast a quick glance in Karola's direction. She sat rigid on the seat beside him, Aislinn in her lap. She was staring at the passing countryside, but her grim expression told him she was too lost in thought to see what surrounded her.

This isn't the wedding day she expected.

Looking away, Jakob set his jaw, determined not to feel guilty. He'd told Karola he was sorry, despite it not being his fault she hadn't received his letter. He'd offered to pay her way back to Germany, even though he couldn't afford to do so and hadn't any idea where he would have found the money. He'd given her a way out. She had chosen to stay. Many women far younger than Karola were never given a choice. Arranged marriages hadn't been uncommon in Steigerhausen. Back in Germany, two of his friends had married girls they'd never met before their wedding days. Wasn't this better than that?

They weren't strangers, he and Karola. They'd loved each other in their youth—a different sort of love than what he'd known with Siobhan, but love all the same. He and Karola had a shared past, as distant as it all seemed to him now. And he would be good to her. He was not an unfair man. He would not expect more from her than any other man, perhaps not even as much as some. No, he had no reason to feel guilty.

"Is it much farther?" Karola asked, breaking into his reverie.

He turned his head to find her watching him. "No. Not far."

"The reverend. He is expecting us?"

"Yes."

She nodded.

Jakob felt a sudden anger. Anger that Siobhan had been taken from him, that he'd been left alone to raise their children, that he needed to marry again. Why did life have to be so hard? Why did so much bitter come with the sweet? Just once, couldn't things go his way?

"Sure, and you know you'll be needing a wife," Tulley Gaffney, Siobhan's uncle, had told him more than once since she died. *"You cannot go on the way you are. The wee ones have need of a ma to care for them, and well you know it, lad. And you'll be needing someone to look after you, too."*

In those first weeks after Siobhan died, women from town had come to the farm to take care of the children. Later, he'd hired a housekeeper, who'd also served as a nursemaid. Three, actually, over the course of several months. Each time something had gone wrong, and the woman had left him in the lurch. Finally, he'd known his only solution was just as Tulley had said: to find himself a wife. He needed a woman who would stay, and a wife couldn't pack up and leave at the drop of a hat.

That only left one question: Who would that wife be?

Dorotea Joki, the twin sister of the Lutheran pastor, had made it obvious she would willingly consider a proposal from Jakob. But Dorotea was cold and stern by nature, and Jakob couldn't imagine putting fun-loving Siobhan's children into her care.

Then there was the young and very lovely Charlotte White, daughter of the town's blacksmith. She'd begun flirting with Jakob even before the proper period of mourning had passed, and while he wasn't immune to her inestimable charms—he was, after all, still a man—he knew Charlotte was in many ways as much a child as Maeve and far more spoiled. Jakob figured he was better off single than he'd be married to her.

Nadzia Denys was the widow who owned the millinery shop in Shadow Creek. She was pleasant enough in nature, though a less attractive woman Jakob had never met—square-jawed, thick eyebrows, gap-toothed, tall and large-boned. But even if he'd been interested in her, she didn't seem to want or need a husband. She was clearly content to remain independent.

One by one, Jakob had dismissed the unmarried women of his acquaintance. Then he'd had that dream, and asking Karola to marry him had seemed the perfect solution. But what if he'd been wrong?

He frowned. Right or wrong, sure or not, what did it matter? It was done now. She was here, and they were to be wed this very morning.

He slapped the reins against the horse's back and clucked with his tongue, asking for more speed.

Karola worried the inside of her lip, her thoughts spinning faster than the carriage wheels.

Her mother was right. Karola had *always* been a dreamer. From the time she was no more than five or six, she'd spun fantasies and made up pretty stories in her head. Her mother had said that every girl had to eventually grow up and put away childish things, but Karola hadn't listened. The worlds she created in her mind were so much more interesting than the one in which she lived.

Her father had said Karola's pride was her greatest fault. "You are the daughter of a baker, not a prince. Beware thinking of yourself too highly, *Tochter*. Beware of thinking yourself more worthy than your neighbors." Her father had predicted her unchecked pride would bring her low.

And so it had.

Surreptitiously she glanced at Jakob. She'd loved him once, or loved the boy he'd been. She hadn't imagined that. It had been real. But that was so very long ago. What did she feel for him now? In Germany, it had been easy to convince herself that she loved him still. But here . . . now . . .

The wagon turned a bend in the road, and Jakob said, "There's Shadow Creek."

She followed his gaze with her own.

"That's the Lady of Mercy Catholic Church." He pointed. "And there's the Holy Shepherd Lutheran Church on the opposite corner."

"That's our church," Maeve said from behind Karola.

"Yeah, our church," Bernard echoed.

Jakob nodded. "Pastor Joki should be waiting for us."

Karola felt suddenly chilled. In a short while, her life would be forever changed. She would be both wife and mother. It was what she'd wanted when she set sail for America, and now it was about to come true.

It didn't take long to reach the white church building with its steeple and stained glass windows.

Through the Shadow Creek Hotel's large plate glass window, Tulley Gaffney saw the Hirsch carriage stop in front of the Lutheran church. He stepped closer to observe Jakob as he took little Aislinn from the woman's arms, then assisted her to the ground.

"Ian," Tulley called to his son who was attending to some paperwork behind the front desk. "I'll be across the street."

By the time he was out the door and had stepped off the sidewalk, Tully saw that Jakob and his bride, as well as his children, had disappeared inside the church. Then he noticed Father Patrick, his black robe flapping against his heels, headed in the same direction as he was.

"A good mornin' to you, Father," Tulley said as the two men drew closer to their destination.

"And a good morning to you, Tulley. It appears there's to be a wedding."

"So it does, Father."

The Catholic priest smiled. "Have you met the bride-to-be?"

"No, Father. Sure, and it hasn't been me pleasure. She was to arrive yesterday by train."

"Then let us not delay."

Tulley motioned for Father Patrick to proceed ahead of him through the church's open door.

The sanctuary was cool and dim. Morning light filtered through colored glass, staining pews and floor in shades of green, red, and gold. Jakob and his bride stood at the front of the church, while his children sat in the front row. Rick Joki, the Lutheran pastor, was speaking to the couple in soft tones. His sister, Dorotea, sat at the organ, her brow pinched.

Everyone looked toward the back of the church at the sound of the new arrivals' footsteps on the wooden floor.

Tulley's gaze went straight to the bride. She had a willowy build, and everything about her—from her wheat-blond hair to her ice-blue eyes to her fair complexion—seemed soft, pale, quiet.

So unlike his niece.

Tulley glanced at Jakob. He had a tender spot in his heart for this young man. He'd been a loving and faithful husband to Siobhan and was a devoted father to their children. A harder worker couldn't be found in all this valley. It seemed to Tulley that Jakob had suffered more trials and heartache than were his due at his age. It was time he was blessed with happiness, and in Tulley's way of thinking, the right wife could bring that blessing.

But I'm wondering if you're after bein' the right one, Karola Breit? It's an odd choice you seem to me now. Will you be bringin' happiness into Jakob's heart?

The priest offered his hand—and a smile—to Karola Breit. "I'm Father Patrick. Welcome to Shadow Creek, Miss Breit."

"Danke," she replied as she placed her gloved hand in the priest's.

"We only learned of your coming a few days ago." Father Patrick looked at Jakob. "Though why you'd want to keep this lovely young woman a secret from your friends is beyond me. The townsfolk would have welcomed her in style if we'd been given a chance."

"We didn't want a lot of fanfare," Jakob answered.

"Maybe not you"—Father Patrick's gaze returned once more to Karola—"but every bride hopes for some. Isn't that true, Miss Breit?"

It seemed to Tulley that Karola grew even more pale as her gaze lowered to the bouquet of flowers she held in her free hand. Her seeming meekness gave him a moment's pause. He couldn't imagine Jakob married to a shy, retiring mouse of a woman.

Dorotea played a sour chord on the organ. "Rikkard, may we proceed? I have other things to tend to at the parsonage."

Faith and begorra, thought Tulley, his attention momentarily diverted from the bride. *That is one cantankerous woman. I'll not be knowing how Rick puts up with her, brother or no.*

Rick Joki—only his sister called him *Rikkard*—cleared his throat. "Yes, shall we proceed?"

"I'll be asking you not to be in such a hurry," Tulley interjected, Dorotea forgotten. "Not until I've said me welcome to the bride." Like the priest before him, Tulley thrust out his hand toward Karola. "Me name's Tulley Gaffney. I'm by way of being a granduncle to the wee ones there." He jerked his head toward the children in the pew behind him.

"Guten Morgen," she said, accepting his welcoming gesture.

Her hand was small within his, as fragile, he thought, as a bird's wing. She didn't seem the type to come from halfway around the world alone. Yet she had. He liked her for that. And if he weren't mistaken, there was intelligence in her gaze—and a bit of gumption in the set of her back.

Aye, I'm thinkin' you're the one for Jakob after all.

Chapter Five

*K*arola clasped the bouquet of wildflowers in both hands as she faced Pastor Joki. Jakob stood at her side.

"Into this holy estate this man and this woman come now to be united. If anyone, therefore, can show just cause why they may not be lawfully joined together"—Pastor Joki paused and glanced toward the witnesses—"let him now speak, or else forever hold his peace."

Karola felt as if her high-collared blouse were choking her.

After another moment's pause, the pastor continued. "Jakob Hirsch, wilt thou have this woman to thy wedded wife, to live together after God's ordinance in the holy estate of matrimony? Wilt thou love her, comfort her, honor and keep her in sickness and in health, and, forsaking all others, keep thee only unto her, so long as ye both shall live?"

"I will," Jakob replied.

But he does not love me. How can he promise that when it is not true? It is not true. He cannot love me because he does not know me. And I do not know him. Mother was right, and Father, too. I do not know this Jakob Hirsch. He is not the young man who left Steigerhausen. He is someone else.

"Karola Breit, wilt thou have this man to thy wedded husband, to live together after God's ordinance in the holy estate of matrimony? Wilt thou love him, comfort him—"

"Nein."

At her strangled whisper, the pastor glanced up from his prayer book.

"Nein." She shook her head, repeating softly, *"Nein."*

"Karola—," Jakob began.

She looked at him, eyes wide, feeling almost as surprised as he sounded. "I cannot."

"Excuse us, Pastor Joki." Jakob took hold of her arm and steered her toward a corner, away from the others. "What do you think you're doing?" Though he spoke in a low voice, his irritation was apparent.

"I cannot marry you, Jakob."

"But yesterday you said—"

"I was wrong."

She couldn't tell if he was confused or frustrated. Probably both.

"So you want to go back to Germany after all? Is that it?"

She shook her head.

"Then what in heaven's name *do* you want?" His voice rose, his patience clearly stretched to the limit.

"I do not know." Karola's heart hammered in her chest at the admission.

Jakob muttered something beneath his breath, then glanced behind him.

Reluctantly, Karola looked too. The pastor, his sister, the priest, and Tulley Gaffney were all watching them, waiting to see what the outcome would be.

She touched his forearm lightly. "Jakob."

He met her gaze again.

"You do not love me, Jakob, and I do not love you."

His eyes narrowed as he drew in a deep breath, as if fighting for control of his temper. "Perhaps not, but that would change with time."

"How can you be sure?"

He scowled. "I just am."

"Because you learned to love Siobhan?"

"Karola, we—"

"Is that not true? Is that not what you said to me?"

With a sigh, he answered, "Yes . . . but I don't see what—"

"I do not wish to marry for other than love, Jakob. You know nothing of me or my life since you went away." She gave her head a slow shake, only now beginning to understand her reasons for stopping the ceremony. "When, since I arrived, did you ask one question about me or what's happened to me or what I might want or hope for? When did you ask about my parents or the people you used to know in Steigerhausen? We have scarcely talked at all." She might have been angry over his lack of interest, she supposed, but she wasn't. Only sad.

"Look, I never meant to make you think—" He stopped, rubbed a hand over his face, then tried again. "It isn't that I don't care. But after I found out you didn't get my letter telling you about the children and everything . . ." He let his explanation trail into silence.

Karola swallowed a sudden lump in her throat. "It is not entirely your fault, Jakob. I am as guilty as you. I believed what I wanted to believe. I even pretended I still loved you after all those years of silence just so I could get away from those who felt sorry for me and those who laughed at me behind my back. I did not know that was why, but it was. Jakob, I did not love you when I left Germany, and I do not love you now. I do not know you, and I do not love you."

Jakob supposed a woman couldn't speak any clearer than that. She didn't love him and she didn't want to marry him. Period.

He wasn't sure how he felt about any of that. All he knew was he'd spent hard-earned money to bring her here—money that couldn't easily be replaced—and now he was still without anybody to watch over his children while he worked the farm.

"Jakob?" Pastor Joki's hesitant voice pulled him back to matters at hand. "Miss Breit?"

They both turned to find the pastor walking toward them.

"The wedding's off." Jakob knew he sounded harsher than he intended, but he couldn't help it.

"Off?"

Jakob felt heat rising up the back of his neck. "Yes, off." So much for not being sure how he felt. He was frustrated, and he was angry. With Karola. With his circumstances. With God.

"I am sorry."

Jakob didn't know if Karola spoke to him or the pastor. He didn't rightly care. "Maeve, you and your brother take Aislinn out to the carriage. We'll be there straightaway."

Dorotea appeared beside her brother. "What will you do now, Miss Breit?"

Karola looked at Jakob, her blue eyes filled with questions. Obviously, she hadn't considered anything beyond her refusal to marry.

"We'll figure it out later," he said gruffly. "Right now, we need to be on our way."

"Good heavens!" Dorotea exclaimed. "You can't mean to take her back to your farm, Mr. Hirsch. Now that you're not to be married . . . Well, what would people say?"

Tulley spoke up. "I'll be offering her a room at the hotel. We've plenty to go around."

Jakob turned, saying in a low voice, "Tulley, I can't afford—"

The Irishman flicked his hand, waving away the words of protest. "We're family, after all. Sure, and it will be our pleasure to have her stay with us."

"Well, then"—Jakob looked at Karola—"I guess it's settled."

In the small parlor of the White home, Charlotte White shrieked with delight. Her best friend, Emma Shrum, had just told her the news about Jakob Hirsch and that German woman. Emma had heard it from her mother, Theodora, wife of the Methodist minister, who had heard it from Laura Gaffney, Tulley's daughter-in-law. In fact, by this time, everyone in Shadow Creek had probably heard the news.

"I knew he wouldn't go through with it!" Charlotte pressed her hands to her breast as she leaned back in the brocade-upholstered chair. "I *knew* he wouldn't get married like this."

Charlotte sounded as if she'd believed that, but in truth, she'd spent the morning in her room, weeping into her pillow. The very idea that Jakob Hirsch would send away for a bride when he had to know—

Emma lifted her teacup from the saucer. "Laura Gaffney said it was *Miss Breit* who couldn't go through with it." She paused to take a sip. "Her father-in-law was there to see it all. He said Miss Breit stopped Pastor Joki right in the middle of the ceremony."

Charlotte's eyes widened. "I don't believe it."

"It's true, whether you believe it or not."

Charlotte considered this news a few moments, then gave a sniff of disdain. "That's what he gets for sending for a mail-order bride."

"But haven't you heard, Charlotte? She isn't a stranger to him. They grew up together in Germany. Laura says they were sweethearts before Jakob left to come to America."

That news caused a sick feeling in Charlotte's midsection.

"Mr. Gaffney has given Miss Breit a room at the hotel until it's decided where she will go. Mother says we must call on her tomorrow. Mother says we must make her feel welcome in Shadow Creek."

"I, for one, have no intention of calling on her." She tilted her chin. "I don't care a whit if she feels welcome."

Emma laughed. "But that's because you're sweet on Jakob Hirsch, and you'd just as soon Miss Breit left town as quickly as she came."

Charlotte *harrumphed,* choosing silence for a change.

Karola sat in the chair near the window of her second-story hotel room, looking out at the steeple of the Holy Shepherd Lutheran Church.

Jakob was so angry.

Could she blame him?

Nein, I cannot.

Nor would she blame herself. Not marrying Jakob was perhaps the first truly sensible decision she'd made in a long while.

But what am I to do now? I did not think of that.

She had no money to speak of, and she didn't want to be sent back to Germany. She knew no one in America except Jakob, and she certainly couldn't ask him for help. Nor could she live forever in this hotel room, depending upon the charity of strangers. So what *was* she to do? Where was she to go?

Her mother's words on that last night at home came to her again: *"Have you asked God what he wants you to do?"*

Someone tapped on her door, interrupting her troubled thoughts, and Karola rose to see who it was. Opening the door, she found Laura Gaffney—whom she'd met when Tulley brought her to the hotel that morning—standing in the hallway, a hesitant smile curving her mouth, a tray covered with a white cloth in her hands.

"I thought you might be hungry."

Karola wasn't.

"Miss Breit, you didn't join us for lunch and supper is still two hours away. You really should eat something."

As much as she wished the young woman would leave her alone, Karola stepped back.

Laura walked to the small, round table beneath the window. After setting down the tray, she turned and regarded Karola, her eyes kind. "Is there anything I can do to make you more comfortable?"

Karola shook her head.

"Papa Tulley should be back with your things soon." Laura offered another gentle smile. "He left for the Hirsch farm about an hour ago. My father-in-law never lets grass grow under his feet if he can help it. He has a heart of gold, that man."

"Mr. Gaffney has been very kind to me, offering me a place to stay."

Laura laughed, a sweet and melodious sound. "He'll want you to call him Tulley. He isn't a man who stands on ceremony." She motioned toward the table with one hand. "Won't you sit and eat while we become better acquainted?"

Karola had hoped Laura would put down the tray and leave, but it seemed that wasn't to be. With an inward sigh, she closed the door, then walked to the chair she had vacated a short while before and sat down.

Laura sat in the opposite chair. "I know what it's like to come here, a stranger. I grew up in Chicago. That's where I met Ian when he was there on business. He swept me off my feet, and we were married in a matter of weeks, much to my mother's dismay." Her gray eyes sparkled. "The Irish do have a way about them. Full of charm and blarney. I found it impossible to resist him." She laughed again. "Although, to be honest, I didn't really try to resist."

Is that what happened to Jakob? Is that why he forgot me? Because of Siobhan's Irish charms.

"I'm sorry," Laura said softly. "Have I said something to upset you?"

Karola realized that her eyes were brimming with unshed tears. She blinked them away, at the same time shaking her head, trying to deny their existence.

"Please forgive me, Miss Breit." Laura rose. "I was thoughtless to barge in and start chattering like a blue jay. You must be exhausted from your journey, and on top of that, you've had a distressing morning."

"You have been very kind."

"Please eat a little and then get some rest. We'll have plenty of time to become acquainted later." With those words, Laura Gaffney hurried out of the room, closing the door behind her.

And good riddance, Jakob thought as he watched Tulley Gaffney's buggy disappearing up the road, Karola's trunk and suitcases strapped to the back.

He turned on his heel and headed for the barn.

What on earth had possessed him to think he should marry someone he hadn't seen in over a decade, all because of a stupid dream? He supposed it served him right, what had happened this morning. The truth was, Karola had done him a favor. She'd saved him from his own stupidity.

Jakob paused as he stepped into the shadowed light of the barn, allowing his eyes time to adjust. The mare in the far stall stomped a hoof, and her filly released a high-pitched whinny. Moving toward them, he felt some of the tension leave his neck and shoulders.

There was something about farming, whether working the land or tending the livestock, that brought him a sense of peace. There was plenty he didn't know in this world, plenty of things that were hard for him to understand. But this he knew: Here was where he belonged. When he stood in this barn and breathed deeply of the familiar scents—the dust and the hay and the animals—he knew he belonged. When he observed the rolling wheat fields, swaying in a late summer breeze, looking like the swells of the ocean, he knew he belonged. Whatever else might be wrong in his life, this much was right.

The dun mare thrust her head over the top rail of her stall and nickered at him.

"Hey, girl." Jakob stroked her forehead. "How's that leg doing?"

With a gentle push, he moved the mare back from the gate, then opened it and entered the stall. She nickered again, this time at the filly who had scurried to her opposite side, startled by Jakob's sudden presence.

He ran his hand over the mare's neck and shoulder, then down her front left leg to the fetlock. She lifted her hoof at his gentle touch, and he inspected the cut he'd been nursing for the past week. The wound was healing nicely.

"You'll be out of here soon." He glanced over the mare's back at the filly. "And you, too, little one."

He exited the stall, then tossed hay into the manger before leaving the barn. Once outside, he glanced toward the house to check on the children. He'd left them in the small fenced yard, playing in the shade of a poplar. One, two, three. All accounted for. And no one was crying. So far, so good.

Of course, it wouldn't last for long. Soon one or more of them would need attention, either because of a fall or a dirty diaper or a fight between siblings. Not to mention suppertime was approaching. He supposed another meal of bread, cheese, and cold meats wouldn't kill any of them.

What was he going to do? He couldn't go on like this. In a few more weeks, the first cutting of alfalfa would be ready. He couldn't be out in the fields from dawn to dusk and tend to the children, too. He'd have to have help.

If he hadn't spent all that money to bring Karola from Germany . . .

Wait a minute. He stopped suddenly. *She owes me.*

He'd paid for her steamship passage and train fare with the understanding that she would become his wife upon arrival. He'd even done the honorable thing when he learned she hadn't received the letter that detailed what had happened to him in recent years—he'd offered to pay her way back to Germany. But she'd refused that offer. She'd refused to go home, while at the same time refusing to marry him. It seemed to him that she got exactly what she'd wanted—to live in America. And he was the one who'd paid for her to have that privilege.

Oh, yes. She owed him plenty.

Chapter Six

*H*ave you asked God what he wants you to do?" Her mother's question continued to plague Karola throughout that first night at the Shadow Creek Hotel, and the answer, when it came, brought her no comfort.

Not only hadn't she asked God what he wanted her to do before she came to America, she hadn't asked him what he wanted her to do in years. When was the last time she'd prayed—really prayed? Not the liturgical prayers repeated as part of a Sunday morning service along with the rest of the congregation, but a heartfelt petition to the Lord.

Years.

As dawn pinkened the cloud-spattered eastern horizon and the sky began to change from pewter to blue, Karola stared out the window at the sleepy town's main street.

"O God, when did I let it happen? When did you become just another obligation in my life instead of my Lord and Comforter?"

The waning of her faith hadn't happened overnight, she realized. It hadn't been a conscious turning away from the God of her father and mother. It had taken time and disappointment and resentment. It had taken pride and stubbornness. Mostly, it had taken neglect. She had ignored God, except for Sundays, and even that had been because it was expected of her to be in church, not because she'd gone to worship him.

Fighting tears of regret and shame, Karola closed her eyes. "Forgive me, Father God. Forgive me for my pride and selfishness and willfulness. Show me what to do now, Lord. I cannot take charity from Mr. Gaffney for long. I must find work and a place to live. Guide me, I pray, and keep me close. Do not allow me to stray ever again." She sat very still for a long while before she made the sign of the cross, whispered, "Amen," and opened her eyes.

Across the street, just west of the Lutheran church, she saw a man, black bag in hand, exiting the building that bore the sign, *Doctor's Office, Andrew Cooper, M.D.* She watched as he placed his bag in a buggy, then climbed in and took up the reins. The large sorrel in the traces didn't wait for a slap on its hindquarters but stepped out briskly, as if sensing a need for urgency.

Karola stepped closer to the window, her gaze moving down the street, suddenly curious for a more thorough look at Shadow Creek.

Next door to the doctor's office was a grocery where a man in a white apron was unfurling a green awning above the large window. Beyond the grocery was a barbershop and then a cigar store, and at the far end of the block stood another church, this one made of brick.

From what she could see of it, the town of Shadow Creek seemed a good one, the merchants successful. The buildings appeared clean and in good repair. Surely she would be able to find some kind of work here. There must be a bakery; perhaps the owner needed help. She had worked beside her father since she was a child, so she had ample experience. Or she could hire on as a cook somewhere. And she was a good seamstress. She made all of her own clothes. There must be a call for that, even in a small town.

Karola turned from the window with a new sense of purpose. She wasn't without options. She was young. She could work hard and make a home for herself. She didn't need a husband. She only needed to keep faith in God.

I will look to you, Lord. I will trust you to guide me. I will never turn away from you again. No matter what tomorrow brings, I will follow you.

Jakob hitched the team to the rail outside the hotel, then lifted Aislinn into his arms while his older children scampered down from the back of the wagon.

"Mind your manners," he cautioned them sternly before leading the way inside.

Ian and Laura were both behind the front desk.

Ian—a slimmer, younger version of his father—grinned when he saw Jakob. "Sure, and we weren't expecting to see yourself in town again so soon. You must've come to see the lovely Miss Breit." His grin broadened. "You'll find her in the dining room, having herself a bite of breakfast."

Jakob scowled, not liking the man's merry tone, as if this were all some sort of joke.

Before Jakob could move on, Laura stopped him. "Let me tend the children while you see to your business."

He chose not to refuse the offer, quickly passing the toddler into her open arms. With a glance, he reminded Maeve and Bernard that they were to behave, then strode away.

His gaze found Karola the instant he entered the dining room. Wearing a dress of lemon yellow, she was seated before a large window. The morning light spilled through the glass to create a halo effect around her upper body. She looked almost . . . angelic.

Remember why you're here.

As she lifted a cup to her lips, Karola glanced toward the doorway. Her eyes widened slightly when she saw him, revealing surprise or distress; he couldn't be sure which. She set the cup down without taking a drink.

He strode across the room and stopped beside her table. "Karola."

"Jakob."

"I need to talk to you."

She looked out the window. "There is nothing more to say. I cannot marry you. I was wrong to think I could. We are strangers to one another, and you do not want a wife."

"That may very well be, but I need one. That's why I sent for you."

He saw her shoulders rise and fall with a deep sigh.

"You *owe* me, Karola."

This drew her gaze back to him. "You would *force* me to marry you against my will?"

He grunted, an irritated sound of dismissal. "That isn't how I do things. The last thing I want is an unwilling woman sharing my home."

"Then what is it you do want?"

He pulled out the chair opposite her and sat down. "I want you to take care of my children. I sent for you because I believed you'd be good to them. I still believe it, despite how bad things went yesterday."

"Jakob, I cannot—"

He felt his temper rising, and his voice rose along with it. "You got what you wanted, Karola. You wanted to come to America. Well, here you are, and I paid for every mile of the journey without getting anything in return. You don't want to marry me? Fine. So be it. But we had an agreement, and since you're the one who reneged, I think it's only fair that you work off the debt you owe me."

She stared at him. "Reneged?" Confusion—and perhaps fear—sounded in her voice.

"It means to break one's commitment, to go back on your word." He drew in a deep breath, trying to calm himself, then blew it out slowly. "I'll give you the same salary as I did the housekeepers I hired last year, and I'll apply it against the cost of getting you here. When the debt's paid off, you'll be free to go if you want. That'd be about right after the harvest is in." After the harvest, he should be able to look after the children himself. He'd have the winter to figure out what he should do next.

"And where would I live?"

He looked up at her soft question.

"Miss Joki is right. I cannot stay under your roof. There would be gossip." A frown pinched her golden eyebrows. "I had thought to find employment in town. If you pay me no salary, I cannot continue to stay in this hotel. And how would I get back and forth each day? I have no horse."

"I already thought of that. There's a small cabin on my land, up the hill from the main house. It was the old homesite. A little bit of work, and it'll be a suitable place for you to stay at night. Not even the worst of the town busybodies could object to that arrangement." He leaned forward, arms resting on the table. "So, what's your answer?"

Karola looked down at her hands, folded now in her lap. She could refuse. What could Jakob do to her if she did? Nothing really.

Or she could offer to pay him back once she found employment. She certainly didn't want to be beholden to him. She even supposed it was fair for him to say she owed him. Regardless of the missing letter that might have stopped her from coming to America, the fact was she *had* come and he *had* paid her expenses.

I did promise God, only this morning, that I would trust him to show me the way.

Of course, this was not what she'd expected when she made that promise. Not even close. She didn't like the idea of working for a man who was angry with her, who held an obligation over her head to get what he wanted.

"Karola?"

She glanced up. Jakob no longer looked angry, she realized. Instead, he looked . . . exhausted.

His next words confirmed the thought. "I need your help. I can't afford to hire anyone else. I spent what I had to spare to bring you here. Once the harvest is in, I'll be able to look for someone else to take care of the house and the children. It's only about five months."

Compassion tugged at her heart. Until harvest was in. That wasn't such a long time.

"The children need you, too."

That did it. The last of her resistance crumbled. "All right, Jakob. I will come to work for you. Until after the harvest."

"'Tis a fine idea," Tulley Gaffney pronounced when he heard the news from Ian. "A fine idea, indeed. 'Twill be a help to them both. More than either of them may know."

"Is that a matchmakin' twinkle I see in your eye, Da?"

Tulley laughed. "Could be. Could be. You know I'd be wantin' nothing but the best for the lad. I loved Siobhan like she was me own daughter, and I'm sorry she's gone, God rest her soul. But gone she is, and 'tis time Jakob found himself a bit of happiness."

"And why is it you're thinkin' Miss Breit can give him that?"

"'Tis a feelin', me boy. Just a feelin'." Tulley winked at his son. "Haven't I always had a way of knowin' these things?"

"Aye, Da. That you have." Ian smiled and shook his head. "But I'd not be too sure about those two. 'Tis a poor beginnin' they've made, if you'd be askin' me."

Tulley rubbed his chin, as if considering his son's words. "You'd be surprised the good that can come from poor beginnings, me boy. I'll be having you remember I said so."

Chapter Seven

————————— ❦ —————————

28 May 1908
Shadow Creek, Idaho

Dear Father and Mother,

I write to let you know I arrived safely in America and am now in Shadow Creek. The ship crossing went without mishap as did the train ride across this vast country. I am still very tired after such a lengthy journey, but it is exciting to be here at last.

I want you to know that Jakob and I are not to be married, but you should not worry. I was not abandoned. It was a mutual decision. I am to have my own place to live, a small cabin near the mountains, and will have employment caring for three small children who lost their mother a year ago.

Jakob is their father.

I know that will surprise you as it did me, but Jakob is not to be blamed. He, too, was surprised that I did not know as he had written to me of the circumstances. Of course, I never received that letter, and I am left to wonder if I would have come if I had known the whole story.

For one more night, I shall stay at the hotel in Shadow Creek. Tomorrow, I shall move into my cabin. I took the opportunity today to become acquainted with the town that is to be my home. The hotel proprietor's daughter-in-law, Laura, was gracious enough to be my guide.

Laura Gaffney is about my age and quite personable. I hope she and I will become good friends. She and her husband, Ian, both work at her father-in-law's hotel. Laura is in charge of the restaurant and is an excellent cook. The Gaffneys have no children, but I recognized the yearning in Laura's eyes when she saw a mother with her children on the street. It was a look that touched my heart, for I have known the same yearning. I have wondered if I will ever have children of my own. I wonder still since I remain without a husband.

Shadow Creek is not much larger than Steigerhausen, but it is dissimilar in every other way. It is laid out in a precise square with three streets running east and west and two running north and south. Nearly all of the businesses are on Main Street, with two church buildings on the east end of town and two church buildings on the west end of town. I will be attending the Holy Shepherd Lutheran Church with Jakob and his children and have already met the pastor. His name is Rick Joki. There is also a Catholic church (the priest is Father Patrick, whom I have also met), a Presbyterian church, and a Methodist church.

Everything is new here by comparison with our country. Shadow Creek was founded, I am told, around the time I was born. The valley is bordered by mountains to the west and east, and the land rolls gently and is rather treeless, except along the streams. Higher up on the mountains, however, there are more trees, and I am told the colors of the changing aspen are beautiful in the fall.

Laura's father-in-law, as I mentioned above, owns the hotel. His name is Tulley Gaffney. He is from Ireland, and I do not believe I have ever met another quite like him. He is tall, even taller than Jakob, and of much greater girth. His hair is bright red, and he has thick, bushy eyebrows of the same startling shade and green eyes the color of the forest meadow where we used to picnic. But it is not only his physical appearance that makes him seem different from others. It is his joyous and quite boisterous nature. There is something contagious about it, I think.

I was introduced to many people today, but I will only share about one more in this letter so that I will have other things to tell you when I write again.

The millinery shop is owned by a widow woman named Nadzia Denys. Her parents and her husband were all from Poland, but she was born in America. Perhaps thirty years of age, Frau Denys is quite formidable. She is sturdy, like the stone wall beyond the Steigerhausen mill, and plain of face. At first when we entered her small shop I thought her unfriendly, for she did not smile. I thought perhaps she did not know how. But then she said to me, "You must be Miss Breit," and I said, "How did you know?" and she said, "Shadow Creek is a very small town." At this point, Laura Gaffney laughed, a merry sound that filled the shop from corner to corner. This, I think, was what caused Frau Denys to smile, and when she did, it revealed a wide gap between her two front teeth. I think this is why she tries not to smile.

Frau Denys makes beautiful hats and bonnets, and there was one especially that I would love to have purchased. You know how much I like pretty hats. This one was made of yellow straw trimmed with sky blue feathers and a large rosette of blue-and-white striped fabric.

Both of the other women encouraged me to try it on, but I declined, knowing I do not have money to waste on something as frivolous as a new bonnet. But it was lovely, all the same.

Before I close this letter, I must tell you that I believe God brought me to America. I know you have worried about me and have prayed for me. Your prayers have been answered, I think. I have asked God to forgive me and to guide me, and I know that I am changed in a way I cannot put into words. Be assured that I am comforted by the words you have taught me all of my life and believe those words and God will help me find the answers I need.

Your loving daughter,
Karola Breit

Chapter Eight

*J*akob wore a bandanna over his nose and mouth as he attacked the thick layer of dust that covered everything inside the two-room cabin. Even so, he tasted the dirt on his tongue and felt it stinging his eyes. He could have used Lance Bishop's help, but his young farmhand was occupied with the children, making sure they didn't get into mischief while their dad was up on the mountainside.

Jakob paused a moment and cast an eye at the roof. He wondered if it leaked in a rainstorm. He didn't see any blue sky peeking through, but that didn't mean water couldn't find a way.

The log cabin had been the first home of Matthew Lewis when he came to this valley to farm in the 1880s. Lewis had done well for himself, and after he married he'd built the main house down below for his bride. Then this cabin had become home to small varmints and spiders. It had remained so after Jakob purchased the farm from Lewis's widow.

Is it a suitable for Karola?

He glanced around the room, then shook off the bothersome thought. Setting his jaw, he went back to work. Suitable or not, it would have to do. Short of having Karola sleep in the barn loft, this was the only place available for her.

Frustration welled inside of him.

Just once! Just once couldn't life deal him a fair and easy hand? Why did it always have to be difficult? He'd watched his father get beaten down by hardship and poverty. That was one reason Jakob had left Germany. He'd wanted to escape the day in, day out adversity of existence in the old country. He'd thought things would be different here.

Things *had* been different, of course. By many standards, he was a successful man. But things had also been painfully similar. Like his father before him, Jakob had lost his wife too young and been left to raise his children alone.

He paused again, cupping his hands over the top of the broom handle and leaning on it. This time his thoughts centered on Siobhan. Oh, what a tumultuous marriage they'd had! Jakob was more reserved by nature; he liked a quiet and peaceful atmosphere in order to reflect and consider the matters of life. But Siobhan? There'd been nothing reserved about her. She'd been like a Roman candle, bursting brightly in the sky, shining light all around. She'd loved nothing more than a good *Donnybrook,* as she'd called their fights.

But Jakob had hated their frequent disagreements, no matter the cause. Until after Siobhan was gone. Then he'd missed them. Strange. He hadn't known he would miss them as a part of missing her.

I wonder if Karola likes to argue.

No, he answered himself immediately. Karola would never like to argue. She was more gentle in spirit, more eager to please.

"You know nothing of me or my life since you went away, Jakob."

She was right, he thought, gripping the broom and returning to work. He didn't know. Maybe she loved nothing more than a good Donnybrook. Maybe she would have made his life miserable if they'd married. He didn't know, and he didn't need to know. As long as she took good care of his children so he could take care of the business of farming, that's all that mattered to him now.

Ida Noonan smiled as she dropped Karola's letter into a leather bag behind the counter at the back of the grocery store. "I'm sure your folks'll be glad to get word from you, Miss Breit. It's good of you to write to them. Gotta be worrisome for them, having you go so far away."

Karola nodded. *"Ja."*

"I was tellin' Henry—that's my husband, you know—that I'd sure hate it if one of our young'ns took it into their heads to go to a whole other country once they're all growed up. Hard enough when they leave Shadow Creek."

It seemed that Karola's participation in the conversation wasn't necessary, so she remained silent.

Ida leaned her forearms on the counter. "Our oldest girl, Elizabeth, she married a fellow from over in Boise. She's expectin' her first baby come fall, and I'm wonderin' how she's gonna manage. She can't stand that mother-in-law of hers, so it isn't like she'll want *her* coming to stay after the baby arrives. Not that I can blame Elizabeth. Mrs. Young is the most busybodyin' woman I ever did set eyes on." She straightened and gestured with a hand toward the rows of grocery items behind Karola. "But it isn't like I can just up and go stay with her for long. Henry, he counts on me to help keep this place runnin'. He's got himself a lot of good qualities, that man does, but land o' Goshen, organized he isn't."

When Ida Noonan paused to draw a breath, Karola grabbed the opportunity to smile, nod, and turn to leave.

Ida didn't let her escape that easily. She bustled out from behind the counter and walked with Karola toward the door. "I hear tell you're gonna look after the Hirsch children."

Karola remembered the words that Nadzia Denys had spoken earlier that day: *"Shadow Creek is a very small town."* It seemed news traveled as quickly here as it did in Steigerhausen.

"I think that's right kind of you, given the circumstances and all. Mr. Hirsch's had a hard time of it since Mrs. Hirsch died. Poor man. So heartbroken he was when he lost her." She clucked her tongue. "Poor, poor man. And those adorable children, left without a mother. They are needin' a woman in the home."

The shop door opened, and two young women—one tall and dark-haired, the other petite with strawberry-blond curls—stepped inside, arm in arm. They were talking softly to one another, their heads close. Their expressions implied they were sharing intimate secrets.

"Oh, look who's here," Ida said with enthusiasm. "Miss White. Miss Shrum. You're just in time to say hello to Miss Breit. She's come here all the way from Germany."

When the more formal introductions were accomplished, Emma Shrum, the dark-haired girl, nodded to Karola. "I believe my mother called on you earlier this afternoon."

"*Ja,* she did. She was very kind."

"Oh, Mother would never think of allowing anyone to remain a stranger for long in this town." Emma laughed softly. "Not even someone who chooses to attend a different church than my father's."

Ida chimed in. "Emma's father is the Methodist minister."

Karola nodded.

Charlotte White tipped her head and her curious gaze rested on Karola. "And what are your plans, Miss Breit, now that you and Mr. Hirsch aren't to be married? Will you move to Boise or elsewhere?"

"Oh, she plans to stay right here," Ida answered before Karola could. "Miss Breit's moving into the old Lewis cabin and is going to care for the Hirsch children. I'm surprised you hadn't heard."

Charlotte looked at the girl next to her, her eyes suddenly narrowed. "No, I hadn't heard. Did you know about it, Emma?"

Emma didn't so much as glance at Charlotte, appearing as if she hadn't heard the question.

"Well," Ida continued, "it's absolutely the perfect plan for all concerned."

Karola hoped the proprietress was right. All she knew for certain was that it was the *only* plan available to her at the moment. And if this wasn't God's will, she would trust him to stop it from happening.

A loud noise, like something heavy hitting the floor, came from another room at the back of the store. It was followed by a man's angry curses.

"Good heavens!" Ida hurried away, calling, "Henry Noonan, we've got *customers*. Watch your language."

"That'll be the day," Emma said softly, a chuckle in her voice. Then, with another smile at Karola, she added, "I'd better see to my shopping or Mother will wonder what's happened to me. Please excuse me."

"Of course," Karola replied.

"I'm sure I'll see you again soon." With that, Emma headed down one of the aisles.

"Good day, Miss Breit," Charlotte said with a definite lack of warmth. Then she followed her friend.

Karola stared after the two young women, who were whispering to one another again. Had there been a time in her life when she'd had someone with whom she could laugh and whisper and share secrets like that?

Ja. Jakob. A long, long time ago.

She turned and left the store, her steps slow and heavy as she headed toward the hotel.

Jakob leaned over the crib and covered Aislinn with her favorite blanket. She slept on her stomach, her face turned sideways on the mattress, sucking on her thumb. Several women in Shadow

Creek had volunteered pointers on stopping the habit, but he hadn't paid them any mind. He figured she'd stop on her own when the right time came.

Turning from the crib, he stepped to the side of Maeve's child-sized bed. With his fingertips, he brushed her unruly red hair from her face, then bent low to kiss her freckled cheek. Maeve murmured in her sleep before rolling onto her side.

"Happy dreams," Jakob whispered. He walked from the girls' room into Bernard's.

The boy had been asleep no more than fifteen minutes, and already his sheet and blanket were twisted in knots and his nightshirt was bunched underneath his arms. He slept crossways on the mattress, his legs hanging over one side.

Jakob gently repositioned his son on the bed. Then he pulled the bed coverings back into place, knowing they wouldn't stay there long. He ruffled the boy's hair with one hand and kissed his forehead. Bernard was oblivious to it all.

Wouldn't it be nice to sleep that soundly? Jakob thought as he left the boy's bedroom and went down the stairs.

He walked out onto the front porch and settled onto one of the rocking chairs as he stared across the valley to the east. The clouds along the horizon were stained red and orange by the setting sun, and the mountains were a deep blue hue.

Jakob sniffed the air, hoping for the scent of rain. Farming, even with the benefit of the Shadow Creek Irrigation Project, was a gambling proposition. The weather always mattered. So far, spring had cooperated, sun and rain coming in their proper turns.

This year, Jakob had nearly half his acreage in alfalfa, the rest in wheat. They were crops that needed no weeding or tilling and relatively little water and thus were easier to raise for a farmer who was short on extra hands. Some of his neighbors had switched to more labor-intensive—and lucrative—row crops, such as sugar beets and potatoes, but Jakob was sticking with the tried and true. Too many unknowns at present for him to add something else.

In the east, the bright colors faded from the clouds, and the sky and earth blurred together, awash in shades of deepening gray as dusk turned to night. The chirping of crickets filled the air, punctuated occasionally by the deep *ribbet* of a frog.

Tomorrow, he would ride into Shadow Creek for the third time in three days. Yesterday, he'd expected to return with a bride. Tomorrow, he would return with a housekeeper and nursemaid for his children.

Maybe that was for the best. He hoped so. He supposed only time would tell.

Chapter Nine

*E*xcept for the rattle of harness and the creaks and groans of the wagon, the ride from Shadow Creek to the Hirsch farm had been a silent one. Jakob's children had been left for a second day in the care of Lance Bishop, Jakob's part-time farmhand. Lance never complained about that particular duty—he said he liked kids—but Jakob wasn't keen on paying him to watch the children when there was so much other work to be done. Thankfully, after this morning he wouldn't have to worry about it. Now Karola would be there.

He glanced sideways at her and wondered what she was thinking. Did she resent him for his insistence that she repay her passage to America, or did she accept the fairness of the situation? He couldn't be sure. It seemed to him there'd been a time he'd known exactly what Karola thought because they'd been of one mind. Or maybe he'd imagined that. It was all such a long time ago.

He slapped the reins against the broad backsides of the horses. "I'll take you up to the cabin first so we can unload your things. Then we'll go back to the house."

From the corner of his eye, he saw Karola nod.

"I hope you're not expecting much. About the cabin, I mean. It isn't big, but it's solid. I cleaned it as good as I could yesterday and brought up a better mattress and an old chest of drawers that used to belong to Mrs. Lewis, the lady who owned the place before us. I expect you'll do all your eating with the family, so I didn't worry about things like dishes and pans and such."

Karola nodded again.

"I figure you'll mostly just be sleeping there. 'Course, if there's anything you need—"

"I am sure it will be fine, Jakob. Please, do not worry about me." She sounded stoic, resigned.

For some reason, that galled him. *She's right. I've got nothing to apologize for. She won't be doing without.*

Jakob pressed his lips together and didn't speak again for the remainder of the way.

The wagon followed a narrow track of road that passed to the south of the main farmhouse before winding up the slope of the mountain. It wasn't long before the cabin—Karola's new home—came into view. Square and squat, the log structure sat in the center of a small clearing surrounded by tall but scraggly pines.

For a moment, Karola recalled the place she and Jakob used to go, deep in the forest beyond their tiny village. She remembered the dim light that had filtered through the thick tree branches. She could still smell the damp air, and see the greenness of everything around them.

And then, unexpectedly, she remembered something else.

Jakob and Karola sat on a large boulder, surrounded by the dense forest and a denser silence. This was their secret place. Since they were children, they'd come here on Sunday afternoons, sharing their hopes and their dreams.

"I could go with you, Jakob," Karola said softly, a catch in her voice. "We could marry first, and I could go with you to America."

"Your father would never agree. You know that. You're too young, and I have nothing to give you yet."

"But it is not fair that I should have to remain here, just because I am a girl! I could work, too, Jakob. I am strong, and I am a skilled baker like my father."

"Karola." Jakob took her face between his hands, then leaned forward and silenced her with a sweet kiss. When their lips parted, he whispered, "It won't be so long before I send for you. I'll work hard and I'll buy my own land, and then you'll join me and we'll grow rich and fat together."

She felt as if she might die from the pain of his going. What would she do without Jakob? He had been her best friend long before she had fallen in love with him. Jakob understood the things her seventeen-year-old heart longed for. He understood her dreams because they were so much like his own.

"Do not cry, mein Liebling." Jakob kissed her lips again, then brushed the tears from her cheeks with tender fingertips. "Do not cry."

Karola did her best to obey. Swallowing the lump in her throat, she reached into the pocket of her skirt and withdrew a small, round photograph of herself. Until this morning, it had been part of a larger family photograph, sitting on a shelf in her father's office at the back of the bakery. Karola had cut out her likeness to give to Jakob.

"It is for your watch." She sniffed. "So you will not forget me."

Rather than take the photograph, he cupped her face with his hands. "I could never forget you, Karola." His voice was deep, his devotion clear. "And you must remember that you are promised to me."

"I will remember. I promise, Jakob. I will always be yours."

The memory of that day and of those whispered promises was not a welcome one. How awful that her mind would betray her in such a way! It would be better to forget all that had passed between them so long ago. That had been another time, another country—even another Jakob and Karola.

As Jakob drew the team to a halt, the door of the cabin opened, and Jakob's two older children spilled through the doorway, followed a moment later by little Aislinn, who was gripping the index finger of a tall young man, bent low to accommodate her as she toddled forward.

"Da!" Maeve rushed toward the wagon.

"Da!" Bernard echoed, hard on his sister's heels.

Jakob jumped down from his seat.

"Mr. Lance showed us the cabin," Maeve said. "It doesn't look like it did before."

"It had better not." Jakob gave his daughter an affectionate pat on the shoulder before turning toward Karola. "Let's give you the grand tour."

Karola stood, and Jakob stretched out a hand to help her down. The memory of that same hand cupping her face with such tenderness made her reluctant to accept his offer, but she had little choice. To refuse might give too much meaning to her private thoughts.

Neither seemed inclined to hold hands longer than necessary. They separated as soon as her feet touched the ground.

"Karola, this is Lance Bishop. He works for me a few days a week."

"Pleasure to meet you, ma'am." Lance bent the brim of his hat.

"*Danke,* Mr. Bishop."

The young man chuckled. "Mr. Bishop's my father, ma'am. I'd just as soon you called me *Lance,* if you don't mind." His grin was lopsided and infectious.

She smiled in return.

Jakob grunted. "Help me get this trunk inside, will you, Lance?"

"Sure thing."

"Maeve, take your sister's hand," Jakob instructed, and the girl obeyed.

While the two men stepped to the back of the wagon, Karola moved toward the cabin. At the doorway she paused and peeked inside.

The main room had a stone fireplace, large enough for cooking, with what appeared to be an oven built into one side. A box in the nearby corner was stacked high with wood, and the scent of pine filled the room. A small table and two chairs were positioned beneath one of the two narrow, curtainless windows, set high in the walls—one facing north, one facing west. The only other furniture was a wooden rocking chair with an oval-shaped table beside it.

Hearing sounds behind her, Karola entered the cabin and walked across to the bedroom. She stepped through the doorway, then off to one side so she would be out of the way as the men carried in her trunk and set it on the floor at the foot of the bed.

The bedroom was as sparsely furnished as the main room. Here there was the brass-framed bed covered in a yellow-and-white quilt, a large chest of drawers, and a long, narrow table set against one wall, a pitcher and basin in its center. The bedroom had one window; it, too, was curtainless.

Jakob cleared his throat, drawing Karola's attention. "Lance is bringing in the rest of your luggage. We'll leave you to settle in. When you're ready, walk on down to the house." He gestured, as if she could see outside. "You can't get lost. Just follow the path down the hillside. It's no more than half a mile or so. We'll have our lunch when you get there, if that's all right with you."

She nodded.

He looked as if he might say something more, but instead, he turned on his heel and strode out of the house.

Karola stayed where she was until Lance appeared with her bags. He set them next to the trunk, then bent his hat brim to her a second time, saying, "Ma'am," before departing. Finally, alone in the cabin, Karola stepped to the bed, sank onto the edge of the mattress, and listened as the silence closed in around her.

Alone . . .

Rejected . . .

Unwanted . . .

Just as she'd been in Germany.

She was supposed to have been a bride by now. She was supposed to have a home and a husband and be looking forward to children of her own. What had gone wrong? Why hadn't it worked out the way she'd imagined? Why couldn't any of her dreams come true?

She felt a stab of guilt. Her newfound trust that God would see her through hadn't lasted much more than a day. Already she was questioning his will for her life. Already she was doubting that he would handle her disappointments.

She sighed heavily. "Help me."

Moments passed, and then a thought occurred to her. *I was the one who stopped the wedding.*

She straightened a little.

That was true. She was the one who had chosen not to marry a man she didn't love. Jakob hadn't rejected her. She had rejected him. Naturally, she had fond memories. Jakob had been her dearest childhood friend, and she'd loved him when she was young. But everything was different now. She was no longer a girl. She was a woman, and she didn't have to think the way she'd once thought. Why, she should be reveling in her freedom. She was no longer a spinster who lived with her aging parents and worked in her father's bakery. She was an independent woman, unmarried by choice, with limitless possibilities in this wonderful new land. Hadn't Jakob come to America with nothing? Yet look at him now. If she applied herself, couldn't she accomplish the same?

Of course she could.

She rose from the bed, lifted her chin, and squared her shoulders.

Harvest was not such a long time away, and this cabin wasn't such a horrid place. She would repay Jakob because it was the right thing to do. But after the harvest . . . well, anything was possible.

Anything.

Chapter Ten

*K*arola's housekeeping duties included the cooking and baking, the washing and ironing, the dusting, sweeping, and mopping. There were beds to be made and mending to be done and eggs to be gathered. But Karola thought all of that would be easy in comparison to her role as nursemaid, particularly when it came to the eldest Hirsch child.

"My ma was prettier than you." Maeve spoke from the doorway of her brother's bedroom.

Karola turned, clutching the just-removed bedding in her arms. She was certain the girl hadn't meant to hurt her feelings, but she was hurt nonetheless. She did her best to hide it. "Do you look like her, Maeve? You are pretty."

Maeve's chin quivered and her eyes grew bright. She shook her head, then without another word, disappeared down the hallway.

Karola sighed.

It was only her first full day working in Jakob's home, but she wasn't off to a great start. Jakob had left for the fields immediately after breakfast, leaving Karola with only a few instructions. It seemed he'd expected her to simply know what to do as well as where to find whatever she needed. But she didn't know what or where. And now it seemed she'd upset Maeve, perhaps made her cry.

Would it be better to pursue the girl or to leave her be? She didn't know. She couldn't be sure, and so she chose the latter because it was easier.

Karola dropped the sheets and blankets into a pile near the door, then took the clean bedding from the chair where she'd placed them earlier and proceeded to make Bernard's bed.

"My ma was prettier than you."

It wasn't wrong for a child to think her mother prettier than others. In fact, it seemed quite natural. The comment shouldn't have hurt Karola this much. But it did.

She smoothed the top sheet with the palm of her hand while worrying her bottom lip between her teeth.

Karola loved being with and caring for children. She'd wanted a large family of her own, partly because she'd hated being an only child herself. She'd longed for brothers and sisters when she was young.

But loving children didn't guarantee Karola the wisdom she would need when it came to dealing with a little girl who missed her mother.

With a sigh, she lifted the dirty linens and carried them out of the bedroom and down two flights of stairs to the laundry room in the basement, where she dropped them onto the growing pile of dirty clothes and bedding.

When *was* the last time Jakob had washed anything? Karola wondered. Then she tried to imagine her father doing laundry. An impossible image to conjure. Gottfried Breit gave no thought to how or why he had a clean white apron to don each morning as he began his workday. Karola doubted he knew how hard his wife labored to make certain he did.

She pictured her mother then, not scrubbing clothes in a washbasin but down on her knees, her worn Bible open on the bed before her. It was the way Frieda Breit began every day, in an attitude of prayer.

I should ask God to help me with Maeve.

Hadn't she read in her Bible that it was the Lord who gave wisdom and that out of his mouth came knowledge and understanding? Of *course* she should ask him for help. She should have done so earlier.

Quickly, she knelt on the cold, stone floor beside the mound of dirty laundry. Closing her eyes, she bowed her head and clasped her hands before her chest.

Lord, help me to help Maeve. I do not know what to do for her or what to say to her. I can see that she is hurting, but I am not wise enough on my own to know what to do. I need your wisdom, Almighty God. For whatever purpose, you brought me to this family. Help me to do your will in my time with them.

She waited for a brilliant flash of understanding, but none came. It seemed she would be forced to exercise patience as she waited to become wise.

Jakob lifted the control gate, allowing water to spill through the opening and rush along the narrow ditch toward the alfalfa fields. He hoped that within two years he'd have all of his land under irrigation. Maybe then he'd be able to attempt a few more profitable crops.

Not that he hadn't done well with the wheat and alfalfa. He had. But he wouldn't mind a little more money with which to line his pockets as protection against future hard times.

He grabbed the shovel from the ground and followed the ditch toward the east.

In his first year in this valley, Jakob had become actively involved in the fledgling Shadow Creek Irrigation Project. He'd spent many evenings poring over government reports and reading agricultural articles in newspapers and magazines. He knew as

well as any of the farmers in this valley—and better than most—
that irrigation wasn't a solution to all of their ills. It couldn't pre-
vent a drought, and it certainly wasn't effective if a farmer didn't
properly grade his land or if he continually spread too much water
on his fields.

Bradley Mason, who owned the section of land to the south
of the Hirsch farm, was a good case in point. Jakob would be the
first to admit that his neighbor had a heart of gold and was generous to a fault, but Bradley was also unbelievably inept when it
came to understanding the mechanics of irrigation. Try though
he might, no amount of cursing had enabled Bradley to force
water to flow uphill, and it certainly hadn't kept him from finding himself mired up to his knees in mud on more than one occa-
sion due to both seepage and overwatering.

To be fair, Jakob had at times applied too much water to his
land, too. Gauging the exact amount of moisture needed was difficult, if not impossible. There were so many variables to consider—the type of soil, the lay of the land, rain or the lack of it,
temperatures, the particular plants under cultivation. Nature stub-
bornly resisted a farmer's attempts to control and regiment it, and
that went for irrigation, too.

Or maybe it was the farmer who was stubborn, Jakob mused.
He remembered the many times his father had stood at the head
of the table, his sons seated to his left and his right, as he quoted
the Scripture: *"Cursed is the ground for thy sake; in sorrow shalt
thou eat of it all the days of thy life; Thorns also and thistles shall
it bring forth to thee; and thou shalt eat the herb of the field; In
the sweat of thy face shalt thou eat bread, till thou return unto
the ground; for out of it wast thou taken: for dust thou art, and
unto dust shalt thou return."*

He paused in his chores to look upward. "So if the land's
cursed, why do I love it so?"

It was a rhetorical question. Jakob anticipated no response
from the Almighty. He'd never been a man who expected God's

intervention in his life. He didn't doubt God's existence or else he wouldn't be so faithful in his church attendance. But from what he'd seen in life, God let men fend for themselves the best they could. People lived and died while God looked on.

Unto dust shalt thou return . . .

Like Siobhan.

It seemed only yesterday that Aislinn had entered the world as Siobhan left it. And at the same time, it seemed decades ago. Jakob had passed those first weeks and months in a fog of grief. He hadn't believed the people who'd told him time would soften the loss, but they'd been right. Time did have a way of healing the wounds.

He turned, looking toward the farmhouse, wondering how Karola was managing with the housework and the children. He hadn't exactly given her an abundance of instructions, nor had she asked many questions. She'd arrived at dawn, her shoulders wrapped in a shawl against the morning chill, and he'd left her in charge with hardly a greeting.

Not a very decent way to treat the woman he'd intended to make his wife. Would he have interacted with her in the same careless manner had they married?

He found the silent question unsettling. He liked to think he was a better man than that. But then, a better man would have done many things differently than he had, especially when it came to Karola Breit. Many things.

With a scowl, he set off toward the alfalfa fields, hoping some hard manual labor would clear his head.

It mattered little to Theodora Shrum that Jakob Hirsch was Lutheran by church membership. By all rights, Dorotea Joki should be the one visiting the Hirsch farm today, but Theodora knew the woman would never lift a finger to make Karola Breit feel welcome in the community, not since Dorotea's chances of snaring the handsome widower had vanished. Therefore, Theodora took it upon herself to do so, bringing with her not only a number of baked goods provided by a few of the women in the Methodist congregation but also her daughter.

Clucking to the horse, Theodora jiggled the reins, asking him for a bit more speed. "We won't stay long," she said above the rattle of harness. "I'm sure Miss Breit has enough on her hands without feeling she must entertain guests."

"Why do you suppose she did this, Mother?"

Theodora looked at her daughter. "Did what, Emma?"

"Why would Miss Breit choose to work for Mr. Hirsch rather than marry him?"

"I don't know." Theodora had wondered that very thing, but she didn't say so to her daughter. "Of course, no marriage should be entered into lightly."

"Charlotte says it was really Mr. Hirsch who changed his mind. She says once he saw Miss Breit again after all those years he realized he couldn't possibly marry her, and so they pretended it was Miss Breit who stopped the wedding so she could be saved embarrassment. Otherwise, her reputation could have been harmed, and Mr. Hirsch is too honorable to do such a thing. Charlotte says—"

"Charlotte White should be reminded that she who goes about as a talebearer reveals secrets." She gave her daughter a reproving glance. "Gossip is a sin, Emma Shrum, and it is unbecoming for a young lady to participate in it. Miss Breit needs friends in Shadow Creek, not enemies."

Emma blushed. "I'm sorry, Mother. I never meant to be unkind."

"Dear heart," Theodora answered gently, "I know Charlotte has set her cap for Mr. Hirsch. Everyone in town knows it. It galls her that he doesn't seem to notice her. Charlotte is used to getting whatever she wants."

"Her parents do spoil her a bit. Especially her father."

Theodora chuckled at the understatement. "Just a bit."

Emma turned to gaze at the passing countryside. After an extended silence, she said, "I've never told her so, but I think Charlotte would be miserable as Mr. Hirsch's wife. They're all wrong for each other."

"And I think you, Emma, are very, very wise."

Karola had begun helping her father in the bakery when she was no older than Maeve, and it was in the kitchen where she was the most confident. But no matter how accomplished the cook, a woman still needed certain ingredients in order to make a decent meal.

She stood in the center of the kitchen, hands on her hips. What was she to make for supper this first night? There was only a little flour left in the pantry and no sugar or canned goods or butter or lard. Karola had a dozen eggs, thanks to the laying hens, and she'd found potatoes and onions in the fruit cellar, along with a basket of apples. In addition, there was fresh milk in the spring-house and beef, pork, and some kind of game in the smokehouse.

Perhaps if she'd gotten an earlier start, the task of preparing supper wouldn't seem so overwhelming to her now, but she'd spent the past three hours washing pots and dishes and scrubbing the kitchen from top to bottom.

It was at the precise moment tears had begun to well in her eyes that the door chimes sounded, announcing visitors. Maeve and Bernard, who had been coloring with crayons at the kitchen table, bolted for the front of the house. With a sigh of weariness, Karola lifted Aislinn from her high chair and followed after the other two.

As soon as she stepped into the hall, she heard a cheerful greeting.

"Hello, Miss Breit. I hope we haven't come at a bad time." Theodora Shrum didn't wait for an invitation. She entered the house, her arms laden, as were the arms of her daughter, who entered right behind. "We come bearing gifts."

The scent of fresh-baked bread filled the entry hall.

"I took a peek at Mr. Hirsch's pantry not all that long ago," Theodora continued, "and I knew you'd need a few days to get organized."

Karola felt a wave of gratitude wash over her. "*Danke,* Mrs. Shrum."

"No thanks needed. Come along, Emma. We'll take all this straight to the kitchen." She walked past Karola, still talking. "Ida Noonan sent one of her chocolate cakes, a real specialty in these parts, and Laura Gaffney made corned beef hash. Mrs. Thompson, the schoolteacher, sent some canned vegetables, and there's a couple of loaves of bread from my kitchen."

Karola fell into step behind Theodora.

"Emma's got some of Dr. Cooper's apple cider, and Mrs. Denys made a pastry the children are sure to love. And just in case, I brought along some butter, flour, and sugar to see you through until you can do the marketing."

Karola glanced over her shoulder at Emma and was rewarded with a smile. Karola returned it.

"Well, my stars!" Theodora stared at the kitchen. "Haven't you been a busy one?"

Karola stopped, not sure what the woman meant.

"You've made that stove look like new again. I've seen the grime that was cooked on it. You must've been scrubbing for hours." She looked at Karola. "I sure hope that man appreciates what you've done here in one short day." She stepped to the counter and set down the tray laden with food.

Thinking of all there was yet to do, Karola shook her head. "I have not done so much."

"Pish posh! Of course you have. It's no easy thing, keeping a home and caring for children. Believe me, Miss Breit, I know."

Embarrassed by the compliment, Karola sought to change the subject. "May I get you something cool to drink, Mrs. Shrum. There is—"

"No, thank you, dear. Emma and I must head straight back to town. Mr. Shrum is practicing his sermon for tomorrow, and he always works up a tremendous appetite by the time he finishes. He'll be wanting his own supper soon enough."

"But you have come so far only to—"

"It was our pleasure. Isn't that right, Emma?"

"Yes," her daughter answered dutifully as she set her tray on the counter beside the other one.

"I do not know how to thank you properly." Karola looked from Theodora to Emma and back again. "I haven't enough words in English."

Theodora smiled. "You speak wonderfully, Miss Breit. And all the thanks I need is for you not to be a stranger whenever you're in town. You come to see me at the parsonage, and we'll have us a nice visit over a cup of tea."

Karola nodded. "I will not be a stranger, Mrs. Shrum."

"Then I expect us to become good friends, you and I." She smiled. "Perhaps I'll even convince you to attend the Methodist church one of these days."

Karola's eyes widened, and both Theodora and Emma laughed. The merry sound lingered in the house long after they left.

Chapter Eleven

31 May 1908
in care of Jakob Hirsch
Shadow Creek, Idaho

Dear Father and Mother,
It is still early on this Sunday morning, and the sun has yet to rise. There is wood burning in the fireplace, taking the chill from the room. I sit at a small table to write to you by lamplight.

My new home is a two-room cabin on a hillside, a not-too-distant walk from Jakob's house. It is cozy, my cabin, and I am comfortable in it. I do hope I can soon add some touches of my own, perhaps new curtains for the windows and a rag rug for the floor, but those will have to wait.

Yesterday was my first day to work for Jakob. He left early to attend to his farming duties and did not return until late in the day. I was somewhat overwhelmed by all that needs to be done in this motherless home, but by the time I returned to my cabin, I felt a sense of accomplishment. Is that prideful? I hope not. I do not mean for it to be. It is simply that I have never managed a home, and it is good to know that I did not fail.

Little Aislinn, who celebrated her first birthday only a week ago, seems to have taken a great liking to me.

Bernard, who is almost five, is mischievous and quite the charmer. For now he follows mostly in his older sister's footsteps, but it will not be long before he branches out on his own. I think he and I will get on well once we become better acquainted.

It is Maeve who concerns me. She is lonely and confused and much too sad for a child of six years. She misses her mother, and who can blame her? I am praying for wisdom so that in the months I am here I will be of some help to her.

I thought of you often yesterday, Mother, as I tried to bring some order to this big house. I am thankful to God for the parents he gave me. I am thankful for the many things you taught me, and I hope you would be proud of me, could you see my efforts.

I have yet to cook a real meal. Yesterday, one of the women from town brought food to us. A good thing, for I had despaired of finding the necessary ingredients in Jakob's bare pantry. I shudder to think what he has been feeding the children in the months he has been without a housekeeper. To be honest, I do not think he noticed what he ate when he came in from the fields. Weariness was etched deeply into his face. (I do not think you would recognize Jakob. He is much changed from the boy you knew. He has even grown a beard.)

It is clear to me how very much he loves this way of life he has chosen. Or do you suppose it is the way of life that has chosen him?

Does that sound like the dreamy girl who left Steigerhausen, Mother? The one you said always had her head in the clouds? It is not. My feet are firmly on the ground at last. I am remembering all you taught me through the years. I think you would be surprised how much remains. You thought I never listened, but I did.

The words have begun to swim on the page. I am tired and find I cannot keep my eyes open any longer. Today is Sunday, and I will go with Jakob and his children to church in Shadow Creek.

Your loving daughter,
Karola Breit

Chapter Twelve

*O*ver her father's objections, Charlotte White had begun attending services at the Lutheran church in the fall of the previous year. It wasn't for theological or denominational reasons, of course, that Charlotte chose to forsake her family's Methodist roots. No, the reasons were quite secular—and personal—in nature.

His name was Jakob Hirsch.

Charlotte was delighted with this beautiful Sunday morning. Warm and sunny, not even a wisp of clouds in the sky, the weather was perfect for standing outside the church, pretending to visit with other parishioners while she awaited Jakob's arrival. She balanced her pink parasol on her right shoulder, making certain the sun was at her back. The light would create a pretty glow through the delicate fabric.

Pink was definitely her color. Everyone said so.

She wished Jakob would hurry. She did so want him to see her like this, framed by the sunlight. Her rose-colored dress was new, as were her gloves and straw hat, and she had taken special pains with her hair.

Now that his ridiculous plans to marry that German woman had proven fruitless, Jakob would *have* to notice her. He still needed a wife. Everyone knew it. And Charlotte was more determined than ever that she would be the next Mrs. Hirsch. Jakob was handsome and he owned the finest home in the valley. One day it would be *her* home.

"Good morning, Miss White."

Distracted, she glanced in the direction of the familiar male voice. "Oh, hello, Mr. Bishop." She hoped he would take the hint and go away.

She knew, of course, that Lance Bishop was sweet on her, and it wasn't that she didn't normally enjoy his attention. In truth, she rather liked flirting with him. It was fun to see if he became flustered by their exchanges. But she didn't feel like playing that particular game this morning. She had bigger fish to fry.

Without another word, she turned her gaze toward the bend in the road that led into town, looking for that first glimpse of the Hirsch carriage.

"How is your mother today?" Lance was either oblivious to her intentional rudeness or ignoring it. "Better, I hope."

"She's about the same." Her mother was *always* about the same, always suffering from one ailment or another, and it became rather tiresome saying so.

"I'm sorry to hear that. And how's your father?"

Charlotte suppressed a groan, still refusing to look at him. "He's well." *Why don't you go over to the Methodist church and see for yourself?*

Lance cleared his throat. "Please give them my regards."

"I will."

She sensed more than heard his sigh of defeat.

But he tried one more time. "Well, I guess I'll go in. Would you like me to escort you to your pew?"

"No, thank you. I think I'll linger outside a little longer. It's such a pleasant morning. But you go on."

After a moment's hesitation, the young farmer moved toward the church doors, as did everyone else who had been standing outside, visiting with their friends and neighbors.

Charlotte began to despair. Time was running out. She really couldn't wait much longer. Then, as she was about to turn, she caught sight of the Hirsch carriage, just coming into view. She felt a little rush of pleasure, glad that she was standing alone, glad she would be the only person Jakob saw as he drew the horses to a halt.

Her pleasure was short-lived, for though she waited, he never glanced her way. He stepped down from the carriage, then immediately took his younger girl in his arms before helping Karola Breit to the ground. He spoke a soft but firm word of caution to his other two children as they disembarked.

Look at me, Jakob Hirsch. Look at me. I'm here, waiting for you.

With hurried steps, Karola led the way up the walk toward the church entrance, clutching a Bible close to her body with her left arm. When her gaze met with Charlotte's, Karola smiled in shy recognition. Charlotte nodded before looking again at Jakob, but he was bending forward, speaking to his son, and the family passed Charlotte without Jakob even seeming to know she was there.

She would have liked nothing better than to hit him over the head with her pretty pink parasol.

Only an idiot wouldn't have known Charlotte's reasons for standing outside the church the way she did.

Lance Bishop was no idiot.

But how did a fella make a pretty girl like Charlotte notice him when she was all moony-eyed over somebody else, especially when the man was Jakob Hirsch?

Lance's one consolation had been knowing Jakob meant to marry Karola Breit when she arrived from Germany. Only now Jakob wasn't going to marry Karola. What would happen if Jakob took a shine to Charlotte after all and decided to ask her to marry him? Lance would lose a friend, mentor, and employer, *and* the girl he loved, that's what. He'd have to sell his land and leave. He wouldn't be able to stay in the valley if Jakob and Charlotte married.

He slumped in the pew as Pastor Joki began to speak, too miserable to listen.

He remembered the first time he'd seen Charlotte White. A newcomer to the valley, he'd brought a plow horse to the blacksmith to be shod, and there she'd been, talking to her father. She was the prettiest creature he'd ever laid eyes on. He'd believed right then and there that she was the girl God wanted him to have for his wife, just as soon as she was old enough to wed and he had a decent house built. Well, at eighteen she was old enough, and Lance now had a house on his forty-acre farm.

But a lot of good that did him when she wouldn't give him the time of day. He didn't want to consider that he might have heard wrong, that maybe Charlotte was the wife *he* wanted rather than the one God wanted for him.

Half a beat behind the rest of the congregation, Lance rose and reached for the hymnal as Dorotea Joki pounded out the strains of "A Mighty Fortress Is Our God."

Jakob sensed the curious gazes from all around the sanctuary. He was tempted to stand up and tell everyone to mind their own business and leave him to his. He didn't, of course.

Besides, could he blame folks for their curiosity? Jakob had kept his marriage plans to himself until shortly before Karola arrived, and just as the townsfolk were getting used to that idea, the wedding was called off. Then, to complicate things, his intended bride became his housekeeper. If he were in their shoes, he guessed he'd be curious too.

He glanced to his left. Karola, seated on the other side of his three children, was listening intently to Pastor Joki. Personally,

Jakob had never found Rick's sermons to be very inspiring, but Karola seemed to think otherwise.

And, come to think of it, she looked mighty pretty with that rapt expression on her face, her blue eyes sparkling with interest, a pale pink glow on her cheeks.

He frowned, suddenly suspecting that most of those curious gazes he'd sensed behind him belonged to men. That notion didn't sit well with him. Why would it? The last thing he needed was for Karola to decide to marry somebody else and leave him in the lurch.

It seemed to Karola that the pastor's sermon had been prepared especially for her. Every word shot straight to her heart. As she listened, she felt exhilarated and encouraged, challenged and comforted, and she was more determined than ever to do what God had brought her to this place to do. She would draw closer to him. She would love and nurture Jakob's motherless children. Silently she renewed her promise that she would keep her eyes on Christ and not be swayed by the things of this world. She would be heavenly minded in all her ways.

When the service ended, she felt ready for anything.

Outside, members of the congregation pressed in to meet Karola. Her head was quickly spinning with names and faces, and she knew she would never remember them all when next she came to town. And while her English was excellent, there were some people whom she simply could not understand, no matter how hard she concentrated on their words.

But Karola *did* understand Charlotte White. Not her words, for she did not speak to Karola. No, it was Charlotte's attentiveness to Jakob that spoke volumes. The way she smiled up at him, her glance both hopeful and coquettish. The way she briefly rested her gloved fingers on his forearm, not long enough to be improper but long enough to subtly declare her intent.

Oddly upset by the gesture, Karola pretended interest in what someone—she hadn't a clue the woman's name—was saying to her.

"Saints be praised!" Tulley Gaffney's familiar voice boomed out. "You're still here then."

Karola turned to see the Irishman crossing the street, coming from the hotel.

The jovial man smiled broadly and winked at her, then looked at Jakob who was standing with Charlotte a short distance to Karola's right. "Sure, and you haven't forgotten you're to eat with us, Jakob. You and Miss Breit and the children."

"Well, I . . . we—," Jakob began.

"I told me daughter-in-law that you'd not forgot and 'twas only that your Lutheran service went longer than the mass." He bobbed his head at Charlotte. "You'll be excusin' us, Miss White, but Laura says I must bring the entire Hirsch family immediately before the food grows cold." He turned toward Karola and offered her his arm. "Come along, Miss Breit. You, too, children. Your cousin Laura's fixed a special treat for you, and 'twould not be good to keep her waitin'."

Karola took his proffered arm, deciding she liked Tulley Gaffney a little more every time they met.

They walked arm-in-arm toward the hotel, Maeve and Bernard running ahead of them, Jakob with Aislinn in his arms bringing up the rear.

"And how are you findin' things at Jakob's farm?" Tulley asked in a conspiratorial voice. Then he laughed. "No, don't be tellin' me. I can but imagine. The man knows his way around the land and his animals. There's no denyin' it. But he's a poor house-keeper and a worse cook. I've seen and tasted for meself. 'Tis a wonder they've not all starved to death before you came to their rescue, Miss Breit. A real wonder."

Karola thought of the bare pantry and the piles of laundry in the basement. "Mrs. Shrum brought us a great deal of food yesterday. The children loved Laura's hash."

"Aye, they would that. 'Tis a favorite."

"Then I must ask for her recipe."

"Glad she'll be to give it to you, too."

They arrived at the front entrance of the hotel moments after the children had disappeared through the doorway.

Tulley motioned for Karola to enter before him. "Laura's in the kitchen. The wee ones will already be with her, if I know them at all, lookin' for sweets. I'll be waitin' here for Jakob."

Karola glanced over her shoulder to discover Jakob had stopped on the opposite side of Main Street and was engaged once again in conversation with Charlotte White.

It surprised Karola how thoroughly she could dislike someone she barely knew. Rather than ponder the cause, she turned and entered the hotel.

In the restaurant's large kitchen, Karola found Laura handing a stack of plates to Maeve. The woman's cheeks were flushed from the heat of the stove, and stray wisps of hair clung to the back of her damp neck.

"Guten Tag," Karola said to announce herself.

Laura glanced toward the door and offered Karola a tired smile. Then to Maeve, she said, "You and your brother set the table now. That's a dear."

"May I be of help?" Karola asked.

"I'm helping Cousin Laura."

"Me, too," Bernard said.

"I was about to carry the food to the table. Perhaps—" Laura stopped abruptly as the color drained from her face.

"Laura?" Karola hurried toward her, reaching to take hold of her elbow. "What is it?"

"I . . . oh, my." She swayed from side to side, looking as pale as a sheet.

Tightening her grasp on Laura's arm, Karola steered her toward a nearby chair. "Sit down."

Laura obeyed the gentle command.

Maeve came to stare at her. "What's wrong?"

Ignoring the girl's question, Karola slid her hand from Laura's arm to her shoulder. "Lean forward. Breathe deeply. Not too fast. That is better."

Laura groaned, the sound nearly inaudible. Then her eyes rolled back in their sockets an instant before her lids closed. She pitched forward.

Karola caught her before she could fall off the chair. "Maeve! Run get your father. Quick!"

Out of the corner of her eye, Karola saw Maeve thrust the plates into her brother's arms before she raced away. One of the plates slid to the floor and shattered.

Moments later, Jakob and Tulley rushed in from the dining room, and at the same time, Ian Gaffney entered through the back door. All three men spoke at the same time.

"What happened?"

"What's wrong?"

"Laura!"

Ian took his wife into his arms and eased her to the floor while Karola went to moisten a cloth in the sink. When she returned, she knelt beside Laura and offered the cool cloth to Ian.

He leaned over Laura and spoke softly as he placed the cloth on her forehead. "Come 'round, love. Hear me? Open your eyes, me darlin' girl."

Laura's eyelids fluttered, and she moaned.

"That's right," her husband said. "Open your eyes now."

Slowly, she did.

Ian smiled his relief. "You've given us quite a scare, love."

"What happened?"

Karola said, "You fainted."

"Fainted?" Laura rolled her head toward Karola. "Don't be silly. I never faint."

Ian released a humorless chuckle. "Then you'll be tellin' us, please, what it is you're doin' here, lyin' on your back on the kitchen floor."

She hesitated before answering. "I haven't the foggiest notion, Ian Gaffney." She frowned as she drew a deep breath. "But I didn't faint. Now, help me up. Our dinner's growing cold."

"The dinner can wait." Still kneeling, Ian lifted Laura into his arms, then stood. "You'll be stayin' in bed until the doctor has a look at you." He glanced toward Tulley. "Da, will you go for Doc Cooper?"

"Aye, I'm already on me way."

Laura began to protest. "Ian—"

"'Tis no use arguing with me, darlin'. You'll not be movin' until the doctor says you may." With those words, he carried her from the kitchen.

Karola felt a hand cup her elbow, and she looked up into Jakob's worried gaze. As he helped her stand, she answered his unspoken question with a slight shake of her head. Then she heard a sob and glanced toward the sound.

There stood Bernard, tears streaming down his face, still balancing the rest of the plates in his arms, shattered pieces of the one he had dropped surrounding him on the floor.

She hurried to him. "Do not be frightened, Bernard. Your cousin will be feeling herself very soon." She hoped she was telling the truth. *Please, God, let my words be true.*

"I didn't mean to break it," he choked out in a pitifully small voice. "It . . . it slipped."

Her heart caught in her chest as she took the stack of plates, set them on the table, then knelt amid the shards and gathered the boy into a close embrace. "The plate can be replaced, Bernard. We know it was an accident. It does not matter that it is broken. Do not cry." She kissed his cheek. "Do not cry."

"Da?" Maeve sounded near tears herself. "Is Miss Karola right? Will Cousin Laura be okay?"

"Yes, she will be."

Karola could only hope Jakob's response sounded far more confident in their ears than it did in hers.

Chapter Thirteen

———— ⚑ ————

*A*s it happened, both Jakob and Karola were right in what they told the children. Laura was perfectly healthy, according to Dr. Cooper.

By the time the Hirsch carriage headed back to the farm, the joyous news was spreading throughout Shadow Creek—Laura and Ian Gaffney were expecting their first child.

Monday morning, as Karola walked from cabin to farmhouse, she paused halfway down the hillside to stare upward, watching the sky as it changed from darkness to light, from gray to blue. She listened to dozens—perhaps hundreds—of tiny finches chirping in nearby trees and saw the limbs bounce and sway as the birds hopped from branch to branch.

Overwhelming joy burst within her, and she smiled, threw out her arms, and spun around in circles.

"Thank you, God, for this day!"

Her mother had often told her there was no joy to compare with the joy of the Lord, the joy of a believer who trusted in Jesus. Karola hadn't understood what she meant then, and she wasn't sure she understood fully yet. All she knew was that she was different. Inside. In her heart.

And she wasn't alone. For years she'd felt utterly alone, rejected, unwanted. But no more. Even in her solitary little cabin in this brand-new land, so far from her parents and the people she'd known all of her life, she'd discovered she wasn't alone. The rejection, the shame, that she'd felt even just a few days before had been lifted from her heart by a divine hand.

Still smiling, she continued down the hillside. "I do not know how you did it, Father God, but I thank you for setting me free."

One of Jakob's dogs trotted over to meet her as she entered the barnyard. She paused a moment to lean down and stroke its head.

"*Guten Morgen.*" Her greeting was rewarded with a rapid wag of its tail.

Catching a whiff of frying bacon, she straightened and looked toward the house. Light fell through the kitchen window in a welcoming glow. But was she truly welcome there? She wondered if Jakob would rush out to do his chores the instant he saw her, the way he had the first morning.

When she entered the kitchen a few moments later, she found Jakob standing at the stove, clad in scuffed black boots and trousers that had been patched at the knees. His red plaid shirt was tucked into the waistband of his pants, but his suspenders hung down at his thighs, as if he'd forgotten to finish dressing in his haste to prepare something to eat. His hair was mussed, his jaw unshaven.

Looking at him, Karola felt the strangest fluttering in her belly.

Jakob cast a glance in her direction as the door closed behind her. "Morning. Care for a fried egg?"

She swallowed hard. "*Ja. Danke.* But let me help you."

"No need. Even I can fry bacon and eggs." He motioned with his head. "Coffee's done perking. Help yourself."

"*Danke,*" she said again, then went to the cupboard, glad for a reason not to look at him and troubled that she needed one.

"Have you got everything you need up at the cabin?" Jakob spoke over his shoulder. "Staying warm enough at night?"

"*Ja.*" She took a large mug from the shelf. "It is quite cozy."

He cracked an eggshell on the side of the skillet. Grease splattered and popped as the egg dropped into the pan. Raising his voice above the noise, he said, "I figured you're going to need to buy some supplies. I know the pantry's in poor shape, and those things the ladies sent out are near gone."

Thank heaven she hadn't had to point this out to him.

Jakob cracked three more eggs in succession. "I should have seen to it the day I brought you out from town, but I guess I had other things on my mind." He reached for the saltshaker. "I'll hitch up the wagon for you whenever you want to go."

Using a dishtowel to protect her hand, she took the coffeepot from the stove. "Whenever it is best for you, Jakob."

"Me? No, thanks. I've made way too many trips into town as it is lately."

She turned to stare at him. "But, Jakob, I know nothing about horses and wagons. I would not know how to control the animals."

His disbelief was plain. "You've *never* driven a wagon?"

"*Nein.* Never."

He muttered something under his breath.

"I am sorry, Jakob."

"It's not your fault." Both his tone and his expression belied his words.

She returned the coffeepot to the stove, the mug still empty. "Father never owned a horse."

"I thought after all this time that—" He gave his head a shake. "I guess I'll have to teach you, but not today. Lance can take you to town when he gets here."

Jakob felt about an inch tall. There wasn't any good reason for talking to Karola in such a sharp tone, and yet it seemed he did it every time they were together. One minute a smile would be lifting the corners of her pretty, bow-shaped mouth, and the next something he said would wipe it away. When she'd entered the kitchen this morning, she'd looked happy. There'd been a sparkle in her blue eyes that seemed to brighten the entire room. Even he'd felt brighter for a moment. It had seemed right that she was with him in that early morning hour. He'd felt an unmistakable desire to kiss her smiling lips, as if there would have been a rightness in that, too.

But it wouldn't have been right. She'd made that clear when she called off their wedding.

Maybe that was why he spoke to her so sharply. Maybe he wanted her to be miserable instead of happy. Maybe he was punishing her. If so, he knew that wasn't fair of him. Karola was doing her best in a less-than-perfect situation. She could have refused to help him out. There wouldn't have been much he could do about it if she had. So why didn't he show her a little appreciation? Had he really become so hardened by the circumstances of life that there was no kindness left in him?

Calling himself several kinds of a fool, he scooped the fried eggs from the skillet and added them to the plates that already held crisp strips of bacon and several slices of toast. Then he carried the plates to the kitchen table. "Let's eat while it's hot."

Karola sat opposite him, her gaze downcast. She looked so sad.

Jakob wished for a way to put the sparkle back into her eyes and the smile back on her lips. At one time taking her in his arms and kissing her would have done the trick, but that wasn't the answer now. Not knowing what else to do, he settled for speaking a brief thanks over the food, then reached for his fork and began to eat. As soon as he was done, he excused himself and headed outside, eager to get on with his morning chores.

Or was his haste really because he wanted to escape Karola's disturbing presence?

Karola was glad to see Jakob go.

His words and tone of voice had hurt. Clearly she was more of a burden than a help because of her inability to drive a team of horses into town. But what caused her the most discomfort was the way her heart had skittered whenever their gazes met, no matter how briefly.

I am not a silly schoolgirl, she reminded herself as she hid her face in her hands while resting her elbows on the table. *I will not act like one.*

Lowering her hands, Karola drew a deep breath. "I would not be here if not for my promise to let you lead me, Father. Do not let me lose sight of my work. Do not let me make a fool of myself again."

"Who you talkin' to?"

With a start, Karola twisted on her chair. Maeve stood near the kitchen doorway, her hair all in tangles, her eyes sleepy pools of green. Her nightgown hit her at midcalf, and her feet were bare.

"I was talking to God," Karola answered.

Maeve frowned.

"I am only now learning to do that. To ask God for help."

"What you need help with?"

"With everything, it seems." Karola knew her smile was sad. "With everything."

One day at a time, Karola restored order to the Hirsch household.

On Monday, she returned from her trip to town with an abundance of foods with which to restock the pantry shelves. That evening, she prepared what she considered her first real meal. It was only a stew made with beef, stewed tomatoes, chunks of potatoes and carrots, and chopped onions, served with biscuits and an apple pie for dessert. But watching Jakob and the children devour the food gave her an enormous sense of accomplishment.

On Tuesday, Karola tackled the task hated by women around the world—the laundry. After a night of soaking soiled linens and clothing in tubs filled with warm water, she hauled heated water from the stove to the basement, then washed each item in a suds bath, rubbing them vigorously against a washboard. She scrubbed and wrung and rinsed and dipped in bluing, then wrung again and starched and wrung again. And finally, she placed the heavy load of damp linens and clothes in a large basket and hauled them up the stairs to hang outdoors on the line.

On Wednesday, she ironed. And ironed and ironed and ironed. And as she did so, she wondered what on earth had possessed her to think she wanted a dozen children when only three and their father could create so much work.

On Thursday, Karola mended. She was glad for a reason to sit for any length of time. Normally, she enjoyed needlework. However, darning a basketload of socks and underwear wasn't the same thing as making a new dress or cross-stitching a pillow cover. To help pass the time, Karola told stories to the children.

On Friday, Karola set to work on the family garden. It was a little late in the spring, but she hoped she would be able to put up canned fruits and vegetables for the family to enjoy through the winter. Maeve and Bernard helped by plucking rocks from the dirt as Karola hoed the soil. Aislinn's contribution was to eat an earthworm while getting as filthy as possible.

Each day of the week, as Karola fell more and more in love with these children, she prayed, asking God to protect her from her own willful nature, asking him to keep her feet firmly planted on the ground and not to act foolishly about Jakob a second time.

Chapter Fourteen

*J*akob had decided Karola should learn to ride astride before she worried about driving a team. She hadn't protested until he gave her a pair of trousers.

"I cannot wear those!"

He'd stared at her. "Why not? They'll be too big, but you can roll up the legs and cinch the waist with a rope."

"I cannot wear them because . . . because they are not proper."

Sounding as impatient as he felt, he'd said, "A woman in trousers isn't so unheard of in these parts. Siobhan wore them whenever she helped me in the fields or when she went riding. You sure can't ride astride in one of your dresses. Unless you plan to hike your skirts up around your thighs, that is."

She'd blushed the brightest shade of red he'd ever seen and had not argued with him further.

Now, seeing Karola's wide eyes as she stared at the horse in the corral, Jakob realized she wasn't merely unsure about the propriety of a woman wearing pants. She was scared to death of the horse itself.

"General's as gentle as a kitten," Jakob reassured her.

Karola glanced up at him, disbelief shining in her eyes.

"Maeve and Bernard both learned to ride on General," he added.

She turned her gaze to where the children were standing nearby. "You did?"

They nodded.

Maeve looked at her as though she were the silliest woman she'd ever seen. "We ride General all the time."

Bernard added, "Yeah. All the time."

Karola looked toward the corral again. "They can ride *that* horse? But he is so big."

"They've been riding him since they weren't much older than Aislinn."

She worried her lower lip with her teeth for a few moments. "You would not allow the children to do anything unsafe."

"You're right. I wouldn't." He paused. "I wouldn't allow you to do anything unsafe either."

Again she looked at him, and it seemed to Jakob there was something new swirling in her blue eyes. Trust, perhaps?

It surprised him that he wanted it to be. He'd given her so few reasons to trust him since she'd arrived in Shadow Creek. He'd demanded and he'd ordered and he'd snapped at her in anger and frustration. He'd even embarrassed her with his hiked-up-skirts remark. No, he had little reason to hope for her to trust him. Yet he did.

As if in response to his private thoughts, she gave him the smallest of smiles. "Then I am ready, Jakob."

He felt a sudden and nearly uncontrollable urge to brush back the stray wisps of golden hair from her pretty face. He wanted to touch the smooth skin of her cheek with his fingertips. He wanted to tell her she looked adorable in a shirt that was much too large and the trousers that were turned up at the hem. Perhaps he would have acted on his desires if Lance hadn't strolled out of the barn right then.

"Hey, boss, ain't you got that nag saddled for Miss Breit yet?"

Jakob took a quick step back from Karola. "Not yet." His

voice cracked when he spoke, and he hoped the young farm-hand—and Karola—hadn't noticed.

Arriving at the corral, Lance smiled at Karola. "There's nothing to riding a horse, ma'am. You just relax and do what Jakob tells you, and you'll be fine. He'll have you ridin' like you been doing it all your life in no time at all."

Jakob opened the corral gate and moved through the opening, then glanced over his shoulder at Karola. Understanding his unspoken request, she followed him, and he closed the gate behind her.

With a soft nicker of welcome, General came toward them. Karola quickstepped closer to Jakob's side—as if she could be trampled by a horse that was moving at a snail's pace!

"He's hoping we'll have a treat for him," Jakob explained. "He's a real beggar, this one. Sugar, apples, carrots, oats, whatever he can get."

General stopped, nickered again, then nudged Jakob's chest with his muzzle.

Jakob patted General's neck. "Nothing this time, old boy." He glanced at Karola. "At one time, according to my father-in-law, General was the fastest horse in six counties. Sweeney used to race anybody who was willing to make a wager, and most of the time, he would come away with the pot, too. But General took a bad fall a few years back, while we were still in Wyoming, and his racing days ended. That's when he became the children's horse."

Tentatively, Karola reached out and stroked General's forehead.

"Nothing ever spooks this fella," Jakob continued, "but it's best not to make sudden movements around any horse. Talk to them as if they understand you. They may not know the words, but they can tell plenty by your voice. If you're calm, they're likely to be calm, too."

A gust of wind raised a dust devil in the center of the corral and a shadow fell across the earth. Jakob looked up, surprised to find broiling black clouds whipping across the sky from west to east.

"Sorry, Karola. We'll have to put off this lesson. Looks like we've got some weather blowing in."

Never in her life had Karola seen such a storm.

The furious wind slammed into the side of Jakob's house, causing it to shudder and shake as if hit by a giant fist. The midday darkness brought by the storm clouds was broken only by blinding flashes of lightning that forked from heaven to earth. The loud, rolling thunder that followed seemed endless.

Seated between Maeve and Bernard on the parlor sofa, Karola tried not to jump at each new bolt of lightning, each new crack of thunder, each new gust of wind. She knew the older children were frightened, and she wanted desperately not to make them more so. Aislinn, on the other hand, seemed to be enjoying the storm. She sat on the floor in front of the sofa, playing with some colored blocks, pausing to look up whenever a flash of lightning brightened the room, then laughing when the subsequent thunder roared.

O God, let it end soon. Give me peace so I will not make the children even more afraid. Let me be like Aislinn, fearless in the face of this storm.

Another flash lit up the parlor, followed almost instantaneously by a deafening clap of thunder. Maeve shrieked and buried her face against Karola's left side. Bernard started to cry and hid his face against Karola's right side.

That's when God answered her prayer. His peace settled over her like a familiar quilt.

"Do not be afraid, little ones," she said softly. "It is only the bad temper of the clouds you hear. They are shouting at the lightning for being so bright. The same way you shout when you are angry at one another." She tightened her arms around Maeve and Bernard. "Would you like me to tell you a story to make you forget the storm?"

"Yes," came Maeve's muffled voice.

"Yes." Bernard's echo was followed by a noisy and very wet sniff.

"All right. Let us see now. What story shall I tell this time?"

Maeve peeked up from her hiding place. "Can you tell us the one about Briar Rose again? I liked it the best."

"If that is what you wish, Maeve, I will tell it. It is a favorite of mine, too."

Lightning flashed again. Thunder shook the house. The children pressed closer to Karola's sides, and she gave them each a smile of encouragement.

"A long, long time ago," she began, "there was a king and queen who had no children, though they wanted a child very much. One day when the queen was bathing, an enchanted frog came out of the water and said to her, 'You will soon have your wish. Before a year passes you will have a daughter.'"

"That's Briar Rose." Bernard's cheeks were still tear-streaked, but the terror had left his eyes.

"*Ja*, but she was not called that until later in the story."

Maeve leaned forward and scowled at her brother. "Just listen."

He stuck out his tongue.

Karola hid a smile.

"Go on," Maeve said.

"The queen did have a beautiful little girl, as the frog had promised. The king was so filled with joy, he gave a great feast and invited nearly everyone he knew. Now there were thirteen fairies who lived in the kingdom and—"

"Da says there's no such thing as fairies and leprechauns and such," Maeve interjected.

"*Ja,* your father tells you the truth. It is make-believe, this story."

Bernard leaned forward. "Just *listen.*" It was a dead-on imitation of his sister.

To hide her amusement, Karola pretended to clear her throat. "Where was I? Oh, I remember. Because the king and queen had only twelve gold plates and there were thirteen fairies, one of them could not be invited. And so the day of the feast arrived. It was splendid in every way. When the feasting was done, the twelve fairies began to bestow gifts upon the baby princess. One gave her beauty, and one gave her virtue, and one gave her riches, and so on. Each gift was more splendid than the one before. But before the twelfth fairy could bestow her gift, the uninvited thirteenth fairy appeared in the banquet hall. She was in a horrible fury."

As if on cue, thunder crashed outside. The children pressed closer but this time didn't make a sound.

"The thirteenth fairy's voice boomed like thunder and frightened all the people. Do you suppose that was the thirteenth fairy we heard? Did she frighten you, too?"

"Yes!" Maeve and Bernard answered in unison, then both giggled.

Jakob stood outside the parlor, listening as Karola told her story of the sleeping princess who would become known as Briar Rose. He was not a man given to flights of fancy—and that included the telling of fairy tales. Still, there was something captivating about Karola's voice.

At some point, about the time the princess pricked her finger and fell into a deep sleep, along with the king and queen and the entire court, Jakob realized the thunder had grown distant. By the time the hedge of briars had grown up around the castle, keeping out all the princes of neighboring kingdoms who sought to find the princess and break the evil spell, the wind had died down. And by the end of the hundred-year sleep, when the last prince found the briars had turned to flowers so he could pass through unharmed, Jakob heard rain splashing against the windows.

He eased forward and looked into the parlor. Karola sat on the sofa, a child on each side. Aislinn, seeming to hang on every word, stood in front of Karola, her hands on Karola's knees. The scene was so much like a family it made his heart catch. A family—not just as his once had been, but as it might have been if only Karola had married him.

"The castle was strangely quiet," Karola continued in a near whisper. "All the prince could hear was his own breathing. Everything in the castle was asleep, from the cook in the kitchen to the king and queen in their royal quarters to the horses in the stables to the doves on the ramparts to the flies on the wall. At last, the prince reached the tower and saw the sleeping princess. She was so beautiful, he could not take his eyes off of her . . ."

Jakob knew how the prince felt. He seemed unable to take his eyes off Karola as well. She looked incongruously beautiful in that oversized man's shirt and the too-long britches. Her pale hair had pulled free from her hairpins and fell about her shoulders in delightful disarray.

"Impulsively, the prince bent down and gave the sleeping princess a kiss . . ."

Hadn't Karola's kisses been as sweet as honey? In Jakob's memory, it seemed so.

"The moment the prince kissed Briar Rose, the spell was broken and her eyes opened. When she awakened, so did everyone and everything in the castle—the king and queen and the courtiers and the cook and the maid and the doves and the horses and the flies. Even the fire stood up and began to flicker under the cooking pots in the kitchen." Karola smiled at the children, one at a time, and they grinned back. "And so the prince and Briar

Rose were married, and they lived happily for the rest of their lives."

Jakob stepped fully into the parlor doorway and applauded. Karola glanced up, wide-eyed, and her smile instantly vanished from her lips.

"Da!" Maeve slid from the sofa and ran toward him. "Did you hear? Isn't it a pretty story?"

"I heard." She threw her arms around his waist, and he gave her back a pat. But his gaze never left Karola. "It's a pretty story. The Brothers Grimm. Correct?"

"*Ja.*" Patches of pink stained her cheeks. "I did not hear you come in, Jakob."

"I didn't want to interrupt the performance."

Bernard ran to Jakob. "I like the part about the frog the best. It was . . . What's the word?"

Jakob tousled his hair. "Enchanted."

"Yeah. En*chan*ted."

Aislinn deserted Karola next, taking a few steps toward her father before dropping to her knees for a faster crawl. As his younger daughter approached, Jakob moved forward, bent down, and scooped her into his arms.

"And you, Aislinn. How did you like Karola's story?"

"Kay-ro!" the toddler cried with glee as she twisted and pointed toward the sofa. "Kay-ro story!"

Up until now, Aislinn's talking skills had consisted of *no, Da-Da,* and plenty of indecipherable babble. But there was no mistaking her meaning now, and for some reason, it seemed fitting to Jakob that this milestone should have something to do with Karola Breit.

He thought to tell her so, but the front door burst open suddenly, revealing a rain-drenched Lance Bishop.

"Jakob! There's been an accident over at the Mason place. A tree blew down in the storm, and Brad's caught under it. I ran into his oldest boy, Tommy, on the way back to my place. We need your help."

"I'll saddle my horse."

Jakob turned his head to look toward the sofa, but Karola was already at his side, wordlessly holding out her arms to take Aislinn. Her eyes were filled with concern. *I will see to the children,* they seemed to say. *You must take care of yourself.*

As he passed his child to Karola, Jakob wished he could take hold of Karola's small but capable hands. He wished he knew the words to tell her how glad he was she was there with him. He wanted to tell her—

"We need to hurry."

Lance's urgency pulled Jakob from his wayward thoughts. With a strange sense of regret, he tore his gaze from Karola. "I'm ready. Let's go."

Chapter Fifteen

he rain had slowed to a drizzle and the wind had died down by the time Jakob and Lance arrived at the Mason farm. Geraldine Mason met them in the barnyard. Her hair was plastered to her scalp; her wet dress clung to her skin.

She grabbed the reins of Jakob's horse. "They're up along Dooley Creek." She pointed with her free arm. "Woodrow's trying to get Bradley free. I sent Tommy to town for the doctor and any help he can get."

"Don't worry, Mrs. Mason," Lance said. "We'll get him home to you. He's gonna be okay."

It was a rash promise, one Jakob wouldn't have made, and he was sorry the younger man had. He'd learned the hard way that things didn't always come out okay, no matter how much a man might wish it so, no matter the effort he made.

"We'll do our best," Jakob said.

She nodded, then released her hold on the reins and stepped back to let them pass.

Putting heels to their horses' ribs, the two men cantered away from the house and up the gentle slope of land toward the tree-lined creek that curled along the southern border of the farm.

They saw the team of horses first, standing idly in their traces, then they saw the fallen cottonwood tree, its roots exposed, stretched across the swollen creek.

Woodrow, Bradley's younger brother, saw them at the same moment. He stood tall and waved. "Here! We're over here!"

Jakob was quick to assess the situation. Bradley—a man close to Jakob's age and about the same height and weight—was lying on the bank of the creek, his left leg in the water, his right leg hidden from view beneath the tree. His face was pale and drawn, his eyes squeezed closed. He was shivering, though whether from cold or from pain or both, Jakob couldn't be sure.

"Thank God you're here," Woodrow said as he approached them.

Jakob dismounted. "I brought my saw." How long would it take to use the two-man crosscut to saw through the thick base of the tree? Maybe too long, judging by the look of the man.

"We were pulling an old stump when the storm blew in." Woodrow couldn't seem to stop talking. "Brad just unhitched the team when a blast of wind hit us. I never felt anything like it before. The horses spooked, and me and Tommy ran after them. Then I heard Brad's shout and a loud noise. Loud as thunder."

Lance and Jakob moved to opposite sides of the tree, as close to Bradley as they could stand, then began to saw.

"I turned"—Woodrow's voice rose above the sound of the saw—"and saw this tree was down and my brother caught under it. I sent Tommy to get help, then tried to dig him out, but the ground's too hard."

Bradley groaned, and Jakob paused to glanced down. His neighbor stared at him with fevered eyes, and Jakob wasn't sure Bradley recognized him.

"Hold on," Jakob said loudly. Then to Lance, in a softer voice, he said, "We'd better work fast."

Karola stood on the front porch, clutching a shawl about her shoulders, watching the angry sky. The wind had picked up again, and the temperature had plunged a good fifteen degrees, maybe more.

She shivered, turned, and went back inside.

She wished she and the children had gone with Jakob. She didn't know the injured man or his wife, but perhaps she could have been of some help. As it was, she could only wait and wonder what was happening. It made the minutes drag like hours. At least the children didn't seem to notice. They were at play upstairs in the girls' room, the storm apparently forgotten.

As she walked toward the kitchen, she prayed. "Father, help Jakob and the others. Give the men strength and wisdom. I do not know what is happening, but you do. I do not know how to pray, but you already know the answers. And, Lord, let me feel your peace again."

Yes, she needed peace—and not only because of the storm and the accident on the neighboring farm.

"I have lost the battle about Jakob, Lord. I have lost my heart to him. I tried not to, but I have. I know I am headstrong and willful and a dreamer. I know I came to America for all the wrong reasons. But I also know you had a higher purpose in bringing me here. I want your purpose, your will to be done." She sighed. "But is it so terrible that I should love him a second time? Really love him. And love his children, too."

She stood at the sink and looked out the window. The clouds were heavy and black as ink, and they raced across the heavens with ferocious speed. The storm seemed to be renewing itself, and a flutter of fear quickened her heart.

Protect him, Lord.

Jakob supposed it was a kind of miracle that they were able to free Bradley Mason so quickly. He supposed it was also some kind of miracle that he stood holding Bradley in his arms while Woodrow went for the horses. Otherwise, it might have been him walking across that clearing.

There was a split second of awareness when the whole world seemed to be enveloped by a searing white light, a split second more when he realized he was flying backward, knocked off his feet by some unseen power. And then all was darkness.

There would never be a time in Jakob's future when he didn't recall awakening to this overpowering, pungent smell. His head ached, and his body felt as if it had been kicked by a mule. As he sat up, he saw a man's boot on the ground a few yards away. It was smoldering. Jakob glanced at his feet. He was wearing both of his boots.

He heard a groan and looked to his right where Bradley lay on his back in the wet field grass, his right pant leg torn and muddied. He, too, had on both of his boots.

Jakob managed to rise, stumbled slightly, then righted himself.

It took him awhile to find another body lying several yards beyond Bradley. It was Woodrow. And suddenly Jakob's mind identified the acrid smell that sickened him: burning flesh. The boot had belonged to Woodrow. He must have been blown out of his shoes by the bolt of lightning that had struck and killed him.

"Jakob? You okay?"

He turned to his left to find Lance sitting on a tree stump, pressing his hands against his temples, his gaze on the ground at his feet.

"I'm all right, but it looks like Woodrow's dead."

Lance pushed himself upright from the stump. "What about Brad?"

"I'm not sure." Jakob moved toward Bradley to see for himself.

Another flash of lightning lit the sky, followed by a crack of thunder. Lance shouted an oath, and Jakob stopped still in his tracks, his mouth gone dry, his heart racing.

We've got to get out of here. I've got to get back to my family.

The children were already in their beds, fast asleep, by the time Jakob returned home. Karola knew something horrible had happened the instant he came through the back door. She rose from her chair at the kitchen table—where she'd been sitting for the past hour, sipping tea and praying—and went to him.

Wordlessly, she placed the flat of her hand against his chest, as if offering strength to his heart. Jakob shook his head, then placed his right hand over hers, trapping it there.

Neither of them moved for a long time.

Finally, Jakob lowered his hand. "Are the children asleep?"

"*Ja.* For some time now."

"I'll walk you to the cabin."

"You do not need to, Jakob. I am able to find my own way."

"No, I want to."

She nodded, deeming it better not to argue.

"I'll get you a jacket. That shawl of yours won't be enough. It's turned cold."

Again she nodded.

Jakob left the kitchen, returning soon with a short coat made of dark blue wool. He placed it over her shoulders. "It's a bit big on you, but it'll keep you warm until we get you home and can build a fire."

"*Danke.*"

They left the house, walking up the hillside with slow, even steps. The rain had stopped, and a break in the clouds allowed a first-quarter moon to peek through, shedding an unexpected light on the path before them.

They were halfway to their destination when Jakob started talking. "He was only twenty-eight. He was young and strong. And now he's dead."

"The man who was trapped?"

"No. His brother. Woodrow." Silence, then: "He was struck by lightning. It could have been any of us."

"Oh, Jakob," she said softly, a tremble in her voice. "How awful."

Thank you for protecting him, Lord. Thank you for not taking Jakob away from his children. And . . . from me.

"You know what I thought? How Siobhan died that suddenly. For no reason. I thought how quickly the people we love are taken from us, and no matter how hard we try to protect them, we're helpless to change things. Life's a series of loss upon loss. That's all life is."

She heard more than loss in his voice. She heard a desperation of the soul, and the sound tore at her heart. She had to blink away tears and swallow a lump in her throat before she could respond. "Do things seem as hopeless to you as that, Jakob?"

"There is nothing secure, nothing safe."

Her heart felt as if it were breaking. "There is safety in God, Jakob. There is hope in him."

"Is there?" His voice had turned hard. "I'm not so sure."

"Oh, Jakob. Doubt anything but that. Doubt anyone but him."

His stride lengthened, anger evident in every step. "Why *shouldn't* I doubt him? Where was he when the storm hit tonight? Where was he when Siobhan died?"

Karola hurried to keep pace with him.

"There's no reason my children should've been left without a mother. No reason. And what about you?" He stopped, forcing Karola to do the same as he spun to face her. "You deserved a family of your own, a husband and children. When I didn't send for you like I promised, why didn't God provide a husband for you?" He stepped toward her, the movement almost threatening. "Your hope was *wasted,* Karola, and so was your trust."

Speechless in the face of his rage, she began to cry, silent tears streaking her cheeks. *God kept me for you, Jakob. Can you not see that for yourself?*

For a moment, they stared at one another. Even the night seemed to hold its breath.

Jakob cursed softly, then took hold of Karola's shoulders. "Were all the men in Steigerhausen blind?" The embers of his rage still burned in his eyes. "Couldn't they see what I see?"

Before she could react, he drew her to him and lowered his mouth to hers.

His kiss was harsh and furious—and like a whirlpool in a river, it sucked her under. She was helpless in the grip of his fiery passion, but she didn't care. Wouldn't have fought if she could. She wanted to surrender completely. She wanted—

With a gasp, she pulled away, frightened by the intensity of her response. She touched her lips with her fingertips, staring at Jakob, eyes wide, her pulse pounding in her ears.

He stared back, unmoving.

She formed his name with her mouth but no sound came.

He shuddered, as though seeing his name on her lips had broken him free from his emotions. He closed his eyes, then opened them again, and the sorrow in his gaze raked her raw emotions.

"I'm sorry, Karola. I'm tired. I wasn't thinking straight." He raised a hand toward her, then let it fall. "My actions are inexcusable. It won't happen again." He glanced up the hillside. "There's the cabin. You'll be all right from here." With that, he spun on his heel and strode into the night.

"I love you, Jakob."

But he was already gone, and her tearful whisper was caught and carried away on the wind.

Chapter Sixteen

12 June 1908
in care of Jakob Hirsch
Shadow Creek, Idaho

Dear Father and Mother,

I hope this letter finds you in good health. I yearn to hear from you, and every day I hope to receive a letter written in Mother's beautiful hand.

I am doing well. I feel more at home in my little cabin every day. As for my work, I have found my way into the hearts of the children, and they are definitely in mine. Even Maeve has decided I am not some wicked witch come to eat her house of gingerbread. I believe she has come to like me, although not as much as Bernard and Aislinn do.

Jakob has begun to give me riding lessons. Can you imagine me on a horse, Father? And once I have learned to ride horseback, he plans to teach me to drive a team pulling a wagon. He says I cannot live out so far from Shadow Creek without knowing how to ride and drive. I am nervous around the horses, although I try to hide my fears.

I feel foolish, being afraid, because both Maeve and Bernard are able to ride, and Aislinn is totally fearless. She sits in the saddle in front of her father and giggles as he trots the horse around the corral. It makes a delightful picture, the two of them. I wish you could see them.

Not all the news is good. There was a tragic accident on a neighboring farm last week. One man was injured during a violent storm, and his brother was killed. The funeral was held a few days ago, and even though I did not know these people, I wept for them. And I weep for Jakob because he seems to be blaming God, not only for this accident but for his wife's death and other losses, too.

I long to be able to help him find a place of peace, to accept God's comfort, but I feel I know too little myself. I read my Bible every morning now, and the words often seem to burn themselves into my very soul. Yet who am I, who walked apart from the Lord for so many years, to tell Jakob how to find peace with him? I feel so inadequate.

I have wondered if I should talk to Pastor Joki. Would I be wrong to express my concerns about Jakob to him? Would that be gossip? Pastor Joki seems to be both wise and kind. He was with Jakob, of course, when Jakob's wife died, so he must know far more than I. I suppose I should keep my counsel to myself.

Please remember Jakob in your prayers. And pray for me as well, that I will hear God's directions.

Now, let me write of other things.

I will tell you about Lance Bishop. He is a young farmer who works for Jakob several days each week. He has his own farm not far from Jakob's but needs additional income as his farm is small and he wants to buy more land.

Do you know what one thinks of as an American cowboy? Then you can imagine Lance Bishop. He is tall and slim and always wears a wide-brimmed hat like one sees in the photographs of the Wild West shows. He is younger than I, perhaps twenty-two or twenty-three, and as fair as Gunther Crosby. He is a little bowlegged, and when he walks, he makes me think of a marionette because his joints seem that loose. (I wonder if my description can paint the picture I mean to convey.) When he is in conversation with a woman, he always tucks his chin slightly downward, causing him to have to look up from beneath his brows. There is something quite charming about it.

Herr Bishop has lost his heart to the blacksmith's daughter, Charlotte White. He confided so to me last night after supper, and my heart breaks for him because Fräulein White has her sights set on another and pays no heed to Herr Bishop. I wonder as I write this if he shared his feelings because he has seen my own heartache over a love that is out of my reach.

Yes, it is true. For the second time in my life I have fallen in love with Jakob. "Too fast," I can hear Mother saying. "You cannot know him any more now than you did two weeks ago."

Perhaps. Or perhaps I have loved him all along. Perhaps I am as foolish as I ever was. I do not know.

I wonder what would have happened if I had married Jakob when I arrived in Shadow Creek, as planned. Would I still have loved him today? Or would my heartbreak have been worse because my husband did not love me?

I wish you were here to advise me. I miss you so very much.

Your loving daughter,
Karola Breit

Chapter Seventeen

*L*ance settled beside Karola on the buggy seat. "You take the reins, ma'am. I reckon you're ready."

Karola glanced toward Jakob, who stood nearby.

"He's right," Jakob said in answer to her silent query. "You're ready."

It was apparent both men had more faith in Karola's horsemanship than she did. She took the reins from Lance, lacing the leather strips through her fingers the way Jakob had shown her.

Please, God, still my shaking hands.

"You'd better get a move on," Jakob said. "You don't want to be keeping those ladies waiting. Miss Joki isn't known for her patience."

Karola nodded. She might be a newcomer to the community, but she had learned a great deal in the past few weeks. One of those things was that Dorotea Joki didn't like her and would like her even less if she were late to today's meeting.

Karola never should have acquiesced to Laura Gaffney's insistence that she be part of the committee. What did Karola know about Independence Day celebrations? But Jakob had been present when Laura asked her, and he'd seemed all for it. The next thing she'd known, she'd agreed to help.

"You are sure you will not need me to watch the children?"

Jakob gave a wry chuckle. "I think I can handle them by myself for one afternoon, Karola."

She hoped her embarrassment didn't show in her smile. Of course he could manage the children for an afternoon. Did she think she was totally indispensable to him? He needed her, yes, but they both knew she was only to stay through harvest, a date that hastened toward her much too quickly.

Since the day of the thunderstorm, something had changed between Jakob and Karola. He'd put up some sort of invisible but impenetrable wall, as if in protection from the love she felt for him.

"Have a good time." So saying, Jakob gave a nod and slapped the horse on the backside with his hand.

The horse moved out at a smart pace, and for a short while, Karola forgot everything but her fear she wouldn't be able to control the animal.

Finally, Lance placed a hand over one of hers. "You're doin' fine, ma'am."

"*Ja?*"

"*Ja.*"

She heard his teasing tone and, strangely enough, began to relax because of it.

"I reckon you know what the Bible says about controllin' a horse."

She glanced at him.

"'Behold, we put bits in the horses' mouths, that they may obey us; and we turn about their whole body.'" He grinned. "You don't reckon the Good Book would tell us somethin' that wasn't true, do you?" He motioned toward the horse. "You control him with that bit, and you can turn his whole body because of it. You remember that."

The last of Karola's tension drained from her. As if seeing it go, Lance gave her one of his irresistible lopsided grins.

"You surprise me, Mr. Bishop."

"Lance, ma'am. Remember? Mr. Bishop's my father."

"Lance." She smiled and looked at the road ahead. "I am Karola, not . . . ma'am."

"Fair enough. Now, why do I surprise you?"

She gave her head a slight shake, wishing she hadn't spoken her thought aloud.

"I reckon you didn't see me as the sort who could quote the Scriptures. Now did you?"

She felt her cheeks grow warm.

"No offense taken, ma'am." He chuckled. "I mean, Karola. Besides, I don't reckon there's anybody in Shadow Creek who would think me a Bible-thumper."

"A Bible-thumper?"

"You know. The overly pious sort who's always talkin' about his faith instead of just livin' it." He shrugged. "But I know who made the world. Look at it." He motioned with his arm at the passing countryside. "I know there's folks who like to think this was an accident, that there's no rhyme or reason to the universe, but I don't see how they can think that way. There was a plan to creatin' all this, and there's a plan for everybody that's born. Readin' the Good Book helps me understand what God's plan is for me."

And me, Father? What is your plan for me?

Sometimes she thought she knew. Sometimes, when she was tucking the children into bed at night or when she sat at the supper table across from Jakob, she thought she was exactly where God wanted her to be. Not just for now, but for always. But how could she know for sure? And if this wasn't where God meant for her to be, if Jakob never loved her in return, how could she bear it?

O God, I want your will, but I also want my own way. Is it possible to have both?

They traveled in silence, both of them lost in their private thoughts, until Lance finally spoke. "You reckon Charlotte will be at this meeting of yours?" The longing in his voice matched the longing in Karola's heart.

She smiled sadly. "I do not know, Lance, but she may be."

Jakob lay beneath the wagon, staring at the axle, wondering if he could repair it or if he should take it to the blacksmith in town. Nearby, Maeve and Bernard were playing tag with Aislinn in the barnyard, their laughter filling the air. Happy sounds.

Jakob turned his head.

Sunshine bathed the yard. His dogs lay in the shade of a poplar, too smart to be cavorting with the children in the heat of the day. Maeve let Aislinn catch her, and the toddler squealed with delight, then darted off in the opposite direction, Maeve and Bernard in mock pursuit.

They sounded happy because they were happy, Jakob realized—and that was because of Karola.

He looked up at the underbelly of the wagon again.

Jakob had brought Karola to America to care for his children, and that was precisely what she'd done. She cared for them, and more important, she loved them. And they loved her in return. They were going to miss her when she left.

Jakob tapped the axle lightly with his hammer.

Why hadn't he considered that before? He'd thought he was so clever, insisting that Karola owed him, forcing her to work to repay the debt after she'd refused to marry him. Now he wondered if he'd made a huge mistake. Had he set his children up for a second loss?

He slid from beneath the wagon and rose to his feet. With both hands, he brushed the dirt from the backside of his britches.

Did you set yourself up, too?

He frowned. Certainly he would be sorry when Karola left. After all, his household hadn't run this smoothly in ages. In less than a month, Karola had managed to put everything in order, keep the Hirsch family well-fed and dressed in clean clothes, and make the children laugh again. So naturally it would be hard on Jakob when she left his employ. Where would he find anyone like her?

Anyone like her . . .

Was there anyone like her?

Eleven days had passed since Jakob kissed Karola. Eleven restless nights since he'd felt her respond to him, then reject him. Pushing him away had been a wise move on her part. Giving rein to their passions would have been a mistake—for both of them. Karola wanted love, and Jakob wasn't willing to give it to her. Wasn't able to give it to her.

Yet there were times he'd swear he could still taste her lips upon his. There were times . . .

It was a dangerous thing, the direction he'd allowed his thoughts to wander. He was determined to stop them, once and for all.

"Come on, kids. I'm hungry. Let's get something to eat."

The planning committee for the Shadow Creek Independence Day Celebration Bazaar held its meeting in the basement of the First Methodist Church at the corner of West and Main, Theodora Shrum presiding.

"Ladies," Theodora called above the visiting voices of nearly two dozen women. "If we could please call the meeting to order." She waited an appropriate length of time. Then, into the newly arrived silence, she said, "I want to thank you all for coming this afternoon. As you know, it takes many hands to put on an event such as the one we have planned."

Laura leaned over to Karola. "Theodora always has big plans. She never thinks small."

"Independence Day is just over two weeks away," Theodora continued, "and I'm delighted to report all of our preparations are on schedule." She glanced to the woman at her right. "Miss Joki, would you report on the food, please?"

Dorotea—as thin as a beanpole and looking more so next to the full-figured Theodora—rose from her chair. She folded her hands and pressed them against the waistband of her skirt. "Thank you, Mrs. Shrum." She cast a cool gaze over the other women in the room. "I've contacted all of the best cooks in our valley and have received promises of fried chicken, baked ham, all kinds of breads and preserves, and plenty of pies and cakes. We'll also have some vegetable dishes and fresh fruits, and Dr. Cooper will be bringing his wonderful root beer."

Laura leaned close to Karola a second time. "What did she ask you to bring?"

"Nothing."

Laura stood quickly. "Excuse me, Dorotea."

The woman sighed dramatically, letting one and all know that she didn't appreciate the interruption—or the use of her given name. "Yes, Mrs. Gaffney."

"I'm sure it's an oversight on your part, but you haven't asked *all* the best cooks. You failed to ask Miss Breit to bring some of her incredible pies."

Karola received an angry glare from Dorotea Joki. She gave Laura's skirt a tug, hoping her friend would stop talking and sit down.

Undeterred, Laura continued, "Perhaps you don't know Miss Breit's father owns a bakery in Germany and that she worked with him until she came to America." She smiled at Karola. "My family and I had the pleasure of joining the Hirsches for supper last Sunday, and if Miss Breit didn't already have a job, my father-in-law would hire her to work in the hotel restaurant in a heartbeat."

Karola's cheeks were flaming by this time.

"Well," Dorotea said stiffly, "I suppose it wouldn't hurt to have a few more pies on hand. Just in case."

Laura grinned as she sat down.

Karola shook her head. "Why did you do that?"

"Because she intentionally didn't ask you. She meant to slight you."

"I did not mind."

"I did. You *are* the best cook in the valley, and once the word gets out, I'll bet your boxed lunch will get the highest bid, too."

"Boxed lunch? What——?"

She was interrupted when Theodora Shrum stood. "Our next report is from Miss White."

Charlotte stepped to the front of the room, then turned to face the gathering of women. "As you all know, my father is once again in charge of the fireworks display, and I can assure you it will be the best ever. He went up to American Falls this week and brought back a wagonload full of boxes. Father says he has enough explosives to light up the sky over Shadow Creek for a solid hour."

There was an appreciative murmuring as Charlotte returned to her seat.

Half an hour later, the meeting was adjourned, and the women began to leave the church basement in groups of twos and threes, excited chatter preceding them. Laura and Karola had just reached the church doors when they were joined by Charlotte White.

"How nice that you could be with us today," Charlotte said to Karola, not sounding the least bit pleased. Without waiting for a reply, she added, "Did Mr. Hirsch bring you?"

"*Nein.* I came with Mr. Bishop. See, there he is, waiting for me now." She smiled as she lifted a hand and waved at Lance, who was standing beside the buggy. He tugged on his hat brim and smiled in reply. "He has been so kind to me, so thoughtful. He is at Jakob's farm almost every day." She lowered her voice. "Not many men are as attentive as Mr. Bishop. Such a gentleman."

Please see how right for you he is and leave Jakob alone.

Karola quickened her strides, hoping it would look like eagerness when all she really wanted was to keep Lance from turning a moony-eyed gaze on Charlotte. Reaching him, she slipped her hand into the crook of his arm. When he stiffened in surprise, she cast him a look that said, *Say nothing!*

"I am sorry you had to wait for me in the heat of the day, Lance. I hope I have not kept you too long." She glanced at Charlotte and Laura. "Did I not tell you how thoughtful he is to me? A fine farm and house of his own to tend to, and still he finds the time to bring me here."

Charlotte stared at Lance Bishop as if she'd never seen him before.

Karola squeezed Lance's arm and prodded him toward the buggy, telegraphing her desire to depart. Wordlessly, Lance obliged, helping her up to the buggy seat before taking his own place.

"*Guten Tag,* Laura." Karola gave her friend a little wave. "Miss White." She nudged Lance in his ribs with her elbow. "We will see you in church on Sunday."

Lance clucked at the horse, and they drove away. It wasn't until they were out of town that he spoke. "What was *that* all about?"

As she recalled the look of surprised discovery on Charlotte's face, Karola chuckled.

Lance gave her a suspicious glance. "You havin' a heatstroke, ma'am?"

"*Nein,*" she answered. "*Nein.*"

"Well, you surefire act like it. What's gotten into you anyway?"

"Miss White."

"What's Charlotte got to do with what you were sayin' back there?"

She placed her fingertips on her cheeks. Maybe she *was* suffering from heatstroke. She couldn't believe she'd lied about Lance Bishop's interest in her. Whatever had possessed her?

"Karola?"

Her laughter forgotten, she answered, "I was trying to make Charlotte jealous."

"Jealous of what?"

The last of her amusement drained from her like the dregs of bathwater from a tub. "Of me . . . and you."

He looked like the horses had kicked him in the head. "Me and *you?*"

She nodded, completely miserable now. It had been a stupid, irrational thing to do. Who in their right mind would believe Lance would prefer Karola to the younger and stunningly beautiful Charlotte White? All Jakob wanted from Karola was for her to watch his children and cook his meals and clean his house. Perhaps that was all any man would ever want from her.

Lance bumped his hat brim with his thumb, pushing it up on his forehead. "You thought if Charlotte believed I was interested in you, she might . . . ?" He let the question drift into silence.

Karola nodded. "It was a foolish thing to do. And it was not honest. I am sorry."

"Maybe you shouldn't be so quick to apologize." He grinned. "Who knows, Karola. This little charade might work if we play our cards right. Charlotte did seem to be payin' attention as we were leavin'." He slapped the reins against the horse's backside. "Yes, sir. I reckon it might work at that."

The time for the first cutting of hay arrived, and for many days Jakob and Lance labored from sunup to sundown, mowing the fragrant alfalfa plants, waiting for it to cure beneath the relentless sun, raking it into rows, then into bunches, and finally stacking and hauling. The men were tortured by a dried mixture of cheat grass and fireweed that climbed up pants legs and drifted down sweaty shirt collars, prickling their skin. They ate the dust that swirled around them and breathed chaff up their nostrils.

Their faces and forearms were sunburned, and their muscles cried out for relief.

Jakob kept an eye on the weather, hoping he wouldn't see rain clouds forming on the horizon. Rain at this time could spell disaster for his crop.

Each day, Karola brought lunch to the two men—ham sandwiches or cold fried chicken, chowchow made by Geraldine Mason or dill pickles preserved by Theodora Shrum, and one of Karola's wonderful desserts, one day a cake, another day a pie. Jakob and Lance would sit in the patch of shade cast by the wagon while they ate, thankful for a brief respite from their work, even more thankful for the delicious food with which to fill their bellies.

Jakob didn't fail to notice the easy camaraderie that had blossomed between Lance and Karola of late, and he couldn't say he liked it much either. They smiled and they laughed and they gently teased one another. It never went on for long. Their behavior couldn't be called inappropriate.

Yet it irritated Jakob as surely as the cheat grass beneath his collar.

Chapter Eighteen

*J*akob stood in the creek, two feet from the bank, casting his line, him against the fish in the cool of a summer morning. It was what he'd been needing. Solitude. Time to think.

"There you are, boy-o!" shouted a familiar voice. "Sure, and I knew I'd be finding you here."

Jakob looked over his shoulder to see Tulley Gaffney strolling toward him through the cottonwoods, carrying a tackle basket over one shoulder, a fishing pole in the opposite hand.

So much for solitude.

"Aye, you're wondering how I knew you'd be fishing." Tulley set the basket on the ground, then sank onto a boulder, huffing slightly from the walk. "'Tis no secret, Jakob. You always come to fish when the haying is done. 'Tis your reward to yourself." Tulley searched through his tackle for the right fly. "Are they bitin' this morning?"

"I've had a few nibbles." He faced the creek.

"'Tis a fine morning for it."

Don't talk, Tulley. Just fish.

A few moments later, Tulley joined him in the creek, several yards upstream.

For a while, it seemed he'd read Jakob's thoughts. He remained silent, casting his fishing line in a practiced rhythm. But it wasn't in Tulley's nature to be quiet for long. "Is it true what I've been hearin'?"

"Is what true?"

"About the lass and Lance Bishop."

Jakob shrugged, pretending ignorance.

"Folks are sayin' there'll be a wedding before the year is out, 'tis that serious. I'd not be surprised, you know. She's a fine girl, that one. A *fine* girl."

Jakob wished Tulley would keep his comments to himself.

"Never have I seen children take to a lass the way yours've taken to Karola. Sure, an' she'll make a fine mother for her own wee ones when the day comes. Don't you agree?"

"Yes." His mind filled with images of Karola, her arm around Maeve, laughing with Bernard, bathing Aislinn . . .

He stopped the flood before he could imagine her with him.

Tulley let a few minutes of silence pass, then said, "I was thinkin' it would be you who married the girl. 'Tis not often I'm wrong about such things. Why'd you let her go, Jakob?"

He stared at the river. "If you'll recall, it was Karola who decided not to marry me."

"Aye, I'm knowin' that, but that was more than a month ago now. Your heart's different than it was then and so is hers."

Jakob turned toward the Irishman. "You don't know what you're talking about."

"Don't I? Sure, and I'm thinkin' 'tis you who's wrong, me boy."

Jakob scowled at him, then reeled in his line, stepped onto the bank, and headed downstream, not stopping until he'd gone beyond a bend in the creek.

Little good it did him.

"So"—the Irishman rounded the bend himself—"this is the way I see it. You lost your darlin' Siobhan, and your heart was after bein' broken, it was. There wasn't one of us who didn't see your heartache, me boy, for we was all grievin', too. And right it was for you to feel that way, I'm thinkin'. She was your wife and the mother o' your children. But Siobhan's gone, and 'tis time for you t'join the livin'."

"Shut up, Tulley."

"I don't think I will. 'Tis words you're needin' t'hear that I've got to say, and say them I'm going to."

"I don't have to listen."

"Are you forgettin' I lost me own wife? I'm knowin' what 'tis like, what you're goin' through, the things you're feelin'. I'm knowin' that you're afraid to risk lovin' again, for fear of losin' a second time. 'Tis worth the risk, Jakob. Love is always worth the risk. Sure, and I'm thinkin' Karola Breit is worth lovin' and that you know it, too."

Jakob ground his teeth to keep from saying anything.

"'Twould be a pity if she were to marry the wrong man, with you lovin' her as you do."

That was too much. He glared at the man. "I'm *not* . . . in love . . . with Karola."

"No?"

"No."

"Well then, I guess it won't be botherin' you when Lance bids for the lass's boxed lunch come Independence Day." With that, Tulley turned and headed back upstream, disappearing quickly from view.

Bothered? No, Jakob would *not* be bothered.

He returned his attention to the creek, concentrating hard on his delivery loop as he silently dared some hapless fish to take the bait.

He hoped when one did, it would put up a long, hard fight. Jakob Hirsch was itching for a good fight.

"It seems to be true," Emma said to Charlotte as she reached for a straw bonnet on display in the millinery shop window. "I overheard Winifred Thompson talking to Ida Noonan, and *she* said—"

"Who could possibly care what those two old gossips have to say?" Charlotte stared into a mirror as she adjusted a silk and feather concoction on her head. "They almost never know what they're talking about."

"Well, you go to the Lutheran church these days. Were they sitting together last Sunday or not?"

Charlotte turned from the mirror. "Mr. Bishop sat with Mr. Hirsch and his family. He's done that before. The two men are friends, and Mr. Bishop works for Mr. Hirsch."

"But he sat *beside* Karola Breit. Right?"

"Oh, what on earth does it matter, Emma? He couldn't possibly be interested in her."

"Why not? Karola's very nice."

Charlotte rolled her eyes. "She's a *foreigner.*" She was careful to whisper, not wanting Nadzia Denys—who had stepped into the back room a few minutes before—to overhear. "She doesn't belong in Shadow Creek, and the sooner she leaves the better. She should hightail it back to Germany, if you ask me."

"Charlotte, that's unkind." Emma's eyes were filled with disapproval.

"Well, it's how I feel." She tilted her chin upward. "I'm entitled to my opinion, just like anybody else."

With a slight shake of her head, Emma returned the straw bonnet to the display in the window. "I'd better get home. Mother is working on the banner for the gazebo, and she said she would need my help with it."

Charlotte knew Emma was making an excuse, but she didn't try to stop her from leaving. The last thing she wanted was to continue this conversation. She waited until Nadzia returned with the hat she'd ordered, then left the shop herself, her mood turned sour.

It can't be true, Charlotte thought as she walked toward home. He couldn't be seriously interested in that woman. Karola Breit was at least five years older than Lance, far too much to be considered a suitable match. And while Charlotte supposed Karola was pretty enough in her own way, she certainly wasn't *that* attractive.

Besides, everybody in town—Charlotte included—knew Lance Bishop had been sweet on *her* since he first came to Shadow Creek. And she had to admit he was cute and kind of charming, and she'd always liked the sound of his laugh and the shy looks he shot her way from beneath his Stetson.

But her sights had been set on Jakob Hirsch. He had the finest house in the valley, and her father said he was one of the best farmers around. He was sure to be wealthy one day. Of course, he *was* thirteen years older than Charlotte, and he *did* have three children to raise.

Lance's image drifted into her thoughts a second time. Lance Bishop—young, handsome, childless . . . and if rumors were true, interested in Karola Breit.

It simply wasn't possible!

Karola was washing the last of the children's breakfast dishes, Aislinn playing with blocks on the floor near her feet, when Lance tapped on the back door, then entered the kitchen.

"Morning, Karola. Jakob back from fishing yet?"

"Nein."

"Fish must be bitin' good to keep him out this long." He took a mug from the shelf. "Coffee?"

"Ja, there is plenty still."

He went to the stove and filled his mug from the coffeepot.

Karola turned her back to the sink and leaned against it while drying her hands on a towel. "I did not think you would be here today."

"I'm not supposed to be. I've been repairing a plow this morning, but I don't have the tools I need. I came to borrow some, if Jakob doesn't mind."

Bored with her blocks, Aislinn rose and toddled over to Lance and raised her arms above her head. "Up! Up!"

Lance chuckled, set his mug aside, then lifted the little girl into his arms. "You're growin' like a weed, Aislinn." He smiled at Karola. "Isn't she? Just since you got here she's changed."

"*Ja.* It is true."

Karola felt a tiny catch in her heart. How terrible it would be when she was forced to leave this place, when she would no longer see Aislinn's adorable face each morning or hear her squeals of laughter as she played with her brother and sister.

How will I bear it? I love them. I love their father. I should have married Jakob when he wanted me for a wife. Now he no longer wants me for anything but tending his children, washing his clothes, preparing his meals. I am only here to pay back a debt. Oh, God, why do I always do the wrong thing? Why do I always make the wrong choices?

With tears stinging her eyes, she turned to the sink and began to dry the dishes.

Lance came to stand nearby. "While I've got the chance, Karola, I want to say thanks for helpin' me out with Charlotte."

She didn't trust herself to speak, so she merely shrugged.

"Did you see her at church on Sunday? She was fit to be tied. I don't think she paid any notice to Jakob at all."

What if Jakob wants Charlotte? What if helping Lance means that Jakob will not have the woman he could love?

But Charlotte would be all wrong for Jakob. Surely he could see that for himself.

Am I an expert on what men want? They do not want me. Even Lance is only pretending.

The lump in her throat grew bigger, and she was completely blinded now by her tears.

"Karola?"

She shook her head.

"What's wrong?"

She choked back a sob.

The next thing she knew, Lance had put Aislinn on the floor and gathered Karola into a comforting embrace. She gripped his shirt in her hands, pressed her forehead against his chest, and wept as he patted her back.

"What's wrong, Karola? You can tell me. What're friends for? Whatever it is, I'll do my best to help. You can count on that. Hey, come on. Dry those eyes. It's okay. It's okay. Stop crying and tell me what's wrong."

She couldn't stop. Her tears had become a torrent. Her throat ached. Her chest hurt. She didn't want to cry. She wanted to be a woman of strong, unshakable faith, like her mother. She wanted to trust God with her future, like her father. But she wasn't and she didn't. At the moment, she had given into despair and the returning belief that she was unlovable, unwanted, unattractive.

In the midst of her misery, Karola barely heard Aislinn's cry of *Da-Da.*

But she heard Lance quite clearly when he said, "Looks like it's fish for supper."

Karola took a step backward and turned to see Jakob standing in the kitchen doorway, a string of trout held in his right hand, his younger daughter now cradled on his left hip.

"What's happened?" His words were as fierce as his scowl.

Karola dashed the tears from her cheeks with her fingertips. "It is nothing."

"Lance?"

"I don't know. She just started cryin' for no reason. Don't know what came over her."

Jakob crossed the kitchen and dropped the fish into the sink. "What are you doing here? Haying's done. You should be tending your own crops." His gaze flicked between Lance and Karola.

"Needed to borrow some tools," Lance answered. "My plow's broke."

"Well, let's get them for you. I'm sure you're in a hurry to get that plow repaired." He passed Aislinn to Karola without a word to her, then headed for the back door.

"I'll talk to you later," Lance said softly before following Jakob out the door.

Jakob was propelled across the barnyard by his own fury. He yanked open the door to the toolshed, stepped inside, then waited for Lance to catch up.

Once the younger man arrived, Jakob said, "Take what you need and bring it back when you're done." He would have left but Lance blocked the doorway.

"You got a burr under your saddle, Jakob?"

"No."

Lance bumped his hat back on his forehead. "No? Who you tryin' to fool? Karola's in the house drippin' like a broken faucet, and you're as grumpy as an old bear who's woke too early from hibernatin', and neither one of you knows why. Don't you think you should figure it out?"

"What *I'd* like to figure out," Jakob snapped, his voice rising, "is what gives everybody in this valley the right to stick their noses into my business?"

"Who's everybody? All I did was ask a simple question."

Jakob swept Lance to one side of the doorway with the back of his hand, then strode out of the shed. "That isn't all you did."

"Don't you think you should figure it out?"

What was there to figure out? He'd seen them with his own eyes. Plain as the nose on his face.

Lance and Karola. Well, why was he surprised? Tulley had been talking about the two of them not more than two, maybe three hours ago. In fact, it seemed the whole town was talking about their budding romance.

So what had Lance done to make her cry like that? Was it because he'd proposed marriage, but Jakob had made her promise to stay working for him until after harvest?

"Sure, and I'm thinkin' Karola Breit is worth lovin' and that you know it, too."

Of course she was worth loving. He'd never tried to say she wasn't. He could understand why Lance would fall in love with her. She was pretty, kind, generous, tender. She worked hard and never complained. She was courageous. She was gentle and loving with the children. What wasn't to love about her?

" 'Twould be a pity if she were to marry the wrong man, with you lovin' her as you do."

But he didn't love Karola, and it didn't matter to him what Tulley or anybody else said. He didn't have it in him to fall in love again.

Jakob stopped walking, raked the fingers of both hands through his hair, then looked around, as if coming out of a trance. He found himself standing not far from Karola's cabin.

When had it all gone wrong? His plan hadn't seemed too complicated when he'd thought it up last winter. He'd needed a wife to care for his children. He'd been honest about that when he contacted Karola. It wasn't his fault his letter of explanation had been lost in the post. How was he to know she'd expected them to love one another after all these years? How was he to know she'd never married because she'd been waiting for him?

He groaned.

He should have known. Just because he'd lost hope along the way didn't mean Karola would. He should have known that about her.

So, all right. Fair enough. She'd called off the wedding, then come to work for him instead of being his wife. Shouldn't that have made things better? He hadn't wanted to marry anyway. Not really. And she *had* promised to stay until after the harvest. That would be far longer than any of the other women he'd hired lasted. Surely by harvesttime he'd be able to find a replacement for her.

No one could replace Karola . . . no one had eyes so blue or a smile so sweet . . . no one had a voice that rang with such music . . .

He scowled at the thoughts. Don't be stupid! Eyes, voice . . . every woman had them. He would find one and he'd do so quickly. He wasn't sure how, but he'd do it.

And if you do, how long will she stay? Three months? Six months? A year? How soon will you need another replacement?

It seemed taking a wife was still the best answer.

"'Twould be a pity if she were to marry the wrong man, with you lovin' her as you do."

He leaned forward, elbows on his thighs, and hid his face in his hands. "I don't love her," he said softly. "I don't want to love her or any other woman." He straightened suddenly, looking upward at the patch of blue sky, fighting the ache that had lodged in his chest. "The price is too high."

Besides, Karola didn't love him. She'd said so herself.

Chapter Nineteen

⚬

1 July 1908
in care of Jakob Hirsch
Shadow Creek, Idaho

Dear Father and Mother,
I am sorry for not writing to you in many days. I go to Jakob's home each morning even before the sun comes up, and each night when I return to my cabin, I am too tired to keep my eyes open.
The heat has not helped. The temperature rises every day to nearly one hundred degrees Fahrenheit. The sun blazes in a cloudless sky, baking the earth below. Sometimes, in late afternoon or early evenings, thunderclouds build on the horizon, but they have brought neither rain nor relief from the oppressive warmth.
I have discovered how completely ignorant I was regarding the difficult life of a farmer. In Father's bakery, our days were much the same, rising early and making the same breads, pies, and cakes. Our work was hard, but we knew what each day would bring. But the farm, I have found, has new and unexpected challenges mixed with the

routine chores of daily life. A horse gets injured. A calf becomes sick. A coyote threatens the chicken coop. And the weather always matters. Always.

Jakob is a good farmer, and he is respected by his neighbors. They come to him for advice about their crops and the irrigation of their land. Jakob studies books, newspapers, magazines, and anything else that will help him increase his knowledge and make him a better farmer. He does whatever he can to assure his harvest will be plentiful and his children well provided for.

Even with the long days of hard work, Jakob never fails to be an attentive father. When we were young and courting all those years ago, it was I who spoke of wanting many children. It never seemed important to Jakob, although he agreed to please me. I knew that even then. But Jakob loves his children fiercely. As he loved their mother.

Does a man who loved and lost a wife ever find room in his heart for another? I am beginning to believe not.

Shadow Creek is preparing for its Independence Day celebration, which will be held in three more days. This is an annual event for the people of this valley, as it is for people in every town and city around this great nation. Maeve tells me that it is great fun, and she and Bernard are almost giddy with anticipation.

All of the businesses in Shadow Creek will close for the day, and there will be a parade and a bazaar in the town's park where a band will play music in the gazebo. There will be a fireworks display after sunset. They even auction the boxed luncheons of the single young ladies and women of Shadow Creek to the highest bids by the unmarried men. I was alarmed when I learned of this but am assured by my friend, Laura Gaffney, that it is a respectable and fun event.

Do you remember when I wrote to you about Lance Bishop and his unrequited love for the blacksmith's daughter? I did something impulsive, thinking I would help him win her affection. Oh, it is too complicated to explain in a letter, but now people believe Lance and I have formed an affection for one another. It is not true. Not the way they think. We are friends. That is all. Lance believes I have achieved what I wished, that Charlotte is seeing him in a new light, and he is grateful. I am not certain he should be. Not yet. I fear the end results may not be what either of us would wish.

I can make excuses. I can say I never actually told a lie, but even that is an untruth. For by my actions and my implications, I deceived others.

Why am I like this? Always rushing ahead, acting on impulse, letting my emotions control me? When will I learn to stop and consider my actions first? I know the answer because I read it in my Bible. The answer is to cease being carnally minded, to stop wanting the things of this world more than I want God's will. "For they that are after the flesh do mind the things of the flesh; but they that are after the Spirit the things of the Spirit. For to be carnally minded is death; but to be spiritually minded is life and peace."

This week I have been reading the book of Proverbs and have seen how much God wishes for his children to be wise and to exercise self-control. I must seem a great failure to him most of the time. Yet he loves me anyway, and for that I am thankful.

Your loving daughter,
Karola Breit

Chapter Twenty

A man could only fool himself for so long.

And when Karola Breit stepped off the back porch that Independence Day morning, wearing a red-and-white striped skirt, a white blouse with billowy sleeves, and a large straw bonnet that sported red, white, and blue ribbons, Jakob knew he could no longer deny one obvious truth: she meant more to him than just a housekeeper and a caretaker for his children. She was more than an employee in his home.

But what exactly was she to him?

The question dogged Jakob as he loaded the back of the wagon with two wicker baskets, Karola's boxed lunch for the auction, a covered tray that held four pies for Miss Joki, and several blankets.

"Is that everything?" he asked Karola as he tethered his saddle horse—the one he planned to race that afternoon—to the back of the wagon.

"*Ja,* it is everything. We are ready."

Jakob lifted the children into the wagon. First, Maeve and Aislinn in their matching white dresses, starched and ironed to perfection. Next, Bernard in his short pants, white shirt, and suspenders. Finally, Jakob offered a hand to Karola and assisted her to the wagon seat, then he joined her there, picked up the reins, and the family headed for Shadow Creek.

The family . . .

Yes, they were like a family, the five of them. And he cared for Karola. Cared for her more than he wanted to admit. Could Tulley be right? Was it love he felt? Had he fallen in love with Karola?

He glanced to his right. She was staring into the distance, a faraway expression on her face. He wondered where her thoughts had taken her.

It was difficult to know. They'd spoken little in the days since he'd found her weeping in Lance's arms. That was his fault. He'd made himself scarce. Isn't that what he did when emotions got the better of him, bury himself in his work?

No wonder she'd looked elsewhere for affection. He'd offered her no other choice.

Is it too late to change your mind about me, Karola?

Even if she could, did he want her to? Did he want her to love him? Moreover, did he want to love her? Hadn't he suffered enough loss in his life?

Jakob detested all the questions and his indecisiveness. It wasn't like him to vacillate this way, to not know his own mind or what he wanted.

What do you feel for me, Karola?

He looked away, as if afraid she might hear his silent question and answer him.

Karola had loved him once, years ago. He knew that was true. But he doubted there was much, if anything, left in him of the young man she'd loved. Chances were, even if he tried to win her heart, she wouldn't want him.

Why would she? He hadn't treated her fairly. He'd made her many promises back in Germany, then he'd disappeared without a trace, without so much as a letter to say, "I'm sorry." There was a whole list of things to call a man who did what he'd done, and most of them weren't repeatable in polite company.

He hadn't done any better by Karola upon her arrival in America.

It's a wonder she doesn't hate me.

But for some reason, she didn't seem to hate him. She had worked hard to make his house a home. She could have punished him, made him sorry he'd forced her to remain, but she hadn't.

"Tell me something, Karola." The words were out before Jakob could stop them.

"Ja?"

He met her gaze. Such soft blue eyes, like a hazy summer day. "Weren't you ever angry at me?"

"Angry?"

"For not sending for you all those years ago. Like I promised I would."

"Oh." She looked into the distance again. "*Ja,* I was angry. I even thought I hated you for a time. But that was long ago."

"Even without the past, I've given you plenty of reasons to be mad since you got here."

The hint of a smile curved the corners of her mouth. "*Ja,* you have."

"So, why not?"

She met his gaze, her eyes filled with patience. Then she shook her head. "I do not know, Jakob. I would be lying if I said I have not been hurt and confused. But I am to blame for my circumstances, too. I had to learn that for myself. Perhaps that is why God brought me to America. So I could grow up."

Jakob was about to ask if she could forgive him for every hurt he'd caused her, but he was interrupted by his elder daughter.

"Look, there's Mr. Lance."

"Hello!" Lance cantered toward the wagon.

Karola smiled and waved. Behind them, the children chorused their greetings. Jakob remained mute, not the least bit happy to see his friend.

"Karola," Lance said as he drew his mount to a walk, falling in beside the wagon, "you look like you belong on a carousel. You're as pretty as a picture." He chuckled. "And I reckon that blush makes you even prettier."

Indeed, her rosy cheeks were pretty. *She* was pretty, from the top of her straw bonnet to the tips of her white shoes. Karola was as close to perfect as any woman on earth could be.

Close enough that there wasn't one good reason why she should give Jakob Hirsch, who was so imperfect, another chance to win her heart. Not after all the mistakes he'd made.

But in that moment, he decided to try anyway.

The road into Shadow Creek was thick with people. They came on foot, by horseback, in wagons and buggies. The mood was cheerful, folks smiling, jesting, laughing.

Karola felt a flutter of excitement. This was her first Independence Day in her new country. It seemed anything was possible today. Anything.

"There's Penny and Vic, Da." Maeve waved at her young friends as Jakob drove the wagon into the shade of a tree behind the schoolhouse. "Can I go play with them?"

"If you promise to keep an eye on your brother."

"Okay. I promise. Come on, Bernard. No, not you, Aislinn. You gotta stay here. Just the big kids get to go."

Karola was about to reach for Aislinn when Lance swung down from his horse and held out his arms to the toddler.

"Here you go, princess." He lifted her onto his shoulders, knocking his hat off his head in the process.

Aislinn giggled as she gripped two fists full of Lance's hair.

Jakob hopped to the ground, picked up the hat, and held it toward Lance. "Don't feel like you've got to hang around with us."

Karola was surprised by Jakob's rudeness, but Lance didn't seem fazed.

"I don't mind." The younger man took his hat from Jakob. "I like being with all of you." Holding onto Aislinn with one hand, he dropped his hat onto her head with the other. "Isn't that right, princess?"

Head and shoulders having disappeared inside the large felt hat, Aislinn's squeal of delight was muffled but unmistakable.

With admirable dexterity, Lance exchanged his horse's bridle for a halter and removed the saddle and blanket from its back, using only his right hand while he held onto Aislinn with his left. Then he tied the horse to the back of the wagon beside the sorrel mare Jakob had brought from the farm.

Karola smiled as she watched, thinking Lance had a way with the little ones. Some day, God willing, he would be a wonderful father to his own children. She could only hope Charlotte White would make them a good mother, if she did, indeed, become Lance's bride.

"Karola."

She glanced down to find Jakob standing beside the wagon, arm outstretched. "Maybe we should get those pies over to Miss Joki."

What on earth was wrong with him? He hadn't seemed out of sorts during the drive to town. In truth, when he'd asked her if she was ever angry, she'd felt a spark of hope because it had seemed they were beginning to communicate, to really hear one another.

"*Ja.*" She took hold of his proffered hand and stepped to the ground.

"Lance, would you mind keeping an eye on Aislinn while I help Karola with these pies?"

"Nope. Fine with me. Go on ahead."

Karola didn't need help. She could have carried the tray of pies with no trouble. But she didn't tell Jakob that.

The town park, located across West Street from the schoolhouse, had been turned into a veritable village of booths stretching around three sides of the park. Some of the booths were filled with food or crafts, others with games to tempt adults and children alike. Triangular flags in varying sizes and colors hung from ropes stretched between booths. Delicious odors—roasted ears of corn, fried chicken, baked potatoes—filled the still, warm air. In the gazebo, the band was beginning to gather, some of the men and women warming up their instruments.

"Do you remember Gretchen Finster?" Karola asked Jakob, breaking the silence that had accompanied her and Jakob since walking away from the wagon.

He looked uncertain for a moment, then nodded. "Yes. She was that skinny girl with curly dark hair. She was engaged to Conrad Elend's son. I've forgotten his name now."

"Otto. He and Gretchen got married not long after you left." Karola gave her head a slight shake. "Gretchen is the mother of eight and not so skinny now."

"Eight?"

"*Ja.* Eight. All girls, including two sets of twins."

"I can't imagine."

At Jakob's smile, Karola felt a lift in her spirits.

"What made you ask if I remembered her?"

"All of this." Karola motioned toward the booths and the people around them. "Otto took Gretchen to Munich for Oktoberfest when they were first married. She said there was a carousel and horse races and tents with lots of food and beer. She still talks about it, all these years later, especially in October. I used to dream about seeing the festival for myself, but of course, I never did."

Jakob stopped walking, forcing Karola to do the same. His hazel eyes perused her with an unsettling intensity. Unconsciously, she pressed a hand against her collarbone, as if to steady the odd fluttering in her chest.

"We'll have horse races," he said, his voice low. "This afternoon. Will you cheer for me?"

Her heart skipped a beat. "*Ja,* Jakob. I will cheer for you."

He looked as if he might say something more, but then he glanced beyond her shoulder and the hint of a scowl returned to his brow.

Karola turned to see Miss Joki marching toward them, clearly a woman on a mission.

"There you are, Miss Breit. Good heavens, you're late. I was afraid you weren't coming. And after Mrs. Gaffney insisted you bring pies for the booth." She stopped, made an impatient motion for them to follow, then spun on her heel and marched in the opposite direction. "Come along, Mr. Hirsch. Don't dawdle with those pies. Time is wasting."

Charlotte and her father left their home on East Street together. Beatrice White wasn't with them. For as long as Charlotte could remember, her mother had been sickly and much of the time was bedridden. Perhaps that was why Edgar White doted on his only child, trying to give her whatever she wished.

Charlotte adored her father in return, even if she would have preferred he engaged in a more refined profession. Still, when he was clean-shaven and his graying hair was slicked back as it was now, he appeared rather dapper for a man of forty-eight, and everyone knew his years in the smithy, pounding hot iron, had made him stronger than most men half his age.

As they made their way toward the park, her father carrying her boxed lunch for the auction, Charlotte glanced up the road leading into town.

"Looking for somebody in particular?"

"No, Daddy."

But she was. She was looking for Lance Bishop on that black horse of his. He hadn't been in services on Sunday, which was unlike him; he was exceedingly faithful in his church attendance. But the Hirsch family and Karola Breit had been present, so Charlotte had spent the bulk of the service staring daggers at Karola's back.

It infuriated Charlotte every time she thought how that woman had stolen Lance's affections. The conniving foreigner. And her an old maid, too!

"I don't see why you're so upset," Emma had said yesterday. "You've never shown any interest in Mr. Bishop before."

"A girl can change her mind, can't she?"

"I don't think you know what you want, Charlotte White. Maybe you should find out before you hurt someone, including yourself."

Charlotte had been stunned by her best friend's words. Why had Emma snapped at her when it was so obvious the trouble lay with that Breit woman?

"Do you know where we're supposed to take this boxed lunch of yours?" Her father's question brought Charlotte's attention back to the present.

"Here, Daddy." She stopped and held out her hands. "Let me take it. I know you're dying to get over to the horseshoes."

Her father grinned. "You comin' to watch? I've got every intention of winning the competition again this year."

"I'll come a bit later. I want to find Emma first." She returned his smile. *And I want to look for Lance, but you don't need to know that.*

"Look who's there, Aislinn," Lance said to the toddler on his shoulders. "Miss White. I reckon it would be impolite if we didn't make sure we said hello to her."

Keeping Charlotte—decked out in her signature pink, parasol resting on her right shoulder—in view, Lance ambled across the green, pretending to see everything *but* her. Still, he knew the instant she noticed him. When he was only a few yards away, he stopped and glanced behind him.

"Good morning, Mr. Bishop."

Hiding a grin, he pretended surprise to see her. "Well, good mornin', Miss White."

Charlotte moved her parasol from her right shoulder to her left. "You must have come to town quite early."

"Yes'm. Rode in with the Hirsch family." He glanced around the park. "In fact, I was looking for Miss Breit. Have you seen her?"

"No."

Her clipped reply was music to his ears. Imagine, he'd been trying for three years to make Charlotte look on him with favor, never knowing all he had to do was show interest in someone else! It wasn't that he didn't know this pretty coquette was spoiled, willful, and as changeable as the weather. He knew. Marriage to her wouldn't be easy. But he remained convinced she was the wife God had picked for him. Of course, the Lord might not approve of his method of finally getting her attention, but it wasn't as if he was doing it to harm her. That should count for something. Right?

He looked at Charlotte again and watched as she composed her features into a charming smile.

"I just dropped my boxed lunch off for the auction"—she motioned toward the booth behind her—"and I have no immediate plans. Perhaps I could help you find Miss Breit. I'm sure you'd like her to take charge of the child."

"Oh, I don't mind lookin' after Aislinn." He lifted the girl off his shoulders and set her feet on the ground. "I'm right fond of her. Aren't I, princess?"

Aislinn giggled and started off in her choppy little run. Three quick strides, and Lance caught her, swinging her up again.

He turned to face Charlotte. "I'd enjoy your company, Miss White, if you've a mind to walk with me."

Chapter Twenty-One

*T*heodora Shrum stood at the front of the bunting-draped gazebo, the band seated behind her. "Now remember. The money raised in the auction today is going to the women's guild, so you men don't be stingy with your bids. You'll be doing a good deed, *and* you'll have a delicious lunch to eat. Not to mention the pleasant company of the delightful lady who prepared it. What more could you ask for?"

The crowd applauded.

"Of course," Theodora continued, "this being a secret auction, you won't know who your lovely companion will be until you win."

Jakob heard the expected murmurs, as if people were surprised by this announcement even though it was the way it was done every year. Not that he'd participated before. While his wife had been living, he'd been a spectator at the auction, enjoying the spirit of the bidding, laughing and applauding as the winning bids were announced.

Last year, he'd been in mourning. He'd brought the children to town, though he'd wanted to be anywhere rather than where folks were having a good time. He couldn't recall if he'd stood in the middle of a crowd like this one or not. Maybe he'd stayed at the wagon, lost in a haze of sorrow.

And this year? Well, this year things were different. He was going to participate in the auction, and he knew exactly with whom he meant to eat lunch. Luckily, he had an inside edge. Only half an hour ago he'd sought out Laura Gaffney, and she'd told him that Karola's boxed lunch was the only one tied around with a single red ribbon.

Theodora Shrum waved an arm in the air. "Could I please have all of our ladies come forward at this time?"

Jakob glanced to his left where Karola stood. "That's your cue."

She looked as if she'd swallowed one of their chickens whole. Her eyes widened and her lips parted.

"Go on." He placed his hand in the center of her back and gave her a nudge forward. "It'll be fun."

He half expected her to call him a liar, but instead, she wove her way through the crowd toward the gazebo, where she joined the other women whose lunches were up for auction.

Theodora waved her hand again and called for quiet. "Now if my handsome assistants will please bring out the boxes that are to be auctioned."

From the booth on the east side of the gazebo came eight men, many of them fathers to the single women gathered there. They balanced identical white boxes on the palm of each hand—identical, that is, except for the ribbons and bows that decorated them. But only one box had a single red ribbon tied around it like a Christmas package.

Thanks, Laura.

Jakob scanned the crowd, looking for his accomplice. But he wasn't exactly pleased when he found her. Laura was talking with Lance, and judging by the way Lance leaned toward her, Jakob guessed she was speaking softly so no one nearby would overhear. Was she, perhaps, also telling Lance about the red ribbon? Surely not. He'd gotten the distinct feeling Laura had been pleased when he asked her to help him, especially since she'd also volunteered to mind his children while he shared the boxed lunch with Karola—assuming he would have the winning bid.

He stuck his hand into his pocket and withdrew the money he'd brought with him. He hoped he wouldn't have to bid more than a dollar, but if Lance were bidding against him . . .

"All right, gentlemen," Theodora called. "Let's begin with this box with the lovely yellow rosette, shall we?" She lifted the lid and looked inside. "Oh, my. What a feast!"

"Fifteen cents," shouted a voice from the back of the crowd.

"I have fifteen cents. Who'll make it a quarter? I promise you, this is exceptional cooking."

"Twenty-five cents," a man on Jakob's left called.

It turned out the box belonged to Emma Shrum, and it went for forty cents to Kevin Cooper, Dr. Cooper's nephew. Kevin had come to work in his uncle's pharmacy while on summer break from his studies at an eastern university. Judging by his expression, he was more than a little pleased when he discovered who his luncheon companion would be.

The auction continued.

Nadzia Denys's boxed lunch went to the doctor. As far as Jakob knew, Andrew Cooper had never bid on a boxed lunch before. Perhaps he'd been inspired by his nephew.

Rick Joki had the winning bid for Aida Gallo's lunch.

Lance bid ten cents on the next box, but it went to a fellow Jakob didn't know.

Several more boxes were sold before Theodora held up the one with the red ribbon. "Who'll start the bidding?"

"Two bits," Jakob said in a firm, loud voice.

Lance immediately shouted, "Forty cents."

"Do you hear that, folks?" Theodora crowed. "We're already up to forty cents, and we've only just begun. Do I hear fifty cents?"

"Yes, ma'am," a man at the back of the crowd replied. "I'll give you four bits."

Panic thumped in Jakob's chest. "Sixty cents." He felt in his pocket again.

"Seventy-five cents."

Who was that guy and why didn't he shut up? He didn't know Karola, and he didn't need to know her. How dare he drive the price so high?

"Eighty cents."

That bid came from Lance, and it didn't make Jakob feel any better.

Jakob closed his eyes. "One dollar."

"Well, bless my soul." Theodora held the box a little higher. "Gentlemen, we have a dollar for this lunch and the company of the lovely lady who prepared it. Do I hear a dollar ten?"

Jakob waited. No voice came from the back of the crowd. He looked toward Lance and found Lance looking at him. The younger man grinned, shrugged, then shook his head.

"I was only trying to put a little spice in this auction," Lance said, and folks laughed. "But I reckon things're gettin' a bit rich for my blood. You win, Jakob."

Theodora declared, "Going once, twice, sold to Jakob Hirsch. And your lovely companion is"—she checked the label on the back of the box—"Miss Breit."

As he made his way toward the gazebo, Jakob felt as if he'd won a million bucks instead of spending the one in his pocket.

Karola wasn't at all sure how she felt about this auction business. It seemed a bit insulting, as if she were a prize hog. It was also somewhat frightful. What if a total stranger had won? Or worse, what if Lance had won? The two of them eating together would have fueled the rumors, and Karola was more than ready for them to stop. She didn't like deceiving people, not even for a good cause. It only made matters worse that *she* was the guilty party who had started the gossip in the first place.

But if truth be told, she would have to confess the auction had been exciting, too. She'd found herself pretending Jakob knew exactly whose box he was bidding for. She'd pretended he'd spent a dollar of his hard-earned money especially for the pleasure of her company.

I have not changed at all. I still have my head in the clouds, no matter how hard I try to keep my feet firmly on the ground.

Having paid his money to the ever-disapproving Dorotea, then collected the boxed lunch from Theodora, Jakob made his way to where Karola was standing.

"Miss Breit," he said with a tip of his head, "I believe you're stuck with me for another meal."

Was he disappointed? Or was he teasing her? She couldn't tell.

"*Ja,* I believe you are right, Mr. Hirsch."

He moved the box to the crook of his left arm, then he offered her his right. "We'll get one of the blankets from the wagon and go sit in the shade by the creek. It'll be cooler there."

"And the children?" She sought their faces in the crowd.

"Laura's going to look after them."

She couldn't help smiling a little. "Oh." She took his arm and he escorted her away.

Smiling, Lance watched Jakob and Karola leave, then turned back to the auction—and leaned forward suddenly. There it was. The box he'd been waiting for. He'd convinced Laura to reveal the identifying decoration on Charlotte's boxed lunch, not that it had been all that hard to extract the information. Laura was a match-maker at heart, and Lance knew it.

The bidding against Jakob had been for show and nothing more, although he'd taken a bit of a risk, going as high as he had. If Jakob had backed out . . .

"And now we have this box with the lovely silver bows." Theodora held it high.

Lance resisted the temptation to offer the first bid. He would bide his time.

Jakob hadn't intended to go far before he settled on the perfect picnic spot. But by the time he stopped and spread the quilt on the ground, the sounds of the crowd in the town park had grown faint.

"It's turned into a real scorcher," he said, glancing through the tree branches at the cloudless sky. When he looked at Karola, he saw her cheeks were flushed from the heat. "Let's stick our feet in the creek so we can cool off a bit before we eat."

She hesitated a moment before she smiled and nodded. "*Ja, that sounds good.*"

Within minutes, they'd both shed their shoes and stockings and were seated on the bank of Shadow Creek, feet in the water. Jakob had rolled his pant legs up above his knees. Karola didn't pull her striped skirt quite so high; she kept the fabric mere inches above the surface of the water, hiding her knees from view.

They looked at one another and, in unison said, "Ahhhh." Then they laughed.

Karola tucked the hem of her skirt between her knees so it wouldn't fall into the creek. Then she reached up to remove her straw bonnet and toss it over her shoulder onto the blanket. She braced the heels of her hands on the ground behind her, leaned back, and lifted her face toward the sky, eyes closed. "This is heavenly."

Jakob had to agree, for it seemed he was seated beside an angel.

"So peaceful," she whispered.

Her throat formed a gentle arc, creamy smooth, and very kissable.

Jakob suddenly felt warmer than he had before he'd put his feet in the water.

"I am glad you won my boxed lunch. I can relax with you, Jakob. If that man I did not know had won instead . . ."

"Lance was bidding, too. He could've won. He almost did."

She lifted her head and looked at him, a tentative smile tugging at the corners of her mouth. "But I am glad he did not."

Jakob was completely confused now. He'd thought Karola and Lance . . .

Looking away from her, he plucked pebbles from the edge of the stream and tossed them, one by one, into the water. For a brief moment, he could see distinct rings on the surface, but then those rings were erased by the current, and it was as if nothing had happened.

It would be nice if life were like that, he thought, if mistakes could be swept away as easily as ripples on the water. It would be nice if he could go back and do things right.

"Jakob?" Karola's hand briefly touched his forearm. "Why do you look so troubled?"

He answered her question with a question. "Do you remember what I asked you on the ride into town?" He met her inquisitive gaze. "If you were angry at me for what I did, for leaving you behind and never sending for you."

She nodded.

"I guess the more important question is, can you forgive me?"

She didn't answer. She simply watched him with those beautiful blue eyes of hers, her thoughts unfathomable to him.

He remembered the day they were to have wed. He remembered the look in her eyes then, too, and he remembered the quiet resolve in her voice as she'd said, *"I didn't love you when I left Germany, and I don't love you now. I don't know you, and I don't love you."*

Strange, the way the memory hurt more than the words themselves had when spoken.

"Karola, I never meant my promises to be lies."

"I know."

"When I came to America, I was full of dreams and full of hope for our future. I believed I could do everything I'd ever promised you, and I thought it wouldn't take very long." He dropped his gaze to the surface of the water. "But at some point, it got too difficult to believe any longer."

"When did you stop trusting God?"

He didn't care for her question. "I don't know what you mean." But he did. He just didn't want to answer her. Besides, this was not the direction he'd meant for their conversation to go.

As if sensing his thoughts, Karola drew her feet out of the water. "Shall we eat?"

"Yes." Jakob was glad for the reprieve. Surely he could find something less personal and more pleasant to talk about as they shared their meal.

If Jakob was irritated by Karola's question about his lack of trust in God, he didn't let on. As they shared their meal, he entertained her with stories about the children and the folks around Shadow Creek and even made her laugh over some of his experiences when he'd first arrived in America. He also peppered her with questions about the old country; about people they'd both known as children, especially her parents; and about the life she'd led in the years after he left Steigerhausen. When she answered his questions, he listened intently, smiling sometimes, shaking his head with a look of sorrow or understanding at others. It reminded her of the long talks they'd had years ago, and her heart was gladdened. Before Karola knew it, more than an hour had passed.

"Guess we'd better go," Jakob said, "before somebody sends out a search party for us."

With a nod, Karola rose to her knees and began to put away the remains of their lunch.

"Karola?"

She looked up to find him kneeling, too, their faces mere inches apart.

"I knew the lunch with the red ribbon tied around it was yours."

She felt a tiny flutter in her heart. "You did?"

"Yes."

Her mouth was suddenly dry.

"Karola"—his voice had deepened—"I'd like permission to kiss you, if you have no objection."

She nodded, then shook her head, then nodded again, unsure which response meant she had no objection. She *did* want him to kiss her.

He leaned forward.

Karola closed her eyes, feeling dizzy—and when their lips met, it seemed all of nature held its breath. The creek ceased to gurgle. The birds ceased to chirp.

I love you, Jakob. I love you. I love you. I love you.

She didn't *want* her feet firmly planted on the ground. She *wanted* her head in the clouds. She wanted to dream and to hope and to soar!

Jakob drew back and sat on his heels, his hands resting on his thighs. He stared at her, a strange fire in his hazel eyes.

Karola's lips tingled from his kiss, and she touched them with her fingertips—just as she had done the last time he kissed her.

"Now I *know* we'd better get back."

His voice was husky; she felt it vibrating in the marrow of her bones.

Moving deliberately but without haste, they reached for their stockings and shoes and put them on. Then they rose in unison. Karola picked up the box that had held their lunch. Jakob folded the blanket and draped it over his arm.

Karola wished he would kiss her again, but instead he led the way along the path back to town.

Chapter Twenty-Two

*S*o?" Lance looked at Jakob over the back of his black gelding. "How was your lunch?"

"Fine." Jakob didn't want to discuss what happened with Karola. Especially not with Lance. Better to change the subject. "I hear you ended up with Miss White's lunch. How'd that go?"

"I think she likes me." A silly grin split Lance's face. "A lot."

Bending down, Jakob reached for the cinch beneath the sorrel's belly.

Lance appeared at the mare's head. "You should thank me."

"For what?"

"For keeping Miss White occupied so you could enjoy your time alone with Karola."

Jakob frowned as he tightened the cinch.

"You know as well as everybody else in this town that Charlotte was all set on bein' the next Mrs. Jakob Hirsch, what with you havin' the nicest house and the biggest farm in this valley. Now I mean to change her mind. I mean to help her see she'd much rather take care of a smaller place so she has more time to spend with me. After we're married, of course."

"But I thought you—"

"Are you *blind,* Jakob? Karola and me are friends. That's all. Just good friends. She's easy to talk to, you know."

Karola had told Jakob she was glad he, rather than Lance, had placed the highest bid for her boxed lunch, but he hadn't believed her. Not really. He'd thought she was trying to make the best of the situation.

And the kiss we shared? What did I think that was?

He'd been trying *not* to think about it. When he did, his brain turned to mush.

"Well, I'll be jiggered," Lance drawled. "You've got it as bad as I do."

"Got what?"

Lance's answer was a soft, knowing chuckle as he returned to his gelding.

Jakob jerked on the stirrup. "Got *what?*"

All right. He *was* attracted to Karola. He'd admitted as much this morning before they left the farm. All right. So he was wondering if he might change her mind about not loving him. She had, after all, let him kiss her. Come to think of it, she might have even kissed him back a little bit. What did that mean? What did he want it to mean?

He pictured Karola seated on the creek bank, her bare feet dangling in the water. He imagined her removing her hat and tossing it behind her. He saw those ever-present stray wisps of pale hair feathering around her face.

He should have kissed her right then.

He'd like to be kissing her right now.

"Quit your woolgathering, Hirsch," Lance said, shattering the images in Jakob's head. "They're about ready to start the race."

I guess Lance is right. I do have it bad.

Balancing Aislinn on her hip, Karola stood near the finish line with the two older children and the Gaffneys—Tulley, Ian, and

Laura. She leaned forward, bending over the rope, and glanced up the straight length of road, trying to spot Jakob among the milling horses and riders at the starting point.

"Sure, and you needn't worry your pretty head," Tulley said. "Jakob's mare has won this Independence Day race every year since he brought his family to Shadow Creek. Exceptin', of course, for last year when he hadn't the heart to even try."

Karola felt a sudden shiver pass through her. A year ago, Jakob had been in mourning for his deceased wife. A year ago, he hadn't wanted to race or to celebrate Independence Day because his heart had been broken.

Could Karola find her own place in his life, or would the memory of Siobhan remain foremost in his mind? She didn't want to take second place to a memory. Perhaps that was her pride rearing its ugly head, but it was the truth nonetheless.

"Karola, I'd like permission to kiss you, if you have no objection."

Why had Jakob kissed her? Was it because he—

"The flag is up," someone cried.

Karola saw the white flag fall. The riders raised a shout as they dug in their heels. The horses shot forward, and the ground vibrated with the thunder of their hooves.

At first, Karola could make out no one in particular. But then two horses began to pull away from the others—a sorrel mare carrying Jakob, and a black gelding carrying Lance.

Voices were raised all around her, people shouting for their favorites. She was shouting, too. "Come on, Jakob! Come on!"

"Faster, Da!" Maeve and Bernard screamed in unison. "Faster!"

Karola saw Jakob and Lance look at each other, their horses neck and neck. She saw the men smile in challenge, then lean forward, urging their horses on. Dirt and dust flew up behind them into the faces of those who followed.

"Come on, Jakob!"

Suddenly, a small boy pitched forward out of the crowd, falling to his knees right in the path of Jakob's mare. A horrified gasp rose from the crowd. A woman screamed. A man grabbed for the boy's arm.

A look of horror on his face, Jakob reined in hard, yanking the mare's head to one side, throwing the horse off balance. As the mare fell, Jakob pitched head over heels to the ground. Then he disappeared from view, swallowed by a cloud of dust raised by the racing horses that had followed him.

"Jakob!" Karola thought her heart would stop.

The horses thundered past her.

"Da!"

At Maeve's terrified shriek, Karola grabbed the girl's shoulder with one hand. "Stay here, Maeve. Don't move." She passed Aislinn to Laura. "Keep them here."

Laura nodded.

Karola wasn't alone as she rushed toward the place she'd seen Jakob fall. Many had done the same thing, and she had to shoulder her way through. "Please let me pass. Let me *through*. Please. Please let me pass."

Dr. Cooper was kneeling beside Jakob by the time Karola broke through the gawking crowd. The doctor held Jakob's wrist between his fingers, checking his pulse.

"Jakob?" She knelt on his other side.

His eyes were closed, his face ghostly pale. There was a gash on his forehead above his left eyebrow, and blood ran from it into his hair.

He lay so still. So utterly still.

She looked up. "Doctor?"

Dr. Cooper's gaze met hers briefly, but he ignored her unspoken question, saying to the crowd in general, "I need to get him to my office. Somebody get a wagon."

God, please do not take Jakob from his children. She quelled her tears. *Please do not take him from me.*

Jakob groaned.

Karola swallowed a sob as she leaned forward. An arm went around her shoulders, and she looked to find Lance kneeling next to her. His expression mirrored her feelings.

Please, God. She turned her gaze back to Jakob. *Please.*

His eyes fluttered open, then closed, then opened again, squinting against the bright sunlight.

The doctor said, "Don't try to move."

Another groan slipped through Jakob's parted lips.

Dr. Cooper put a hand on his shoulder. "Lie still. We're getting a wagon so we can take you to my office for a closer look."

"The boy?" Jakob's voice was weak.

"He's okay," someone in the crowd answered. "His pa pulled him out of the way in time, thanks to you."

Jakob focused on Lance. "My horse?"

"Can't say for sure, but I think she'll be okay." Lance attempted a grin. "I was winning, you know. Fair and square, too."

"Next year." Jakob let his eyes drift closed. "Wait until next year."

Alone in the doctor's examination room, eyes closed, Jakob lay on the table, trying not to take any deep breaths. It hurt too much when he did.

"Cracked a few ribs," Dr. Cooper had told him as he'd stitched the wound in Jakob's head.

Not to mention a dislocated shoulder, plus a sprained wrist and ankle. And if the room didn't stop spinning and pitching, he was going to lose Karola's boxed lunch all over the doctor's pristine floor.

He heard the door open. Just the notion of looking to see who it was seemed too much to bear.

"Jakob." It was Karola's soft voice.

"Yeah."

"May we come in? The children need to see you."

"Sure." With effort, he willed his nausea to stop and his eyes to open.

Karola entered the room, holding hands with Maeve and Bernard.

"Hi." Jakob managed a wooden grin. "Some spill, huh? Wish I could have seen it."

"Are you okay, Da?" Maeve's voice quavered.

"Sure. No worse than that time you fell out of the tree. Remember?"

Maeve nodded but looked unconvinced.

Another wave of dizziness made his stomach roll, and he had to fight to keep his eyes focused on the children. "Isn't it about time for the watermelon-eating contest?"

Bernard glanced at Karola. "Is it?"

"I do not know."

Jakob clenched his hands into fists. "Karola, maybe you should take them back to the park. Bernard had his heart set on entering. I'll be along as soon as the doctor's done with me. You know how long that can take." With his eyes, he tried to communicate the urgency of his request. If he got sick, he didn't want the children to see it. They were scared enough as it was. "No point the kids being stuck here when they could be having fun with the others."

She seemed to understand. "Come, Maeve, Bernard. We will go now."

"Don't worry about me. I'm fine. Just a little shook up." Jakob swallowed hard. "Bernard, you eat lots of watermelon. Hear?"

"I will, Da."

He was relieved when the door shut behind Karola and the children. He didn't have enough strength to pretend any longer.

He closed his eyes and, forgetting himself, took a deep breath. The pain in his side was sharp and as hot as a red poker.

Why couldn't this have happened *after* the harvest? He couldn't be laid up now. There was too much work to be done.

One bad year. It only took one bad year to lose it all.

Tulley Gaffney insisted that Jakob, his children, and Karola stay overnight at the hotel.

Relief swept through Karola when Dr. Cooper agreed with Tulley. "Better not subject him to that ride home just yet. Tomorrow will be soon enough."

"I've got work to see to," Jakob argued, wincing from the effort.

Dr. Cooper gave him a pointed look. "You'll be lucky if you can walk by tomorrow, my friend. You can forget any farmwork for a few weeks. Get what rest you can for tonight."

Lance settled matters by offering to see to the evening and morning chores.

And so, after the fireworks display, Karola put the children to bed in one of the second-floor rooms of the Shadow Creek Hotel, across the hall from the one occupied by their father. Karola shared the room with them, though she slept little, her mind replaying again and again the horrible moment when Jakob had tumbled to the ground and disappeared beneath the racing horses.

That horrible moment when she'd feared she might have lost him forever.

Chapter Twenty-Three

By morning, the pain in Jakob's head had intensified rather than lessened. His cracked ribs made every breath torture, and the crutches the doctor gave him were of little use since his dizziness made standing upright impossible. His right hand was useless as well, too weak from the sprained wrist to hold on to the crutch.

Dr. Cooper frowned as he cleaned his eyeglasses on a cloth. "I'd like you to stay in town so I can observe you for a few more days."

"We can't stay. I've got a farm to run."

"Jakob, you can't take care of yourself right now, let alone see to the farm chores."

"We're going home," he replied through clenched teeth.

Dr. Cooper sighed. "You're making a mistake." With that, he left the room.

Jakob closed his eyes as despair washed over him. He knew the doctor was right. He was as helpless as a newborn kitten, but he couldn't stay in town. Able or not, the animals had to be fed and the cows milked. Lance could keep up with many of the chores, but he couldn't be expected to do them all. Not and run his own place, too.

Jakob must have drifted into sleep, for when he opened his eyes again the light in the room had shifted and he found Karola seated beside his bed, watching him with a worried gaze.

"The doctor says you insist on returning to the farm?"

"Yes."

"You cannot even stand yet."

"I know, but it'll pass."

"He says your recovery will take time, and that you need rest. You cannot be alone, Jakob. You cannot see to your . . . personal needs." She sat a little straighter in her chair. "I have given this matter some thought overnight. I have prayed about it, and I believe there is only one answer."

He frowned.

"I will move into your house so I may be there when needed, by you and the children."

Jakob remembered Dorotea Joki's indignation on their erstwhile wedding day. He could imagine the hue and cry if Karola moved in to nurse him.

Karola was one step ahead. "We will marry first. Then no one can think ill of the arrangement."

"Marry?" The room spun again, and he was forced to close his eyes to fight back the accompanying nausea. "You said yourself we don't love each other . . ." The throbbing pain in his head and in his side made it difficult to think straight, made it hard to figure out what more he should say. It seemed he should argue with her, that he should set the record straight, that he should—

"Jakob, you cannot manage alone. I can help you. You brought me to America to marry you, to tend your home and your children and to be a wife to you. Is that not right?"

"Yes, but . . ." He opened his eyes for a moment, but his vision was blurred and he couldn't make her out clearly.

She rose from the chair. "Then it is settled. I will tell the Gaffneys, and then I will send for Pastor Joki."

"You said yourself we don't love each other."

Ja, Karola had said such a thing, but the words were no longer true. Not for her. She loved Jakob desperately. She had even accepted that if he could never love her in return, if she always took second place to the memory of Siobhan, then so be it. She would learn to be content with things as they were, not as she wished.

Wasn't that as it should be? Didn't the Bible talk of living for others rather than for self? Didn't it speak of learning to be content, no matter the circumstances of life? Wasn't her joy to be found in the Lord and not in the world?

Such were her thoughts on that Sunday afternoon as Rick Joki spoke the marriage vows. Jakob hadn't the strength to go to the church, but he'd been adamant about not lying in bed like an invalid while he took a wife. So they were married in the lobby of the Shadow Creek Hotel, Karola looking slightly rumpled in the same white blouse and red-and-white striped skirt she had donned before leaving the farm the previous morning. Their witnesses were Jakob's children, the Gaffneys, Lance Bishop, Dr. Cooper, and Dorotea Joki, who had accompanied her brother across the street, invited or not. Except for Maeve and Bernard, who were wiggling with excitement—"You're gonna be our new ma!" Maeve had exclaimed when she heard the news—the mood was solemn. No rings were exchanged, the ceremony was brief, and when it was done, the groom was quickly assisted out the door and into the back of the wagon before he lost consciousness from the pain.

Laura gave Karola a hug. "Will you be all right?"

"Ja."

Laura wiped tears from her cheeks as she stepped back. "Oh, Karola, this wasn't the wedding you should have had. I wish—"

"We are married," Karola interrupted quickly. "That is all we wished to be."

"He cares for you. Remember that."

Karola nodded, then turned away before her own tears could form. To her dismay, she made immediate eye contact with Dorotea.

"Mrs. Hirsch." The woman made the name sound more of a condemnation than a congratulation.

Karola lifted her chin slightly. "It was good of you to come, Miss Joki."

Dorotea *harrumphed,* then turned on her heel and marched out of the hotel lobby.

"I apologize for my sister," Rick Joki said as he took hold of Karola's hand. "She gets moodier as she grows older."

"It is all right."

"No, it isn't, but I thank you for being forgiving."

Karola nodded, then turned toward Tulley, who was next in line.

Like the pastor before him, Tulley took hold of Karola's hand, but he added a kiss on her cheek. In a low voice, he said, "Sure, and I knew the moment I laid eyes on you that you were going to make Jakob a fine wife. A fine wife."

"I hope so."

"I'll have you listening to me now, Karola Hirsch. I loved my niece, don't you know, but Siobhan was no saint. She was a woman, subject to the same faults as the rest of us. I'm glad for the time she had with Jakob. I'm glad for the children that were born to them. But 'tis after being time for Jakob to find happiness again, and I'm thinkin' you'll bring it to him. I'm thinkin' he'll bring you happiness, too."

I will be happy. Her vision blurred with tears. *If only he can love me.*

Charlotte saw Lance standing beside the wagon, holding the reins to his sleek black gelding in one hand. She quickened her footsteps, wanting to reach him while no one else was around.

When he saw her, he bumped his hat brim with his knuckles, pushing it higher on his forehead, and grinned. "Afternoon, Miss White. I didn't figure on the pleasure of seeing you today."

"Is it true? Did Mr. Hirsch really marry Miss Breit?"

Lance's smile faded. "It's true."

Charlotte glanced toward the hotel entrance, trying to ascertain her feelings. Not all that long ago she'd thrown a fit when she heard Jakob planned to marry Karola. But after yesterday . . .

Well, it was too confusing. That was all she could say.

Lance took a step toward the sidewalk, drawing her gaze. "I don't reckon I'll make it into town for a spell. I'll be helping out extra at the Hirsch place until Jakob's back on his feet."

"Oh?"

Slowly, his lopsided grin reappeared. "But maybe you'll come callin' on Mrs. Hirsch, and I'll happen to be there at the same time."

"Maybe." Her heart pitter-patted in her chest.

"Then I'll look forward to it, Miss White." He tugged on the brim of his hat, pulling it down on his forehead so that it shaded his eyes again. "I'll look forward to it."

Merry voices spilled through the hotel doorway, growing louder. Charlotte took a quick step backward, then turned toward the sounds as Karola stepped into view.

"I just heard the news," Charlotte said with a smile. "I wish you happiness."

Karola hesitated briefly, then returned the smile. "*Danke,* Miss White."

Charlotte looked beyond Karola's shoulder. "Where is Mr. Hirsch? I'd like to give him my congratulations."

Lance chuckled. "He's been right here all along."

"What?" She turned, saw Lance motion toward the wagon with a jerk of his head, then peered over the side of the conveyance to see Jakob lying on a bed made of blankets, his eyes closed. He looked ghastly.

In contrast, there stood Lance . . . tall and lean and strong.

Suddenly, Charlotte didn't feel the least bit confused.

Chapter Twenty-Four

n the pale light of dawn that spilled through the parlor window, Karola stared at the words she had written.

Dear Father and Mother,
Jakob and I were married yesterday.

She didn't *feel* married. She didn't know what she felt, other than tired, but she most assuredly did *not* feel married.

She crumpled the slip of paper in her hand.

I will write to them another day.

She put away her writing materials, closed the top of the small writing desk that had once belonged to Siobhan, then rose from the chair and left the parlor. As she climbed the stairs, she listened for the voices of the children, but heard nothing. The house remained peaceful and still, all inhabitants asleep—save one.

Karola entered Jakob's bedroom and went to stand at the foot of his bed.

Our bedroom, not Jakob's alone. Our bed.

She toyed with the words in her mind, testing them to see if they rang true. They did not.

Jakob lay on his back. Even in sleep his face was etched with pain. He'd been restless throughout the night and had moaned softly whenever he'd sought a new position, which had been often.

Karola hadn't slept at all.

It had been her wedding night, her first night spent in this room, and although her groom had been unaware of her presence, she'd been very much aware of his. She'd even blushed as she slipped into bed beside him last night; she'd felt the heat in her cheeks as if it were the noon sun on her face.

"You said yourself we don't love each other."

A wedding night with an unconscious groom who did not love her. No wonder she didn't feel married. No wonder she wanted to cry.

Jakob shifted, groaned, then opened his eyes. She moved toward him.

"*Guten Morgen,* Jakob," she said softly.

"What time is it?"

"Almost six."

"Lance here yet?"

"*Nein.* Not yet. Is there something you need?"

He stared at her for several heartbeats before answering. "I need to use . . . the bathroom."

Last night, Lance had assisted Jakob to the lavatory. He had also helped Jakob undress and get into his nightshirt. But Lance wasn't here now, so it was up to Karola to take care of her husband.

That was, after all, the reason he'd married her.

"I am able to help you. Together we will get you on your feet and to the other room."

He nodded. Sweeping the top sheet aside, he raised his left arm. "Take hold with both hands and pull slow. Let me do the rest."

It didn't seem the best way to Karola, but she did as he said. She held her breath as she helped him, wincing whenever he did, hating his pain, wishing she could take it from him.

When he was at last upright on the side of the bed, she asked, "How are you doing?"

"I've been better." His eyes were closed, his face pale. "Just give me a minute."

He sounded angry, and her heart sank. Was she already failing him?

Jakob drew in a breath in that slow, careful way he'd learned since the accident. The pain in his ribs was acute. His shoulder was tender, and his head throbbed. But he didn't feel as dizzy as he had the day before, and the nausea seemed to have lessened. He tried forming a fist with his right hand. Useless. He suspected his ankle was about the same.

He opened his eyes and looked at Karola. She wore a dressing gown of lemon yellow. Her hair was tied back from her face with a ribbon, and it had a morning-disheveled appearance that was delightfully attractive.

He was injured, not dead.

She was his wife.

And she'd married him to be his nurse, because he'd made her feel obliged to him.

If he'd had the strength, he would have sworn a blue streak.

"Are you ready?" Karola asked.

He nodded.

She stepped to his left side.

"No"—he motioned toward the pair of crutches in the corner—"I'll need one of those blasted things for under that arm. You'll need to brace my right side."

She retrieved a crutch as ordered.

His pain was increasing. He needed to use the toilet. And he felt guilty for snapping at his bride.

His bride . . . more like his indentured servant.

A marriage between them hadn't seemed so wrong when Karola was in Germany. It had seemed practical and sensible. He'd been able to convince himself he was doing the right thing for all concerned because he'd had no feelings for her beyond a few fond memories.

Now that he'd come to know her anew and afresh, this marriage of convenience seemed all wrong for them both. He wanted her to see him as a man, as a husband, not as a patient. He didn't want a nurse, and he most definitely didn't want a wife who was with him because she had a debt to pay. He wanted to be more to her than that.

"Jakob?"

"Yeah," he growled, gripping the crutch with his left hand. "I'm ready."

Karola was about ten inches shorter than he, and she probably weighed a good seventy pounds less than he did. He tried not to lean too hard on her, but his right ankle wouldn't bear much weight at all, so he wasn't very successful. Still, they somehow managed to reach the bathroom without either of them stumbling or falling down.

He rested his left shoulder against the doorjamb. "I can handle it from here," he announced through clenched teeth.

She gave him a doubtful look but didn't argue. Instead, she carefully slipped from beneath his arm and stepped backward into the hall. After Jakob moved out of the way, she closed the door.

He sagged against the wall, defeated.

He shouldn't let himself care about Karola. He couldn't afford to let her work her way into his mind, into his heart. There was danger in caring, danger in loving.

Too late. It's way too late.

Chapter Twenty-Five

---

8 July 1908
Shadow Creek, Idaho

Dear Father and Mother,

I write to share surprising news. Jakob and I were married three days ago.

The ceremony was officiated by Pastor Joki, the Lutheran minister. My friend, Laura, her husband, Ian, and her father-in-law, Tulley Gaffney, were present, as were Lance Bishop (I wrote to you about him in a previous letter), the pastor's sister, and Dr. Andrew Cooper. And the children were with us, of course.

After moving my things to the main house, I was surprised to discover I missed my little cabin. It had become home to me, and I am feeling unsettled. The feeling will pass, I know. My place is with my husband and his children.

I love them all so very much.

Jakob was in an accident during the town's celebration of the American Independence. He was badly hurt, but Dr. Cooper said there will be no long-lasting damage. However, the mending is not quick enough to suit Jakob. He is not used to being idle, and it chafes on him.

I think it strange, the winding path I took to become Jakob's wife. Marriage is what I wanted for so many years, and then I did not want it when I could have it, and then I could not have it when I wanted it again. Now, here I am, married to the man I first fell in love with more than a dozen years ago.

God has been kind and merciful to a daughter who has problems with both listening and waiting.

There are many things I would ask you, Mother, if you were here. I would be glad for your advice and I am sorry for all the many times I rejected it in the past. At least I have found guidance in God's Word, and I pray I will not make too many mistakes along the way.

One mistake I made, although I did not realize it until today, was that I expected God to remove all storms from my life once I gave my heart to him. Or at the very least to take me out of any storm the moment I ask him to do so. I am like little Aislinn, demanding my own way with tearful cries, expecting my heavenly Father to do as I demand, if only to stop the noise I am making.

Too many of my life storms are of my own making. That I see now, too.

I love and miss you both. I still have not received any letters from you, and I grow worried. Please write to me soon.

Your loving daughter,
Karola Hirsch

Chapter Twenty-Six

───────────── ❧ ─────────────

*J*t wasn't nearly as difficult to milk cows as Karola expected. Lance was a patient teacher, and Karola soon felt confident enough to attempt the milking on her own.

"You need not come so early tomorrow morning," she told Lance before he left on Thursday evening. "I can do this myself. You are already doing so much for us."

"You sure, Karola? 'Cause I don't mind if you need me to be here."

"*Ja*, I am sure."

Karola had discovered that the barn was a peaceful place at dawn. The air smelled of sweet alfalfa hay and the more pungent scent of animal dung. The quiet was disturbed only by the sound of the milk cows chewing their cud while they swatted flies with their ropelike tails.

Sitting on the stool, her head close to the cow's warm side, Karola squeezed the cow's udder. Milk squirted into the bucket with a steady *poosh, poosh, poosh.*

Father God, what am I to do to help Jakob? He grows more short-tempered by the day. Is it because of me? Am I doing something wrong? I am trying hard to be a helpmeet, as your Word says I should be, but it is difficult to know what to do for him.

I do not feel like his wife. The only time we touch is when I must help him out of bed or to sit up so he can eat. I know he is in pain and I know he is frustrated that he can do so little for himself.

She rested her forehead against the bovine, her hands momentarily still.

But there must be more wrong between us than that. Sometimes I think he does not even see me. And sometimes I think he resents me. Can it be that he feels trapped by the circumstances? Was I wrong to suggest marriage? Did I do it not to help him but to get what I wanted?

Karola released a deep sigh.

O God, when will I become more like Jesus? Why do I continue to be willful and headstrong? Why do I act first and pray later? You must grow tired of seeing me act the way I do, of hearing me pray the same prayers time and again.

Father, I feel so helpless. Show me the way.

She hoped for a bolt of understanding to strike her, illuminating her situation and revealing exactly what she must do. None came. But she did feel more at peace by the time she finished her chores in the barn, and for that she was grateful.

On her return to the house, she heard pitiful mewling sounds coming from beneath the back porch. Bending over to peer under the steps, she discovered a small calico kitten no more than two weeks old.

"Little one"—she knelt down—"what are you doing under there alone?" Lifting the kitten, Karola pulled it to her chest, cradling it with both hands. It immediately fell silent as it searched for something to latch onto and suckle. "Where is your mother?"

She tried to see further beneath the porch but it was too dark. Silent, too. No other meows. No threatening hisses from a mother cat who feels her litter threatened.

Karola stood and glanced about the barnyard. The kitten began its mewling again, and she knew she must feed it. She couldn't let it starve. But how on earth was she to get milk into the stomach of a tiny kitten? It wasn't old enough to lap milk from a bowl. She could pour milk down its throat with a spoon, but she suspected that wouldn't work.

Perhaps Jakob would know what to do.

Still holding the kitten against her chest, she hurried inside.

It was surprising how loud a creature this small could be. If Jakob was sleeping, he would certainly be awake by the time she reached the bedroom.

He was.

"What have you got there?" he asked the moment Karola stepped into the room.

As if he couldn't tell by the sounds it made.

"It seems to be orphaned," Karola answered. "It is hungry, but I do not know what to do."

"An eyedropper."

"What?"

"You can get milk into it with an eyedropper." He motioned her closer to the bed. "Here. Give it to me. There's an eyedropper in the cabinet in the bathroom. Top shelf. After you find it, go get some milk. Not much. It can only eat a little at a time. And the milk needs to be warm."

Karola placed the mewling kitten into Jakob's outstretched left hand, then turned toward the door.

"You might as well know that the chances aren't good it'll survive. It'll probably be dead before the week's out."

She nodded but didn't look back at him.

In the bathroom, she found the eyedropper exactly where he said she would. She placed it in the pocket of her apron, then hurried downstairs, where she warmed some milk in a saucepan.

By the time she returned to the bedroom, Maeve, Bernard, and Aislinn—awakened, no doubt, by the kitten's cries—had joined their father on the bed. He sat upright now, his back propped with pillows, and the children were crowded around, making sounds of admiration, asking if they could hold the kitten, wanting to touch it.

"Not yet," Jakob answered patiently. "It's too little."

Karola's heart was in her throat as she observed them. She felt like an outsider, and she didn't want to be. She longed to be part of them. Really a part of them.

Jakob looked up and saw her standing there. "Here's Karola. Let's get some food in this noisy thing's belly so it'll quiet down."

Karola moved into the room. She set the cup of milk on the stand next to the bed, then withdrew the dropper from her apron pocket and offered it to Jakob.

He shook his head. "You'll have to do it. My hand's still not steady enough." Wincing from the effort, he slid to his right. "Sit here beside me."

"I can do it, Da," Maeve said. "I can do it."

"Not this time. Maybe tomorrow, if it's doing okay. But don't get your hopes up."

As Karola took possession of the kitten again, she remembered something Jakob had said to her the night Woodrow Mason was killed: *"No matter how hard we try to protect them, we're helpless to change things. Life's a series of loss upon loss."*

How terrible to have so little hope, so little faith, to expect disaster to strike at any moment, to await it almost as if it were his due. She could see that was how it was for him. She wished she could touch him, touch his heart, and help him find the truth. To show him there was hope. That there was a place of safety, right in the middle of any storm.

"It is going to be all right, Jakob," she said softly. "You will see."

There was something about the way Karola said those words that almost had Jakob believing them.

After giving her a few instructions, Jakob leaned against the pillows at his back and observed as Karola dripped warm milk down the hungry kitten's throat. He saw her tender smile at the kitten's eagerness and heard her soft laughter as milk dribbled down her wrist and onto her apron.

He hoped the kitten wouldn't die, for he knew Karola would be as disappointed as his children would be. He didn't want that. Not for any of them. He was tired of disappointment and heartache.

"Maeve," Karola said softly, "please go and get that wicker basket on the back porch. That small yellow one. Bernard, could you go to the basement and bring up some of those rags we keep under the worktable?"

"What for?" Bernard asked, already sliding off the bed.

"She needs a place to sleep."

"It's a girl?" Maeve also moved to obey. "How can you tell?"

Jakob grinned. "Yes, Karola. How can you tell?" He'd bet dollars to buttons she hadn't a clue how to tell the sex of a kitten, and even if she did, it was nigh unto impossible to tell with one this young.

If Karola knew he was teasing her, she didn't show it. "Just look at her adorable face. She must be a girl." Karola gave her head a firm nod for emphasis.

As soon as the two older children darted off, Jakob said, "You know she's going to need frequent feeding. You've already got your hands full as it is."

"I know." She met his gaze. "That is why I mean to put her basket in here. Then you can see to her throughout the day."

"Me? I'm no nursemaid for a kitten."

Karola smiled. "You have been needing something to occupy your time."

"Cats don't belong in the house. They belong in the barn. We never—"

"I am sure the children will be glad to help you take care of it. Maeve can bring you the milk, and Bernard can change the rags in the basket so that it stays clean."

"Listen, Karola. I—"

"Bitte."

That one little word stopped his protests. *Please.* How could he deny her? She asked so little of him. He'd given her even less. "I suppose I could do it."

"Danke!" Her eyes were bright with joy.

Then she leaned forward and kissed him, and Jakob wasn't sure who was more surprised—he or, from the look on her face as she pulled back, Karola herself.

Chapter Twenty-Seven

*J*akob was drowsing in the afternoon heat when Tulley burst into the bedroom.

"There's himself, lyin' about like a man o' leisure."

Jakob sat up, blinking away the fog of sleep.

Tulley settled onto a chair near the bed. "The doctor says you're doin' well, all things considered. 'Tis glad we are to hear it." He frowned. "Though I'd not know you were improvin'. You have the look of a man who's been on the receivin' end of a prize-fighter's gloves."

"Thanks."

Although Jakob still suffered from too-frequent headaches and had to move with care, he *was* much better. The most frus-trating thing about his recovery was the persistent weariness that dogged him. He supposed it had a lot to do with the blazing heat of the past few days, but that didn't make it any easier to endure. He wasn't used to being idle. He hadn't spent this much time in bed since those robbers in Wyoming nearly killed him.

At least he was more mobile than right after the accident. He was grateful for that. He'd even eaten his breakfast downstairs this morning, despite Karola's objections.

Tulley gave his head a slow shake. "Father Patrick says we must take the little potato with the big potato in this life."

Jakob knew he was supposed to gain encouragement from that bit of Irish wisdom.

"Sure, and I've been sent to bring the wee ones back to town with me for a few days. Laura's missin' their company, she is. She's told me I'm not to be takin' no for an answer." Tulley raised a hand. "I've already talked to your missus—she was hanging out the laundry when I rode up—and she had no objection, so there'll be no arguing from you now, will there?"

Jakob glanced toward the window. The curtain had been drawn in a futile attempt to keep the room cool—and so he couldn't see outside. Even so, he could imagine Karola in his mind's eye, standing at the clothesline, the large wicker basket at her feet, her apron pocket filled with clothespins, her hair caught beneath a kerchief.

The image changed suddenly, and he saw her as she'd been last night. Clad in a prim, white nightgown, her hair loose and flowing about her shoulders. She'd stood near the window, bathed in the light of a full moon, holding the kitten near her cheek, murmuring softly to it, loving it. Her expression had nearly broken his heart, it had been so wistful.

He'd wondered what she was thinking, if she longed for another place. He remembered wishing she would hold him and whisper to him and love him like that.

"Would there be anything you're needin' to say, me boy? You have the look of a man with much on his mind."

Jakob turned his gaze on his good friend. He was tempted to pour out his confusion and frustration. After all, it was Tulley who told him he was in love with Karola before he knew it himself. Who better to help him make sense of things?

But Jakob wasn't the sort to share confidences easily, and so he let the moment pass.

Perspiration trickled down Karola's spine and dampened her bodice beneath her arms as she hung the last load of laundry on the line. Long strands of hair had slipped free of the kerchief she wore on her head and were now plastered against her neck. The glare of the relentless sun, reflecting as it did off the white bedsheet, nearly blinded her.

She hoped Jakob would give his permission for the children to return to town with their uncle Tulley. She was exhausted from long days and relatively sleepless nights, and she would be thankful for a brief reprieve of even a few chores.

Oh, but that was terrible. The children weren't a chore. They were a delight, and she loved them with all her heart.

She turned from the sheet on the line, wiping her forehead with the back of her forearm before bending to lift the basket. As she straightened, she saw a horse and buggy approaching up the drive. She assumed it would be the doctor. He'd promised to look in on Jakob today.

But it wasn't Dr. Cooper. It was Charlotte White, looking as fresh and pretty as wildflowers in a mountain meadow.

If she'd felt exhausted before, now Karola felt old and dowdy.

"Hello," Charlotte called as she drew in on the reins, stopping beside Tulley's carriage.

Karola set the basket on the ground, then walked toward the buggy. "*Guten Tag,* Miss White." With her fingertips, she pushed damp hairs from her face.

"My mother sent me with a cake. She thought Mr. Hirsch might enjoy it. She said to apologize because it won't be as good as one of yours." As she disembarked, Charlotte glanced at the other carriage. "Is Laura here? If I'd known she was coming, I would have joined her."

"*Nein.* It is Mr. Gaffney who came. He is with Jakob now."

Charlotte's gaze scanned the barnyard until it came to rest on Lance's gelding in the corral. With feigned nonchalance, she asked, "Is Mr. Bishop with them, too?"

Amazing, how that one question—and the apparent motive behind it—served to brighten Karola's mood. "*Nein.* He is in the fields." She turned toward the house. "Please come inside, Miss White. It is too hot to stand here in the sun."

She returned to where she'd left the basket, lifted it, then waited for Charlotte to catch up so they could walk to the house together.

"How fortunate you are to have Mr. Bishop's help," the younger woman said as they stepped onto the back porch.

"*Ja,* he is a good friend to us." Karola set the basket near the door, then motioned for Charlotte to enter the kitchen before her.

"And how is Mr. Hirsch feeling?" The question seemed almost an afterthought.

"He is better."

Charlotte handed the cake plate to Karola. "You will give him my regards."

"Of course."

"We were all very frightened for him when he fell." Charlotte glanced toward the back door. "I don't suppose Mr. Bishop will be back anytime soon."

"I cannot say."

Charlotte looked crestfallen.

Karola hoped for Lance's sake that Charlotte's feelings for him were genuine and lasting. Lance had his heart set on this young woman, and Karola knew only too well how it felt when one's heart's desires were shattered by unrequited love.

"Please, sit down, Miss White, and we will become better acquainted. *Ja?*"

Jakob thought the house too quiet without the children. The silence left him too free to ponder his troubles. He hadn't enough cash reserves for the doctor bills and the extra work Lance was putting in. And the weather. If they didn't get some rain soon . . .

Then there were his feelings for Karola. One moment, he was confident he could win her love and trust. She'd kissed him, after all. But then he'd begin to doubt. After all, why should she love or trust him?

No reason I can think of.

Yes, it was too quiet, and definitely too hot. He couldn't bear the upstairs bedroom another minute.

Moving slowly, he shucked his nightshirt and struggled into a clean, sleeveless undershirt and a pair of trousers. He was winded by the task, like an old man who'd smoked one too many cigars in his lifetime.

He rested a few moments, seated on the side of the bed, then rose and shuffled toward the door. He paused when he caught sight of his reflection in the dressing table mirror.

Tulley was right. He looked like a prizefighter had worked him over good. The stitches the doctor had taken in the cut above his left brow looked like barbed wire poking out of his forehead. He was overdue for a haircut, his cheeks were gaunt beneath nine-day-old stubble, and dark circles underscored his eyes.

With a grunt of disgust, he moved on. Out of the room. Down the stairs. Along the hall and through the dining room.

Just before he reached the door into the kitchen, it swung open and Karola stepped through, stopping the instant she saw him.

"Jakob, what are you *doing?*"

"Coming to the kitchen."

"You should have called for me. I would have brought you whatever you needed."

"What I need is a change of scenery."

Karola pushed the kitchen door open again. "Are you hungry? Miss White brought a cake."

"She was here?" He moved forward, anxious to reach one of the kitchen chairs.

"*Ja.* She came while Mr. Gaffney was with you." Karola took a pitcher of tea from the icebox and poured some into a glass, then brought it to the table and set it before Jakob.

"Thanks." He took a long drink of the sweetened beverage.

She moved to sit across from him. "Lance will be sorry he missed her."

"Better if that courtship doesn't work out. She'd make him a poor wife."

"That is what I thought, too, at first. But now . . ." She shook her head. "I think perhaps Lance sees something others do not."

"You're too generous, Karola. Charlotte White thinks only of herself and what's best for her. Besides, she's been unkind to you since you got here."

Karola shook her head slowly.

"How can you deny it?"

"Perhaps I understand her. She is young and headstrong. Not unlike I was at her age."

"You were never anything like her."

"Was I not?" A gentle smile curved her pretty mouth. "I think you have forgotten, Jakob, the girl you knew in Germany. I was willful, stubborn, and impatient. And most determined to have my own way."

Jakob studied her a few moments—the delicate curve of her small ears, the rosy blush in her cheeks, the calm light in her blue eyes. "You *are* different." He leaned forward, wondering at the change. "Even from when you came to Shadow Creek."

"*Ja.*" It was her turn to study him in silence.

He felt as if she were able to look past the surface into the darkest corners of his soul. He couldn't say he liked the idea.

"Jakob, why are you angry with God?"

He started at the question. "What do you mean? I'm not angry with God."

"But you are."

He scowled.

"Jakob . . ." She leaned forward and touched the back of his hand that still held the glass. "I am your wife. You can tell me what is in your heart."

My wife . . .

Yes, she was married to him, but she didn't love him. She'd married him out of obligation, perhaps pity.

"Tell me, Jakob. *Bitte.*"

"Well, if I'm angry, can you blame me?" Was it pain or the heat or his own frustration that caused him to snap at her? He didn't know. Didn't even know if he cared. "Don't I have good reason? Look at what's happened. I just start getting back on my feet after a bad year, and *this* happens. Why can't I have a long stretch of good luck for a change? Don't I deserve it? And what about you? You came all this way from Germany, only to end up in a marriage that makes you more servant than wife. Don't you deserve better than that?"

"Nein." Karola withdrew her hand. "I used to think as you do, but I have come to understand the only thing I deserve, all anyone deserves, is eternity in hell. That I will not get what I deserve makes me grateful to God for everything I receive." Her gaze dropped to her hands, now folded in her lap. "Because of Christ, I am grateful even for the hard things, Jakob. Or at least, I am learning to be. I am trying to be."

"I'm one of those hard things, aren't I?"

She didn't answer, only watched him with sadness in her eyes of blue.

He felt condemned by the look. "I'm going back to bed." Jakob turned toward the door.

Stop him! Karola thought, and the urgency of those two words, heard so clearly in her mind, caused her to jump to her feet. "Jakob, wait!"

He hesitated, but didn't look over his shoulder.

"Do you know how often you do that?" she asked, pulse pounding in her ears.

Now he turned. "Do what?"

"Walk away rather than talk to me. Or get angry and change the subject."

He opened his mouth, as if to object, then closed it without speaking.

Ask him, that small voice demanded, and she felt compelled to speak the words that formed suddenly in her heart.

"Jakob . . . where do you stand with Jesus?"

He frowned. "I don't know what you mean."

She hadn't known the answer for herself until she came to Shadow Creek. How could she explain it to him?

He shook his head. "I'm too tired for this conversation."

"But it is important." She took a step toward him. "It is the most important thing of all." *Even more important than you learning to love me.*

"Later, Karola—" He turned again to leave. "We'll talk about this later."

Not later, Jakob. Talk to me now. Do not turn your back on Christ. Do not turn it on me.

But he had already disappeared through the kitchen doorway, and Karola was left with a disquieting sense of failure.

Chapter Twenty-Eight

*L*ance sat on his horse, stopped in the shade of a large cottonwood, his gaze grimly locked on the water flowing in the canal. It was too low. Much too low. They were only halfway through the growing season. If they didn't get a break in the weather soon . . .

"Lord, I reckon we could use some of that rain you pour on the just and the unjust."

He turned his mount's head and started toward the house.

He was bone weary. There was no denying that. He was putting in twice as many hours at the Hirsch place as he usually did. Other neighbors had pitched in, too, of course. Folks were like that in this valley. They helped when they were needed. Lance had seen it time and time again. God-fearing folks they were. Most of them lived the gospel message rather than just listening to it on Sundays.

His thoughts turned to Charlotte. Not that thinking about her was anything out of the ordinary. He thought about her real regular like, and he felt more than a little impatience about getting their courtship started.

Last night, before Lance returned to his own place, Karola told him Charlotte had been to the Hirsch farm and had asked about him.

"That's a good sign, isn't it, Lord?"

Lance had to confess he was finding it more and more difficult to listen for God's still, small voice over the hard hammering of his heart. He couldn't rightly say what the Lord was telling him to do next about that girl. He was certain she was meant to be his wife—what he couldn't be sure of yet was the timing of it. He'd like it to be sooner rather than later. Didn't the Bible say it was better to marry than to burn?

His gaze moved across his neighbor's fields to the two-story house in the distance.

Lance wondered how long it would have taken Charlotte to forget her silly crush on Jakob if not for the pretense Karola had concocted. And it had worked, too. Charlotte hadn't paid Lance any mind until she'd thought somebody else might be after him.

Suddenly, he frowned.

Wasn't that the same sort of wrong thinking that got Abraham and Sarah into trouble? They accepted God's promise, then took matters into their own hands to make it come true. He felt a pang of apprehension. Was that what was going on? Was he trying to help God along, making things happen when he wanted them to?

"Lord, if that's what I've done here, I reckon I'm sorry. It wasn't what I meant to do. It—"

He stopped himself, knowing the words weren't true. It was exactly what he'd meant to do. Hadn't Karola expressed doubt and remorse almost as soon as she put the ball into motion? Hadn't she realized it was a lie and said so to him? It had been Lance who wanted to continue.

Well, it wasn't like they'd done anything inappropriate. He hadn't kissed her or even pretended to court her outright. They'd been friendly with each other, and in the course of it all, they'd become real friends. If some folks took that to mean more than was there, was that his fault?

Yes.

Remorse swept through him.

"Are you sorry you got caught," his father would have asked him, "or are you sorry you done it?"

Sorry I done it, he answered silently as he reined in his horse. Then he tilted his head and stared at the blue heavens.

"I mean it, Lord. I'm sorry. I know what I want, and that's Charlotte. But I want you more. I want your will to be done. So don't you let me go runnin' down my own path. I'm askin' that, Lord. Help me stay on the straight and narrow and not go givin' in to my own desire. I reckon that'll be best for everybody concerned. Forgive me for makin' Karola my accomplice. Bless her and Jakob and help them find happiness together."

He looked straight ahead, nudging his horse with his heels.

"And send rain, Lord. Please send the rain."

"Well?" Jakob stared hard at the doctor.

"You're doing better than I expected," Dr. Cooper said, still holding the stethoscope against Jakob's chest. "But you've got a ways to go." He straightened, then leaned back on the chair beside the bed.

"I'm tired of just lying here."

The doctor freed the stethoscope from his neck and dropped it into his black bag. "Jakob, it takes a good six weeks for bones to mend, longer for them to heal completely. If you do too much too soon, you'll pay for it with pain for a longer period of time."

"I've got a farm to run! I can't keep depending on neighbors to do things for me. I've already done too much of that over the last year."

"Nobody's doing anything you wouldn't do if it happened to one of them."

"Can I or can't I get back to work?"

Dr. Cooper sighed as he stood. "I suppose there's no reason you can't do what your body will tolerate, long as you stop when it gets to be too much." He squinted at Jakob. "Do you understand what that means? It means *stop* when you know you should."

"Will you tell Karola what you said? She has a tendency to . . . want to do everything for me."

"Doesn't hurt a man to be coddled by his wife now and again." Dr. Cooper grinned. "You should be enjoying yourself."

Maybe he should be, but he wasn't. Lying here in this too-hot, all-too-quiet bedroom gave him too much time with his thoughts. Time to think about all the things that had gone wrong and were still going wrong. Time to consider the mistakes he'd made, the opportunities he'd missed, the people he'd failed. Time to worry about the weather and the bills. Time to—

"I'd best be going." Dr. Cooper gripped the handle of his bag and lifted it off the foot of the bed. "I'm on my way to the Ferguson place. Lettie's expecting again. The baby could arrive any day."

"What is that? Number five?"

"Six."

"That's a lot of mouths to feed off that little patch of land of Quinn's."

"Indeed. Well, they seem to manage." The doctor stepped away from the bed. "Remember what I said. Don't rush what you're not ready to do. And make sure that binding stays tight."

"I'll be careful."

"See that you are."

Jakob lay still, listening to the descending footsteps until they faded into silence. Then he pushed the sheet aside and rose from the bed to dress. Better to get a few chores done now, before the heat of day settled over them. Even without the children to care for, Karola had been up at the crack of dawn.

He closed his eyes.

Things weren't good between them, and the fault lay squarely on his shoulders. It wasn't how he'd meant things to be. He'd had some sort of notion that he'd be able to win her love once they were wed.

More than once he'd thought about telling her he loved her, but those words kept sticking in his throat. He even knew why. If he didn't say them, if he didn't confess his love to her, then it wouldn't hurt if he lost her—or if she couldn't love him in return.

"Do things seem as hopeless to you as that?"

He remembered the night she asked him that question, the night Woodrow Mason was killed by lightning. He remembered the moonlight breaking through the clouds, illuminating the path before them, as he escorted Karola to the cabin. He remembered the soft quaver in her voice when she spoke.

"There is safety in God, Jakob. There is hope in him."

What gave her that kind of assurance? What made her so confident? Maybe she hadn't suffered enough, lost enough, to have her confidence shaken. Maybe life hadn't dealt as harshly with her as it had with him. Was that why she could be so sure?

"Where do you stand with Jesus?"

For some reason, he knew that question also held the answer. Therein lay her confidence and her hope. He knew it, but he didn't understand it.

He took his shirt off the hook and put it on, moving stiffly and not without discomfort. His trousers were next, and then his boots.

"Where do you stand with Jesus?"

What kind of thing was that to ask a person? What did it mean? Standing with Jesus. As if that were possible.

Lucky—as the kitten had been dubbed—suddenly announced it was feeding time, and for a change, Jakob was glad for the noisy cry. It broke the chain of his thoughts, rescuing him from further uncomfortable contemplation.

He went to the basket and lifted the kitten from the bed of towels, holding it in the palm of one hand. With his other hand, he grabbed the eyedropper, then headed out of the room and down the stairs. In the kitchen, he put a small amount of milk into a saucepan on the stove.

Lucky protested the delay in feeding by raising the volume of her meows.

"Keep up that racket, cat," Jakob grumbled, "and your luck's gonna change."

But in contrast to his harsh words, he gently pressed the kitten into the curve of his neck as he'd seen Karola do numerous times in the past few days.

Lucky immediately quieted.

Did love often hurt like this? Karola wondered as she watched her husband from the doorway.

Tears stung her eyes, and she backed out of the room before he could see her, carefully closing the door as she went. She turned, walked to the porch steps, and sat on the top one.

"O God, what am I to do? My heart is breaking."

A soft answer drifted to her, as though carried on the gentle breeze. *Trust me.*

She covered her face with her hands, her elbows resting on her knees, and fought down the myriad emotions threatening to swamp her. She was a failure as a Christian, let alone as a wife. She never seemed to react as she was supposed to. She was impatient and impulsive. Every time she read her Bible, words would pierce her heart, and she would be certain they'd changed her. And then she'd go right out and behave the same old way.

Even now, she was thinking more about herself than about Jakob. That's why she was crying. Because she wanted him to hold her as tenderly as he'd been holding Lucky. Because she wanted him to desire her the way a husband was supposed to desire a wife. It didn't matter to her that he was injured and in pain, that just breathing was difficult for him, that he had come within mere inches of death's door less than two weeks before. All that mattered to her was what *she* wanted.

Trust God.

Be patient.

Wait.

Some days, she felt she could do those things. But at other times . . .

"At other times," she whispered, "I want to be loved."

You are *loved, my daughter.*

She no longer fought her tears. It would have been useless to try.

The doctor was right, Jakob decided as he lay in bed that night. It had been too soon for him to return to farmwork. Even doing the simplest chores had caused an increase in pain that was nearly unbearable.

But there was something worse than physical pain, and that was the memory of Karola, sitting on the porch step, her back to him, weeping into her hands. Of course, when she finally came into the house, she hadn't let on she'd been crying. She'd smiled at him, albeit sadly, pretending nothing was amiss.

And he'd pretended, too, never telling her he'd seen her grief. What a pair they were, Karola so sad, and Jakob the cause of her unhappiness.

Things just kept going from bad to worse.

Chapter Twenty-Nine

For several days, Karola wallowed in self-pity and self-blame. Depression clung to her like a heavy shawl over her shoulders. She knew she should talk to Jakob about her feelings, but she couldn't make herself do it. It was fear that stopped her—what if she made matters worse between them? What if he never loved her as she loved him?

On Saturday morning, Karola rose from bed before dawn, dressed hastily, took her Bible from the nightstand, and walked up the mountainside, not stopping until she was winded from the climb. Then she sat on the ground beneath an aspen.

"I cannot go on like this, Father. Help me."

With her eyes closed, she drew in a long, deep breath, then set her Bible on its spine in her lap and let it fall open. Releasing her breath, she opened her eyes and focused her gaze on the right-hand column of the right page. The first heading read: *Psalm 13.*

"How long wilt thou forget me, O LORD? for ever? how long wilt thou hide thy face from me? How long shall I take counsel in my soul, having sorrow in my heart daily? how long shall mine enemy be exalted over me?"

"How long, Lord?"

Like King David, she felt forgotten. Forsaken. Even knowing God loved her, even knowing he was near to her, hadn't driven away the depression, hadn't lightened her spirit or allowed hope to return. She was impatient for his answer. She wanted him to rescue her from the distress that overwhelmed her. Now.

"Consider and hear me, O LORD my God: lighten mine eyes, lest I sleep the sleep of death; Lest mine enemy say, I have prevailed against him; and those that trouble me rejoice when I am moved."

That's what she had felt these many days. She would sleep the sleep of death.

"But I have trusted in thy mercy; my heart shall rejoice in thy salvation. I will sing unto the LORD, because he hath dealt bountifully with me."

Karola grew still as the final two verses replayed in her mind: *"But I have trusted in thy mercy; my heart shall rejoice in thy salvation. I will sing unto the LORD, because he hath dealt bountifully with me."*

Something new resonated in Karola's heart. Not the despair of King David but his faith and trust, his word's of rejoicing, his recognition of God's goodness to him.

"'Yet I will rejoice in the LORD,'" she said, recalling a favorite verse of her mother's, one Frieda Breit had quoted often. "'I will joy in the God of my salvation. The LORD God is my strength, and he will make my feet like hinds' feet, and he will make me to walk upon mine high places.'"

The meaning behind those words was suddenly clear to her. Rejoicing wasn't the product of feelings. It was a *decision,* a choice of her free will.

She lifted her gaze from the pages of her Bible and stared down the mountainside. She couldn't see the farmhouse or outbuildings from here, but she knew where they were. She pictured Jakob asleep in their bed.

"Father God, I rejoice that you are sovereign. I do not know the plans you have for me, but I do know that they are for my good. You have dealt bountifully with me. You have saved me, and I am grateful for your love. Grant me your wisdom to speak what you would have me speak, and to be silent when you would have me silent. I give you myself, my marriage, and my husband. I choose to trust you. Father, you are merciful and long-suffering, especially to those who call upon the name of your Son, Jesus."

She closed her eyes a second time, savoring the sweetness of God's presence.

How she wished she could share this with Jakob. She wanted him to understand the comfort to be found in God's Word. She wanted him to savor the presence of the Lord the way she savored it now. She knew that sharing this—more than anything she might want for her marriage or for her husband—was of utmost importance.

It is more important for Jakob to love you, Father, than for him to love me.

It was almost painful to think those words. It was hard to let go of what she wanted so dearly.

"Karola?"

Half expecting she only imagined Jakob's voice, Karola opened her eyes. She hadn't imagined it. There he was, perhaps ten yards away.

"Are you all right?"

"*Ja,*" she answered as she stood. "But you are not."

Pale as a ghost, his face was etched with pain. He hugged his side with one arm.

"What are you doing here, Jakob?"

"I came to talk to you." He shortened the distance between them, and as he drew near, Karola saw beads of sweat dotting his forehead.

"How did you know where—"

He shrugged. "I watched from the bedroom window as you came up the mountain."

"I thought you were asleep."

He was silent for what seemed a long time before he softly said, "I always know when you leave the bed."

She flushed, oddly embarrassed by his confession.

Jakob gave her what passed for a smile before he sank to the ground near where she'd sat moments before. "I hope you didn't want to be alone." He leaned against the aspen's trunk and released a soft groan.

"*Nein.*" She sat beside him, a quarter turn around the tree. "I am glad you are here, Jakob." *I was praying for you. For us.*

"I've been doing a lot of thinking the last few days."

She dared to look at him. He was watching her, his expression grave.

"You said I'm angry at God. You said I always walk away rather than talk to you. You said I was without hope."

"I am sorry, Jakob. I say too much. I should not—"

"No. That's the way I am. You've got nothing to be sorry for. You were just saying what you see."

Karola worried her lower lip.

"Are those the reasons I make you so unhappy, Karola? Or is it something more? Don't try to tell me you're not unhappy because I know better. I've seen you crying."

He'd seen? She hadn't meant for him to. She'd tried to hide it. She didn't want to add to his troubles. "It is not you, Jakob. I am unhappy with myself."

"Yourself?"

"*Ja.* Sometimes I forget what is important, what is right. That is what makes me unhappy."

Wordlessly, Jakob took hold of her left hand with his right.

Karola looked down at their laced fingers, and her heart fluttered at the unexpected contact.

Jakob saw her look of surprise and wondered if he'd dared too much by taking hold of her hand. Still, he didn't let go.

"Are you sorry you married me?" He steeled himself against her answer, but he needed to know.

Tears flooded her eyes, and she shook her head.

It was obvious he'd stuck his foot in it again. Quickly, he said, "I wouldn't blame you if you *were* sorry. You've struck a poor bargain in me."

"Oh, Jakob. I am not sorry we are married. How could I be?" The tears that had welled moments before now streaked her cheeks. "I love you."

She said the words so softly—and so reluctantly—he wasn't sure she'd said them at all. But she had said them, and the sweet words were like a healing balm on an open wound.

Fresh tears slipped down her cheeks. "I hope someday you may learn to love me, too."

"It's too late for that." Jakob had trouble getting the words out around the emotion crowding his throat. When they did come, they sounded almost gruff.

Hurt flickered in her eyes, and she tried to pull her hand from his.

He tightened his grip. He wasn't about to let her go. Not now. Not ever. "It's too late to learn to love you, Karola, because I already do."

With a gentle tug, he pulled her across his lap so he could hold her in his arms. After all, it was where she belonged. He didn't care about the pain in his ribs the action caused. He needed to embrace Karola. He wanted to kiss the bride he loved, the bride who loved him in return.

Sure, and there was nothing Tulley Gaffney enjoyed more than being proved right. And he knew he had been when he saw Karola and Jakob that Sunday morning. Oh, he was sorry Ian and Laura were still at mass. He'd have liked them to see this, too.

"We have missed you so much!" Karola gave each of the children a tight hug. "The days have been too long, and our house is too quiet without you there."

"I'm thinking the quiet did you both some good." Tulley grinned. "I do believe there's new color in your cheeks, Mrs. Hirsch. Have you forgotten to wear your bonnet when out in the sun?"

Karola blushed scarlet at his words. Unable to help himself, Tulley gave a conspiratorial wink to Jakob, and bless him if Jakob didn't blush, too.

It was all Tulley could do not to laugh out loud.

Jakob cleared his throat. "We'd better get over to church. I hate walking in after the service is started."

"You'll be staying for dinner after. Laura won't be taking no for an answer and neither will I."

Karola glanced at Jakob; Jakob glanced at her. The tenderness in their eyes was like a physical caress.

Aye, it did a man good to see how things had worked out between those two. Of course, Tulley had known 'twas meant to be the first time he set eyes on the lass. They'd just needed a wee bit o' help, and he'd been glad to provide it.

"Go on with you." Tulley grinned from ear to ear. "You'll be keeping the good reverend waiting, and I'll not be having Pastor Joki accusing me of interfering with his services. You come to the hotel after, and we'll have us a bite to eat. I'm thinking 'tis corned beef and hash on the menu today."

'Twas a good thing, indeed, to help two people find love. Sure, an' Tulley Gaffney couldn't have been more pleased with himself.

"Mornin', Miss White." Lance removed his hat as he spoke, then raked his fingers through his hair, hoping Charlotte wouldn't notice he needed a trip to the barber.

"Well, good morning, Mr. Bishop." She smiled at him, squinting her eyes against the morning sun. "We haven't seen you in town lately."

"Been a bit busy, between my place and the Hirsch farm."

"Karola told me what a help you've been to them." She lowered her voice slightly. "I was out to visit her earlier in the week. Did she tell you?"

Now, that sounds promising. "Yes, she told me. I'm right sorry I missed seeing you for myself."

She fluttered her eyelashes at him. The little flirt.

Swallowing a grin, he said, "I was wondering, Miss White, if I might sit with you this morning."

"I suppose that—" She broke off abruptly, then said, "Look who's here. It's the Hirsches."

Lance turned to see the whole family—Maeve and Bernard leading the way, Aislinn in Karola's arms—coming toward the church. Jakob moved slowly and stiffly, but otherwise, he looked a whole lot different than when he and Lance had talked a couple of days ago. Stronger, less bowed beneath the weight of the world.

And Karola? He'd always known she was pretty, but this morning she positively glowed.

"Well, I'll be . . ." Lance spoke beneath his breath, grinning. Only one reason he could think of for such a change in them both.

Folks began to gather around the Hirsches, greeting Jakob with warm words and pats on the back.

"Good to see you, Jakob. We've been keeping you in our prayers, me and the missus."

"Can't believe you're up and about so soon. It's a miracle. That's what it is."

"Must be the nursing of this pretty wife o' yours. I know she shore would make *me* feel better."

"You know, Jakob. There's easier ways to get a gal to marry you than by throwing yourself under a herd of galloping horses."

Laughter erupted over this last comment.

"Why, they're in love!" Surprise laced Charlotte's soft words.

"I reckon they are at that," Lance replied.

"Does it bother you?"

He looked at the young woman beside him. She appeared uncertain, almost fearful. "Nope. Does it bother you?"

Her eyes widened a fraction, and then a smile slowly lifted the corners of her mouth. "No, Mr. Bishop, it doesn't bother me. I'm delighted for them. I hope they'll be very, very happy."

"Good." He offered her his elbow. "Maybe we'd best go inside now."

"Yes." She slipped her gloved fingers into the crook of his arm. "Let's do."

It occurred to Charlotte for the first time that Lance Bishop was interested in *her,* not her pretty face or her stylish dress or the way she wore her hair or even the fluttering of her eyelashes in his direction. On the Fourth of July, when they'd shared her boxed lunch, he'd listened whenever she spoke, giving her his full attention, and he'd seemed to care about what she said.

Seated beside Lance in the third pew, Charlotte cast a surreptitious glance in his direction. He'd removed his hat upon entering the church, allowing her a nice look at his profile. It was a handsome profile, too, especially today when he was freshly shaven and his hair was slicked back.

Something told her that Lance wouldn't be easily manipulated. Charlotte was used to getting what she wanted, often through her own wiles. But the old tried and true wouldn't work with Lance. She wouldn't change his mind with a winsome smile or a flirtatious toss of her head. She didn't know how she knew that, but she did. Oddly enough, she was relieved by the discovery.

Another thing occurred to Charlotte as she watched him. Lance truly found what Pastor Joki said interesting. He *wanted* to be here, to listen, to sing, to pray. He actually *enjoyed* being in church. And not so he could be sociable. The look in his eyes told her that.

She turned, following Lance's gaze toward the pulpit, wondering if the pastor just might have something to say to her, too. Anything seemed possible today.

Jakob marveled at how changed he felt this morning. Amazing what a difference twenty-four hours could make in a man.

He glanced at his wife, seated beside him in the pew, and acknowledged the difference in her, too. Karola looked happy. Truly happy.

"Thank you for making us one," she'd whispered last night, cloaked in the darkness of their bedroom. Somehow Jakob had known she'd thought him asleep, that her words had not been for his ears but for God's.

Now, Jakob considered her words of thanks to the Almighty, considered how deeply she believed God's hand was in everything, that it was God who had brought them together. He rather envied her confidence, a confidence he saw even when she was fearful, even when she was unhappy. A confidence Jakob didn't have.

"Where do you stand with Jesus?"

Why had she asked him such a thing? It wasn't as if he didn't believe in God and Jesus and the Holy Ghost. He did. He'd been raised in the church, same as Karola, and it never would have occurred to him *not* to believe. He knew the liturgy and the hymns and even a psalm or two. So he considered God rather distant, someone to be reckoned with on Sundays and when dying. That didn't mean he didn't believe. He just figured while here on earth, a man had to do the best he could by the sweat of his own brow.

Where was God, after all, when Jakob had saved and scrounged so he could come to America? Where was God when Jakob slaved in that awful factory in New York, or when he'd been robbed and beaten in Wyoming? Where was God when he'd plowed the fields of his farm and dug the irrigation ditches with the sun blistering his back?

Or when his young wife lay dying, leaving him with three children to raise on his own?

With you.

Jakob stiffened, then looked around, halfway expecting to find someone whispering near his ear. But everyone nearby was dutifully listening to Rick Joki, their eyes trained on the pulpit.

Jakob frowned, deciding he'd better do the same.

Chapter Thirty

25 July 1908
Shadow Creek, Idaho

Dear Father and Mother,

Yesterday, I received six letters from you. Six! I stayed up late into the night reading them. In truth, I read each of them more than once.

How joyous to see Mother's familiar handwriting and to read your words of wisdom, Father. I could close my eyes and hear your voices speaking.

It was wonderful to hear the news of Steigerhausen. I imagined myself there with Father in the bakery as people came and went. Please tell Frau Struve I was delighted to learn of the arrival of her healthy son. And tell Ilse Engels I adore the drawing of her dog you sent to me. Maeve asked to hang the drawing on her bedroom wall, which she promptly did when I agreed.

In your first letters you thought me already married; in the latter you thought me alone. You had not heard Jakob and I were wed. In an odd and wonderful way, it seems we have always been together. God has blessed us *with a love for one another that floods my heart with joy. I am grateful for each new day.*

Jakob is mending from his accident, and although he remains impatient for the healing to be complete, at least Dr. Cooper says Jakob need not fear any permanent damage. This past week, he has resumed many of his daily chores. He still cannot do heavy lifting, and he continues to move with care. But he is greatly improved. I see his frustration over those things he cannot do as yet but am learning not to interfere. He does not like to be coddled.

It remains dreadfully hot in this valley. There has been little rain this summer. The mountains and the uncultivated lowlands have turned brown, withering beneath a blistering sun. The earth is dry and cracked. The streams and irrigation canals are running low. I see Jakob's frown when he looks at the clear blue skies and know he is as worried as every other farmer.

I long to be able to ease his worries, but I know only God can do that, and Jakob has not yet learned to give his concerns to the Lord. I try to exhibit patience, although it is not one of my natural attributes.

Our friend, Lance Bishop, the young man who works for Jakob, has begun courting Charlotte White. It was all the gossip in town yesterday. Frau Noonan, the postmistress and owner with her husband of the grocery in Shadow Creek, took great pains to tell me everything she had heard and seen about the couple. I tried my best to dissuade her, but she is not easily stopped once she has begun.

I hope to have a portrait taken of my family this fall, after the harvest is in. I heard of a fine photographer in American Falls, which is not so far away that we cannot go and return in the same day. I would so very much like to send you a photograph so you might see Jakob and me and the children. You would quickly understand why I am so happy in my role as wife and mother.

Maeve's sixth birthday is nearly upon us. She will enter school when the new session begins. I have been working with her on her reading and spelling. She is bright and learns quickly.

The lessons are good for me, too. I am told my English is excellent, but I know I sound quite foreign because of the way I phrase things. It is not so for Jakob. You would not know he lived in Germany until he was twenty. By the way he speaks, you would think he was an American from birth.

Bernard has been the first of the children to call me Mama. I cannot express the joy I felt the first time he said it, for I feel as though it is true, that these are my children. I suppose it shall take Maeve a little longer. She remembers her mother and misses her still, and although we have grown closer with each passing week, I must be patient. Oh, there it is again. My need for patience. Learning to wait.

Aislinn no longer walks with uncertain steps the way she did when I first arrived. Now she races about everywhere. She has two more teeth, and although much of her chatter is still a mystery, she adds new words to her vocabulary almost daily. She is a delightfully happy child.

I pray that some day you will come to visit us in America, to see this vast and wonderful country that is now my home and to meet the family God, in his bounty, has given me.

I remain your loving daughter,
Karola Hirsch

Chapter Thirty-One

———————— ⚜ ————————

ou tell better stories than that, Karola," Maeve said as she closed her *McGuffey's First Eclectic Reader*.

Karola smiled at the girl. *"Danke."*

Maeve set the book aside, then rose onto her knees and leaned her forearms on the sofa back.

It was afternoon, and the house was quiet. While Bernard and Aislinn napped in their rooms, Karola and Maeve had settled into the parlor, Maeve on the sofa, Karola at the writing desk. Jakob was in the barn.

"What's that you've been reading?" Maeve pointed at the open Bible on the desk.

"I am reading from the gospel of John."

"Can I read it instead of this?"

"It might be a little hard for you yet, Maeve. The English, it is ... well, different, from what we speak today. I struggle with it myself." That was an understatement. It would have been easier if she read from her German Bible, but Karola was determined to persist. She was in America now. She would read English like everyone else.

"Please." The girl slid from the sofa and came to stand beside her.

Karola stroked Maeve's hair, filled with wonder at the bond forming between them. "I suppose you may try if you wish." She turned the open Bible toward the girl and placed her index finger on a passage. "Here. This is where I was reading."

"'Let not your heart be . . .'" Her face scrunched up and her mouth pursed as she concentrated.

"'Troubled,'" Karola supplied.

"'Troubled.' *Ye?* What's that?" She glanced up.

"It is another form of the word *you*."

"Why don't they just say *you* then?"

Karola laughed softly. "I have wondered the same thing."

"'Ye . . . believe . . . in God, believe also in me.'" She looked up a second time. "Believe in who?"

"In Jesus."

"Like what we learn in church?"

"*Ja.*"

"Oh." Maeve considered this a moment or two, then slid the Bible back to Karola. "Why don't you read it to me? It must be a real good story 'cause you're always readin' it."

Karola smiled again, noting the sleepy look in the girl's eyes. She suspected if she read aloud to her, Maeve would soon be napping like her brother and sister. "Come. We will sit on the sofa together."

Maeve led the way. Within moments, the little girl was leaning against Karola's side, Karola's arm around her shoulders, while the Bible lay open on Karola's lap.

"I will try to tell you the story in words you will understand. *Ja?*"

"Sure. Okay."

Speaking slowly, translating the words first in her mind, Karola began. "Jesus said, 'Don't be troubled. You trust God, now trust in me. There are many rooms in my Father's home, and I am going to prepare a place for you. If this were not so, I would tell you plainly. When everything is ready, I will come and get you, so that you will always be with me where I am. And you know where I am going and how to get there.'"

Maeve sighed and nestled closer.

"'No, we don't know, Lord,' Thomas said. 'We haven't any idea where you are going, so how can we know the way?' Jesus told him, '*I* am the way, the truth, and the life. No one can come to the Father except through me. If you had known who I am, then you would have known who my Father is. From now on you know him and have seen him!'"

Karola stroked Maeve's hair. *Please, Father, let this precious child come to know you now, while she is young. Don't let her wait, as I did, until after she is grown.*

"Philip said, 'Lord, show us the Father and we will be satisfied.' Jesus replied, 'Philip, don't you even yet know who I am, even after all the time I have been with you? Anyone who has seen me has seen the Father!'"

Karola knew Maeve slept now, but she didn't stop her recitation, for the words were precious to her, too beautiful not to speak aloud now that she'd begun.

"'If you love me, obey my commandments. And I will ask the Father, and he will give you another Counselor, who will never leave you. He is the Holy Spirit, who leads into all truth. The world at large cannot receive him, because it isn't looking for him and doesn't recognize him. But you do, because he lives with you now and later will be in you. No, I will not abandon you as orphans—I will come to you. In just a little while the world will not see me again, but you will. For I will live again, and you will, too. When I am raised to life again, you will know that I am in my Father, and you are in me, and I am in you. Those who obey my commandments are the ones who love me. And because they love me, my Father will love them, and I will love them. And I will reveal myself to each one of them.'"

"And does Jesus reveal himself to you, Karola?"

She released a tiny gasp of surprise as her gaze left the page and she turned. Jakob stood in the parlor doorway. Their gazes met, locked.

He stepped into the room. "Does he?"

Her heart skipped erratically. "*Ja,* he does."

"How?"

She saw a yearning for understanding in his face and wanted desperately to supply the answers. *Help me, Father.*

Jakob sat on a nearby chair, his gaze never leaving hers. "How?"

"It is hard for me to put into words."

"Try."

"He reveals himself in his holy Word." She touched the Bible in her lap. "And in a voice, though not one I hear with my ears." She moved her hand to her breast. "I hear it here, in my heart."

Jakob leaned toward her, his brows drawn together. "What does that voice say to you?"

"That he is near to me. That he is my portion forever. That he loves me." She mirrored Jakob's action, leaning toward him. "That he loves you, too."

Jakob wasn't a man given to shows of emotion, but he felt suspiciously choked up, and he couldn't even say why.

"*Jakob . . . where do you stand with Jesus?*"

Karola hadn't asked that question of him again, yet it echoed in his mind, in his heart, ever persistent, demanding an answer from him.

"*Where do you stand with Jesus?*"

He still wasn't sure what it meant. He only knew he wanted the same peaceful assurance he saw in his wife.

"Karola . . . would he reveal himself to me if I asked?"

Joy, unlike anything he'd ever seen, shone in her eyes. "*Ja,* Jakob, he would."

"You look like you're feelin' better," Lance said as the two men rode toward the alfalfa fields the next morning.

"I do. Believe me, I do."

Jakob's answer wasn't related to his health alone. This feeling went deeper. It was as if a great burden had been lifted from his back yesterday afternoon, as if a curtain had been drawn back from a window, letting in the light of day. And with the light had come unexpected joy.

He'd actually caught himself humming while shaving this morning. Jakob *never* hummed.

He couldn't say what precisely had happened to make him feel this way. There hadn't been a bolt of lightning in the parlor or a voice from above rattling the eaves of the house. There hadn't been a flash of supernatural knowledge or wisdom. Yet he'd known things had changed, that *he'd* changed. Suddenly he'd known he was in right standing with the Lord.

He'd almost said something to Lance when the younger man arrived at the farm that morning. He had a feeling in his gut Lance would understand. But in the end, he'd kept it to himself, not knowing what to say.

"I talked to Brad about helping us with the second cutting." Lance's easy conversation intruded on Jakob's thoughts. "I figured we'd need one more hand, what with the doctor tellin' you to take it easy a few more weeks. Even if you are feelin' better."

Jakob nodded, though at the moment he felt he could do the work of two men.

After a short silence, Lance continued. "I went into town last evening for supper." A pause, then: "At the Whites'."

Jakob raised an eyebrow. "Is that so."

"Yep. It was real good. Mrs. White was ailin' so she didn't join us, but Mr. White and I got on right well. Better than I expected, to tell you the truth. You know how he dotes on his little girl."

"And how about Miss White? Did you get along with her, too?"

Lance grinned. "She was right friendly."

Jakob laughed. Hard to believe he'd been burning with jealousy only a month ago, afraid Lance meant to steal Karola right out from under his nose. But back then, Jakob had been a man without hope.

Today, he had hope.

Today, he figured nothing could shake his world again.

"Tell me everything." Emma's eyes fairly sparkled with curiosity.

Charlotte was only too glad to comply. She cast a quick glance around the hotel restaurant, making certain no one was seated at the nearby tables, then leaned toward her friend. "He told Daddy his intentions were honorable. He hopes I'll agree to marry him when the time is right and if Daddy agrees to the match."

Emma's eyes widened. "He actually said that in front of you?"

"No, silly. I was out of the room at the time."

"Then how—"

"I was listening from the hall, of course." Even as she said it, Charlotte felt an odd pang. But why should she feel bad about such a thing? "I had to know what they said to one another, didn't I?"

"Oh, Charlotte." Emma's sigh was heavy. "You shouldn't eavesdrop."

She knew her friend was right, although that knowledge had never troubled her before. And it irked her that it did so now. "You would have done the same in my place."

Emma shook her head, and Charlotte knew it was true. Emma wouldn't have done such a thing. And neither should she.

She leaned back in her chair as unfamiliar sensations warred within her. Guilt. Regret. And just a tinge of shame.

Why on earth should she feel ashamed? It wasn't as if listening from the hallway was among the seven deadly sins or something. Her father and Lance had been talking about her. How else was she to know what they said if she didn't listen? She couldn't come right out and ask them, for pity's sake.

Still, Charlotte decided, if such an opportunity presented itself again, she would not listen in. She didn't care at all for the way she felt now.

"I'm sorry, Charlotte." Emma looked truly repentant. "I didn't mean to judge you. It isn't my place."

"That's all right. You're forgiven."

They exchanged smiles. Emma was always quick to apologize, and Charlotte was always quick to forgive. They knew this about one another.

"Do you think you'll want to marry Mr. Bishop when he actually asks you? Do you love him?"

Charlotte considered the question a few moments. "I don't know." A shiver ran through her, a mingling of fear and anticipation—with a dash of curiosity about the mysteries of marriage thrown in. "His smile does make me go a little weak in the knees. Is that love, do you suppose, Emma?"

"Maybe. I've never been in love so I can't say for certain. Now that you've captured the heart of one of the valley's most handsome bachelors, I may never know. I'll probably end up a spinster."

Charlotte looked at her friend, and suddenly it mattered a great deal that Emma was happy. "I won't hear of it, Emma Shrum. Once I'm married, I'll devote all of my attention to finding you a suitable husband. I promise."

Emma laughed softly. "Well, not all. I should imagine Mr. Bishop will want *some* of your attention."

Charlotte blushed, oddly pleased at the thought. *And I shall want some of his as well.* She smiled, even more pleased at that prospect, then decided to change the subject before Emma asked her what she was grinning about and she utterly embarrassed herself.

Chapter Thirty-Two

August arrived without any change in the weather. The skies remained relentlessly blue and clear. Not even one small rain cloud to give the farmers a glimmer of hope.

The Shadow Creek Irrigation Project board of directors and members met at the schoolhouse on the afternoon of August the fourth to discuss the situation. Jakob returned from the meeting three hours later, looking more grim-faced than when he'd left.

"The Fergusons' well's run dry," he told Karola as he hung his hat on a peg near the door. "They've been hauling water from a creek about half a mile away, and that creek's barely more than a trickle."

"But Mrs. Ferguson has only just delivered their new baby. How will the family manage without water nearby?"

"They won't. Quinn says Lettie and the children are going to live with her parents in Pocatello for now. He plans to stay on here until he sees if his crops wither and die. If they do, then he says he'll let the bank take his place and good riddance."

"Oh, Jakob. What will happen to them? Six children and no home. Is there nothing anyone can do?"

"Few bankers hold with excuses for not repaying a loan.

Quinn knew that when he mortgaged his farm. It's the risk every farmer takes when he borrows money on his land."

She touched his shoulder. "And if it rains?"

"Rain could save the Ferguson farm, if it comes soon." He shook his head slowly. "We all need the rain to come soon."

Karola wanted to ask if their farm was mortgaged, but she couldn't bring herself to do it. He hadn't shared such matters with her, not even after they were married. She wasn't certain she had a right to ask.

She turned toward the stove. "I have kept your supper warm for you."

"I'll go up to see the children first. Have they been in bed long?"

"Not long."

He turned and left the kitchen without inviting her to go with him. The omission hurt. It felt like rejection. They'd been close since the morning they declared their love to one another, even more so in the days since Jakob had given his heart to the Lord. Her husband had walked with a lighter step, and the worry lines on his brow had eased. He'd sought her company at every opportunity. Now his worry lines were back, and Karola felt him withdrawing from her.

"I am being oversensitive," she whispered, but it did little to improve her spirits.

She busied herself, filling a plate with the food she'd prepared and pouring a large glass of cold milk. She set both plate and glass on the kitchen table, then sat down and waited for Jakob's return.

Jakob stood at the side of Aislinn's crib, staring down at his younger daughter. Enough light from the dying day fell through the west-facing bedroom window for him to see her cherubic face, the tiny thumb in her mouth. She slept in her favorite position, diapered rump stuck in the air with her knees tucked beneath her.

What would become of her if he were to lose this farm? He didn't want his children raised in poverty as he was. He'd come to America to escape that. He'd worked long and hard. Circumstances had slapped him down more than once, but he'd pulled himself up and fought on. Finally, here, in this valley, he'd succeeded. He'd made a good home for his children. He'd done everything possible to provide well for them.

But there wasn't anything safe and secure. Wasn't that what he'd said to Karola not all that many weeks ago? He knew as well as any—and better than most—how suddenly a man could lose what mattered to him. Money could be stolen. Good health could vanish. A wife could die.

Karola's reply had been that there was safety in God, that there was hope in him. And he'd come to believe what she'd told him. So why had the fears and doubts returned to haunt him? Why couldn't he trust God with this farm, with the future, with his children? What had happened to the indescribable joy he'd felt only a week before? Was it all a mist, an illusion?

No, God was real. The fault had to lie within himself.

He reached down and traced the side of Aislinn's face with the back of his fingertips.

There were others worse off than the Hirsches. He recognized that. Although his resources were stretched thin and he was in debt to the doctor, they had food in the pantry and smokehouse. They had a sound roof over their heads and plenty of wood stacked and ready for winter. The farm wasn't mortgaged; no banker was waiting to foreclose.

Not yet. But if the drought continues, if we lose this year's crops, if...

It could all go wrong so quickly.

"Jakob?"

He turned toward the sound of Karola's voice. She stood in the doorway to the girls' room, hidden in the gathering shadows of nightfall.

"Your supper grows cold."

What if something were to happen to Karola? If I was to lose her . . .

Jakob had loved Siobhan. Their marriage had been volatile and often stormy, but their love had been real. Yes, he'd loved his first wife.

But *love* seemed an inadequate word to describe what he felt for Karola. His feelings were more complex. It was as if she'd become a part of the very air he breathed. His love for her was a hunger deep inside him. Without her—

"Jakob"—her soft voice came to him like a caress—"do not worry."

Easier said than done, Jakob had discovered. Much easier said than done.

Charlotte closed the door of her mother's bedroom, then went downstairs to the parlor where her father was seated, reading a newspaper.

"Mother's asleep," she said as she entered the room.

He glanced up and nodded.

"Daddy?" She knelt on the floor next to his chair and rested her forearms on his left thigh. "What happened at that meeting this afternoon? You haven't said a word about it since you came home."

"Nothing for you to trouble yourself about, Charlotte. Mostly just grown men talking about the weather, the same way farmers always do."

"But it's serious, isn't it?"

"Yes. The drought's serious. It could ruin more than one family in this valley. Quinn Ferguson is sending his wife and children to Pocatello, and he may not be far behind them. They could well lose their farm before this month is out."

Charlotte didn't know the Fergusons well, and normally she wouldn't have given their troubles a second thought. But she discovered, with some surprise, that she felt truly sorry for them. "Perhaps Emma and I should take them a food basket."

"That would be good of you." He stroked her hair, the way he'd done when she was a little girl. "Very good of you."

She waited as long as she could bear, then asked, "Was Mr. Bishop at the meeting?"

Her father nodded.

"Is he in danger of losing his place, Daddy?" The thought frightened her. If Lance lost his farm, what would he do? Where would he go? What if she were never to see him again?"

Her father's smile was tolerant, and she read understanding in his eyes. "I don't know, Charlotte, but I have a feeling that young man will not be easily defeated in whatever he endeavors to do. I don't think you need to be afraid for him."

Charlotte hoped with all her might that what her father said was true.

Chapter Thirty-Three

———————— ❦ ————————

*Y*ou look ... radiant," Karola told Laura as the two women sat in the hotel's kitchen.

It was Thursday, and Karola had come to town with Maeve and Aislinn to purchase a few supplies at the mercantile as well as to pay a visit to her friend. Bernard had chosen to stay at the farm with his father who was repairing the corral fence.

"I feel wonderful." Laura smiled. "And I'm so happy about the baby."

That was apparent to Karola. There was a sparkle in her friend's eyes and a glow in her complexion. Obviously, pregnancy agreed with her.

Laura patted her stomach. "I can't believe how much more energy I have today than I did only a week ago." She sighed, a contented sound, then smiled. "It's a relief to be done with that awful morning sickness, I'll tell you."

Karola felt a twinge of envy. How wonderful it must be to carry a child beneath one's heart. How greatly she longed for it to happen to her.

"Your time will come."

At Laura's soft words, Karola felt color warm her cheeks. "I should not be impatient. Aislinn is so young yet."

"Father Patrick loves to quote a verse to expectant mothers. It says, 'As arrows are in the hand of a mighty man; so are children of the youth. Happy is the man that hath his quiver full of them.'" Laura placed both hands on her abdomen. "Ian and I are delighted to have this little one coming at last. We feared there might never be an arrow in our quiver."

Would Jakob think it a blessing if he and Karola had a child? She didn't know. They hadn't spoken of it. She knew he loved Maeve, Bernard, and Aislinn, but he hadn't said he wanted more.

Of course, there'd been no possibility of Jakob siring children with her until quite recently.

She felt her cheeks grow even hotter at the thought, and she rose quickly from her chair, then walked to the kitchen doorway where she glanced into the dining room, empty except for Tulley and the two girls. The three of them were sharing a plate of cookies, fresh from the oven.

"Karola, is something on your mind? You seem distracted."

She turned toward Laura. She shook her head, but the words came of their own accord. "I do not know if Jakob wants more children. We have not spoken of it." She felt close to tears. She was determined not to let them fall.

"Oh, Karola. Why would you newlyweds speak of such things? You're only married a month. You're still becoming acquainted in many new ways." She laughed softly. "I remember what it was like for us. Oh, the mistakes we made that first year. Our many silly misunderstandings because we didn't know how to talk to each other."

"You and Ian?" She returned to her chair and sat down.

"Of course. All couples go through a period of adjustment, even those who love each other to distraction. It's all the more difficult for someone like Jakob, who naturally keeps his thoughts so deep inside himself."

Karola thought of the many times Jakob had turned away rather than talk to her. She'd thought that had changed. She'd thought, now that they were truly man and wife, Jakob would share every thought, every emotion. Apparently, she'd expected too much too soon.

Wasn't that always the way she was? In a hurry. Impatient. Willful.

Here I am again, Father. Forgive me. Help me to wait and to listen. I know Jakob loves me. Let us learn how to talk to one another. And when he is silent, help me to respect that, too, and not be hurt by it, as if everything were about me.

Unaware of Karola's silent prayer, Laura went on. "I suppose Jakob is as worried as everyone else about the drought."

"*Ja,* he is worried, but he tries not to let me see. It does not work. I see anyway."

"Can you bring me that hammer, Bernard?" Jakob pointed to the object near the corral gate.

"Sure, Da." The boy ran to obey.

"Few more years," Lance said, "and he'll be helping you with just about all the farming chores. I reckon you won't be needin' extra help then."

"I reckon." Jakob wiped beads of sweat from his forehead with the back of his arm.

Bernard returned with the hammer. Lance lifted the new board, holding it tight against the post, and Jakob hammered it into place.

"What else can I do, Da?"

Jakob glanced toward the house as he straightened. "You think you could get us something to drink? Some ice from the icebox in a glass of water sounds real good about now."

Bernard grinned. "I can do that!" Then off he ran again.

Lance slipped through the corral rails. "Havin' Karola here sure has made a world of difference in your kids. They're happy again."

"She's good with them, and they love her."

"What's not to love? She's a special woman. Only a blind man would fail to see that."

Jakob frowned. Did Lance regret not pursuing Karola with a little more diligence? The younger man had said he only felt friendship toward her. Still—

"Maybe next year," Lance continued, "folks'll be saying the same thing about my wife."

"*Your* wife? Are you saying you've proposed to Charlotte?"

"Not yet." Lance leaned his back against the corral and hooked the heel of one boot over the bottom rail. "But I told Edgar White I mean to ask for his daughter's hand when the proper time comes. He didn't have any objections, and I think Charlotte's willing. Or she will be."

Jakob gave his head a slight shake. He would have stuck a rusty nail through his hand before marrying that girl.

Lance sighed. "I reckon it'll never be dull around our place once we're hitched."

"I hope you know what you're doing."

"I do. I knew she was God's chosen wife for me the first moment I laid eyes on her, though she was way too young back then. I been prayin' about it ever since, waiting for God to say the time's come. I've got a feelin' it's getting close."

Jakob wiped his forehead with his sleeve again. If what his friend said was true, if he and Charlotte were going to be married, then he hoped Lance was also praying hard for an end to this drought. Charlotte wasn't the type to do well in want. She was too used to having her every whim handed to her. Edgar must spend close to half of what he made in his smithy on Charlotte's new frocks alone.

Bernard came out of the back door, carrying two large glasses filled to the brim. Water sloshed with every step the boy took. Jakob wondered what sort of disaster awaited him in the kitchen but decided to check on it later.

"They're real cold, Da," Bernard said as he drew closer.

"That's good, son. Thanks." He took the glasses, then handed one to Lance. Both men took a long drink, nearly draining the glasses of their contents.

"Can I go check on the pups?" Bernard asked when his father looked at him again.

Jakob nodded. "Yes, but you don't get too close to them. Daisy's a bit snappish yet. I don't want her biting you just because she's protecting her babies."

"Okay. I'll be careful."

Lance waited until the boy had disappeared into the barn before he said, "New litter, huh?"

"Born last night. Three of them." He tilted the glass to his lips again, finishing the last of the water. Then he held the cool glass against his forehead and closed his eyes. "This heat better break soon."

"Yeah, I've been keeping a steady stream of prayers going."

Before he could stop himself, Jakob muttered, "And what good has it done?" He regretted the words instantly and expected Lance to upbraid him for his lack of faith.

He didn't. "I don't know what good it's done, Jakob, or what good it will do. But that isn't the point. I pray 'cause God says I'm supposed to pray. He says I'm to do it without ceasing. Can't say I'm that constant, but I do my best. I gotta trust him to answer those prayers in his way, not my way."

Jakob peered at Lance, recognizing how rock solid the younger man's faith was. Maybe it was why Jakob had always liked his company. Because he'd seen something different in him. That same sort of something different he'd seen in Karola.

He wondered if anyone would ever think the same thing about him, that Jakob Hirsch was a man with a rock-solid faith and that he was different because of it.

Lance set his empty glass on the ground. "Let's get the last of these rails up."

Jakob nodded, placed his glass beside Lance's, then grabbed the hammer and headed for the corral.

The two men worked in companionable silence and with a rhythm born from familiarity. They were just about to hammer in the last rail when a childish scream pierced the air.

"Da! Da, *help!*"

The horse trotted along the road, raising a cloud of dust behind the carriage wheels. Aislinn was asleep on the seat beside Karola before they reached the road that ran north to American Falls. It took longer for Maeve, who kept up a steady chatter from the rear seat for the first fifteen minutes of their journey. Then her voice began to taper off until at last she fell silent. A glance over Karola's shoulder confirmed the older girl slept, curled on her side, an arm thrown over her eyes.

"How precious they are," Karola said softly. "Thank you, Lord."

Her gaze returned to the road as she pondered her new life. When she arrived in Idaho, she couldn't drive a carriage or ride a horse. She'd never managed a household or been the mother to three children. She didn't know how to milk a cow, had never gathered eggs or saved an orphaned kitten. She'd never shared a home with anyone besides her parents or known the intimacies of the marriage bed.

"How different things are now. How different I am. How good you have been to me, Lord. How good you have been to us."

She drew in a deep breath and let it out, renewing her determination to be patient. With herself. With Jakob. And most assuredly, with God. She *would* learn to wait on him.

She felt the quickened stride of the horse, a sure sign they were drawing close to home. She lifted her gaze—and felt her breath catch in her throat. A pillar of thick smoke roiled above the next rise in the road.

It could only be coming from one place.

O Lord, not the house.

"Maeve, wake up! Sit up and hold on." She looked behind her, watching as the befuddled girl obeyed. "Hold on, Maeve." Then she placed one hand on Aislinn and with the other slapped the reins against the horse's rump. The carriage shot forward.

Jakob! Bernard! God, keep them safe!

Coughing, Jakob stumbled backward, trying to escape the dense smoke and the heat of the fire.

After getting his son to safety, Jakob and Lance had managed to rescue the two horses that had been in separate stalls as well as the new litter of puppies and their mother. Now all they could do was stand back and watch as the hungry flames consumed the barn and everything in it, the smoke and ash rising skyward. Jakob hoped the fire wouldn't spread. If it drifted toward a dry field or sparks landed on the roof of the house . . .

The sound of cantering hooves alerted him to his wife's return seconds before he heard her alarmed cry.

"Jakob!"

He spun around.

"Jakob!" Karola tumbled out of the carriage, Aislinn in her arms. Her gaze moved from him to the barn, then back to him. "Where is Bernard?"

Jakob pointed toward the steps of the house where the boy sat, scared but unharmed.

"What happened?"

Before he could answer, a loud crash caused him to turn toward the barn again. A billow of sparks shot out of the loft and the open doors below it.

Lance cried, "Everybody back! It looks about to collapse."

His words proved prophetic. Within minutes, the roof sank toward the ground, accompanied by creaks and groans and a series of popping sounds. The blazing walls tumbled inward, like

254 *Promised to Me*

a house made of cards, large and square one moment, thinner and flatter the next.

Jakob felt as if he'd been flattened too.

The barn. The tack. Tools. Grain and straw and hay. Lumber. All of it gone.

He heard Karola's soft weeping, and he glanced toward her. Aislinn was still clutched in her arms, and Maeve was cuddled up against her side, holding on to Karola's waist for dear life.

Doom, as dark as the smoke filling the air, settled over him. Doom . . . and anger.

No one said anything for the longest time. They simply watched as the fire turned the barn into rubble. It wasn't until the blaze died down—and the danger of it spreading was over—that Jakob turned toward his son, still seated on the porch steps.

"You go to your room and stay there until I come up."

Karola shivered at the steel-hard sound of the words.

Bernard—face pale, eyes red, cheeks streaked by tears—shot a beseeching look in Karola's direction. She wanted to go to him, to comfort him, but to do so would be to interfere with her husband, so she did nothing. Bernard turned and went up the steps, shuffling his feet, his chin drooping to his chest.

Karola looked at Jakob and felt another shiver of dread. "Maeve, take your sister into the house, please." She set Aislinn on the ground. Maeve grasped the toddler's tiny hand and led her away. After the girls had gone inside, Karola turned to her husband. "What happened? How did the fire start?"

"Bernard took matches from the kitchen. He was playing with them in the barn."

"Oh," she said, a breathless word.

"Once the fire started, he didn't call for us right away. He tried to put it out himself so he wouldn't get in trouble. By the time he yelled for help, it was too late to do anything but save the animals and get out ourselves."

She thought of what might have happened to Bernard or Jakob, and it made her feel ill. Pressing the palm of one hand against her abdomen, she turned to look at the debris that had once been the barn.

"Do not be too hard on him, Jakob. Do not discipline him in anger. He has had a terrible fright."

"A *fright?* Karola, he burned down our barn! He could have burned down a lot more."

"He is only a little boy. It was an accident."

"He has to be punished."

She sighed. "*Ja,* but he also needs forgiveness, Jakob. He needs your grace."

"What he's going to get is my hand on his backside, and it may as well be now." He spun on his heel and strode toward the house.

Karola began to weep again. Silent tears, this time, slipping down her cheeks. The truth was, she felt her faith shaken by these events. She wanted to ask God, "Why this? Why now?" She felt afraid of the future, of what tomorrow might bring, and was ashamed because of it.

Oh, ye of little faith.

She knew she should go inside. She should see to Maeve and Aislinn. They were frightened, too. They couldn't possibly understand it all. The barn had burned. Their brother was being punished. Their father was angry.

"I reckon it'll be all right."

She turned at Lance's words. She'd forgotten he was there.

"No matter what, Karola, it *will* be all right. It could've been a whole lot worse. No matter what happens tomorrow, the good Lord's still holdin' you, Jakob, and the children in the palm of his hand. He's holdin' us all there."

"I know," she whispered, even though it didn't seem true just now.

Late into the night, Jakob lay on his side, his back toward Karola—as hers was toward him. The open bedroom window let in the acrid scent of smoke still hovering in the air all these hours later. He could taste the ash on his tongue. Or was it the anger he tasted?

Why had this happened? Now, of all times, when he was facing the loss of his crops to the drought. Now, when they had little money put aside to see them through. How was he supposed to trust God, to have hope instead of expectations of calamity, when something always went wrong? Karola had told him to forgive Bernard, to show his son grace. Well, where was *God's* grace in this?

He remembered the despair he felt after his fall off the horse. And here he was again. Wasn't he supposed to be different somehow? Where was the joy he'd felt only a week ago?

Restless, Jakob got out of bed and went downstairs. In the kitchen, he lit a candle and set it on the table, then he took the farm accounts ledger from the shelf where he kept it and placed it on the table near the candle. He sat on the chair but didn't open the book. He didn't need to. He knew what the columns of figures said.

They were in trouble.

A nagging feeling told Jakob he wouldn't find answers for that trouble in his accounts book. He should look in the Bible, as he'd seen Karola do. But he didn't know where to look.

Then he should pray. At the very least, he knew he should pray. But he felt empty of words, powerless to express what he wanted to say.

"What do you want from me, God?"

He doubted that was the best way to begin, and he stopped before all the anger could erupt from within. But his mind couldn't be silenced, and it repeated the question.

What do you want from me?

Did Jakob expect an answer? He wasn't sure. But one came.

Know me.

The words didn't bring Jakob comfort. If anything, they made him more restless than before.

Chapter Thirty-Four

***T**he house was as quiet as a tomb.

Bernard had been forbidden to leave his room except for meals and to use the lavatory. Taking their cue from their father's dark mood, Maeve and Aislinn remained in their room without being told.

At lunchtime the day after the fire, Karola fed the children without calling for Jakob to join them. Poor Bernard wilted in his father's presence, so ashamed was he for what he'd done. She thought the boy might be enticed to eat if Jakob wasn't at the table. It didn't work. Bernard only played with his food.

After the children returned to their rooms, Karola went outside. Pausing on the top porch step, she shaded her eyes with her hand and looked across the barnyard. The black rubble still smoldered in a few places. Lance had promised to help clear the site on Saturday, but Jakob hadn't wanted to wait. He was already sifting through the debris, looking for anything that might be salvaged, his face and arms blackened by soot.

"Jakob."

He straightened and looked toward her.

"Lunch is ready."

He gave his head a shake, then returned his gaze to the ground.

Karola went down the steps and crossed the barnyard. "Jakob." She stopped at the edge of the rubble. "You did not eat breakfast. You must eat something now."

"There's too much to do."

"You will make yourself sick if you do not rest awhile. You are not that long recovered from your fall."

"I don't have time to rest, Karola." He straightened again, this time scowling at her. "You don't have any idea the trouble we're in."

"Then you should tell me."

"I don't want you to worry."

Exasperated, she said, "How can I not worry with you acting this way?"

"You don't understand."

Karola took a deep breath, trying to control her sudden anger. He was being bullheaded. He was pulling away from her again, the way he used to. He was keeping things bottled up inside and excluding her.

She took another deep breath. "I will get a pair of gloves and help you. Two will make the work go faster."

"You can't help me." He motioned with his hand, a gesture of dismissal. "Your skirts might catch fire from a live spark."

"I can tuck my skirts into my waistband."

"No."

"Then I will put on a pair of your trousers."

Jakob shook his head. "Karola, I'd rather be alone."

"But you are not alone. I am with you, and God is with us. Do not shut us out because of this misfortune."

"You and God aren't going to get us a new barn." He slapped a blackened glove against his chest. "*I've* got to figure out a way to do that."

She knew her disappointment must be evident on her face. "Where is your faith, Jakob?"

He swore.

She'd never heard Jakob use such a word.

All of a sudden, he stepped from the rubble and walked past her, striding toward the house.

Karola hesitated only a moment before following him. "Where are you going?"

He didn't answer as he dropped his gloves on the back porch, then went inside. In the kitchen, he stopped to wash up in the kitchen sink.

"Jakob?"

He turned around. "I'm going to the bank. I'll need to get a loan." He raked damp fingers through his hair. "I don't even know if Mr. Mindel will consider it. Not with the drought. Not with everybody in this valley in need. But we've got to get a barn up before winter, and that'll take money we don't have."

"We should pray, Jakob. I know God will provide."

"*How* do you know?"

"Because we are his. Because he is good. Because we can trust him. He kept you and Bernard safe yesterday. You could have been hurt, either of you—even killed—but you were not."

"There's other ways to be hurt besides physically. If this place is mortgaged and we lose this year's crops ..." He left the sentence unfinished as he headed across the kitchen toward the dining room door.

"Jakob!" She followed on his heels. "We *must* trust God."

He stopped outside the parlor and spun to face her. "God helps those who help themselves. Isn't that what the Bible says?"

"*Nein,* that is not what it says. It says his strength is perfected in our weakness. We are helped when we recognize we can do nothing without him."

"Well, it seems to me *I'm* the one who labored for every cent that paid for this place. It was by *my* sweat the fields were tilled every spring and the crops were harvested every fall. It'll be by *my* sweat we keep this place, if we do."

Karola stared at him, heartbroken and furious at the same time. "Jakob Hirsch, have you so soon forgotten what Christ accomplished for you? You have made him too small in your eyes. Do not be arrogant and prideful. Ask him for help. Pray and ask."

"You'll have to do the praying, Karola. You're the pious one in this marriage. I've got to take action."

Jakob regretted the things he'd said. He hadn't meant to lash out at Karola. None of this was her fault, and he shouldn't have acted as if it was. Still, he didn't apologize to her before leaving for Shadow Creek. He might be sorry, but that didn't change their circumstances.

He was halfway to town before he realized the darkness around him was caused by more than his mood. Black clouds rolled across the heavens, driven by a steady wind from the west. He pulled in on the reins and stared upward as he sniffed the air.

Rain? Did it smell of rain? Or was that wishful thinking?

Know me.

In the wake of that small voice in his heart came the shame. It hit him so forcefully he thought it would knock him from his horse.

Trust me, Jakob.

Karola was right. He *was* arrogant and proud. He had made the God of the universe small in his eyes.

"Although the fig tree shall not blossom, neither shall fruit be in the vines; the labour of the olive shall fail, and the fields shall yield no meat; the flock shall be cut off from the fold, and there shall be no herd in the stalls: Yet I will rejoice in the LORD, I will joy in the God of my salvation."

He wasn't sure where the words came from, but he knew they were true. And suddenly he understood. God wasn't to be praised because things went well. God wasn't to be praised because he gave his children what they wanted. He was to be praised because of who he is. Jakob was to know him and praise him, no matter what.

"O Lord, I'm sorry."

He heard the rumble of a distant thunder. It seemed as if God were answering him.

"Show me what to do next."

Karola had fallen asleep on the sofa while reading her Bible. It was the thunder that awakened her.

She sat up, then stood and walked to the pàrlor window. The trees around the house were swaying in the wind, and the sky above them had turned black with clouds.

Rain! It was going to rain!

She hurried to the front porch where she leaned over the railing and looked up. Yes, those were most definitely rain clouds. She could smell the moisture, a clean, beautiful fragrance, long absent from this valley.

"Thank you, Lord!"

Lightning flashed above the mountains in the west, followed shortly by the crack of thunder. She stood there, listening as the sound rolled toward her, enjoying the wind in her face. Then she remembered how frightened the children had been the last time there'd been a thunderstorm. Quickly, she returned indoors and climbed the stairs.

Just as she reached the second floor, another crack of thunder rumbled across the sky. Before the sound died away, Aislinn came scurrying down the hall toward Karola, Maeve close behind her.

Karola lifted Aislinn into her arms. "Did the noise frighten you?"

Aislinn nodded.

"Do you want me to tell you a story?"

"Yes," Maeve said without hesitation.

Karola smiled at the older girl as she brushed a hand over her hair. "We'll go into your brother's room. That way we won't be disobeying your father. All right?"

Maeve nodded, then turned and opened Bernard's bedroom door. "Karola's gonna tell us a—" She stopped. "He's not here."

"Not here?" Karola stepped into the bedroom and looked around.

Maeve was right. Bernard wasn't in his room. At least not in plain view. Karola checked under the bed and in the wardrobe, just to be certain. He wasn't either of those places. Karola set Aislinn on the floor, then went out into the hall and to the bathroom.

"Bernard?"

But the bathroom was empty, and there was no answer to his name.

Louder, she called again, "Bernard."

Oh, that boy. He was going to be in terrible trouble if she didn't find him before his father returned.

"Help me look for him, Maeve. He must be hiding from us."

"I'll find him," Maeve assured her. "I know all his hiding places." And away she dashed.

Karola lifted Aislinn into her arms again. "Bernard, please answer me. It is all right. I am not angry with you. But you must answer me. Bernard."

Father God, make him answer me. Help me find him.

"Bernard! Answer me."

An hour later, Karola and Maeve had searched the house and yard, and during that time, the rain had begun to fall, first lightly, then in torrents. The storm mirrored her growing panic.

Bernard was gone.

Jakob hadn't gone to town. He hadn't gone to the bank to ask for a loan. Instead, he'd turned off the road and ridden into the midst of his wheat fields. He'd ignored the storm, mindless of the wind and lightning and thunder. He'd stood on the land he had plowed, the land he still hoped to harvest in the fall, and he'd given it to God. He'd given his home and his lands, his wife and his children, and finally his pride. He'd surrendered every piece of himself that he knew he'd been holding back and asked God to show him if there was more to be given that day.

He wasn't sure how long it had been raining before he realized he was drenched clear through to the skin. Rain. Blessed rain. An element Lance said God poured down upon the just and the unjust—and the latter was surely him.

Jakob turned his face upward and opened his mouth. The rain tasted of hope, but he knew the hope had risen from within his spirit.

Grinning, he grabbed the pommel and swung into the saddle, then jabbed the horse's ribs with his boot heels and rode hard toward home.

When he cantered into the barnyard fifteen minutes later, he saw Karola near the corral, as soaked as he was, struggling to harness the horse to the carriage.

"Karola!"

She spun around. Her eyes widened. "Jakob!" She ran toward him, holding up her sodden skirt, the hem blackened with mud. "Jakob, Bernard is gone. We have looked everywhere and cannot find him. His wooden soldiers are gone, too. I think he has run away."

Jakob's first instinct was to shout orders at his wife, then rush off to find his son. But something stopped him.

"What are we to do?" There were tears in her voice.

Jakob dismounted, took hold of Karola's hands in both of his, and answered, "First, we pray."

Chapter Thirty-Five

Karola stared at Jakob, trying not to show her surprise. And as she looked at him, she realized this was not the same man who rode away in anger and desperation. Something had changed in his heart. She felt her terror begin to dissipate, and when he bowed his head, squeezing her hands as he did so, she felt calm replace the fear.

"Father"—Jakob's voice was barely audible above the falling rain—"I don't begin to understand the reason things happen, but I know I've given everything I own to you. I gave it all up and I promised to trust you with it. So if this is a test, I'm asking you help me pass it."

Help me, too, Jesus.

"We don't know where our son is, Lord. If he's run off because I was too hard on him, help me find him so I can ask his forgiveness. Keep him safe. Don't let any harm come near him."

Joy at hearing her husband praying such words warred with the fear she felt for their son. *O, Jesus, do not require Bernard of us.*

"Now I'm asking for a clear head, God, and for wisdom each step of the way. You're our only hope, of that I'm sure. Amen."

"Amen."

Jakob released one of her hands and placed his free hand on the side of her face. "I'm sorry for the things I said to you before I left. I'm sorry for the way I behaved. Forgive me?"

Nodding, she swallowed the lump in her throat.

"After we find Bernard, we'll talk more about it."

Again she nodded.

"Don't be afraid."

She shook her head. How could she be afraid after seeing this change in Jakob? Whatever had happened, she thought it a miracle. And if she could see one miracle, why not expect two?

"Now I—" He stopped as Lance rode into the yard.

Their friend looked at the two of them, standing in the rain. "I don't know why, but I had the strongest feelin' I needed to get over here."

"It's Bernard," Jakob said. "We can't find him. He's not in the house."

"What do you want from me?"

Jakob was silent for a moment, then said, "We'll hitch up the carriage for Karola so she can take the girls into town and get more help. It'll be dark all too soon, and this rain doesn't look like it's going to let up."

"*Nein!*"

Both men looked at her.

"Jakob, I must go with you. He is my son, too. I must look for him. I could not bear the waiting."

"All right, Karola." Jakob gave her a slight smile of encouragement before turning toward Lance. "You take the girls to the Mason place first. I know Geraldine will be glad to look out for them while Bradley rides into town to form a search party. Tell folks we'll get bells to ringing when he's found." He rubbed his chin. "When you're done at the Mason farm, Lance, you go check up the mountain. He might've headed for the cabin. Karola and I'll look for him to the west of here."

"Jakob," Karola said. "We must take dry blankets for when we find him."

"You're right. I'll get some extra slickers and wrap a couple of blankets in them. Lance can take one with him and we'll take the other."

Karola was about to turn toward the house when Jakob suddenly pulled her into his embrace. With his mouth near her ear, he said, "I love you, Karola."

"We will find him, Jakob. I know we will find him." She kissed his cheek. "I love you, too."

The darkness of night was fast approaching, made earlier than normal by the black clouds that wept upon the earth without ceasing. Jakob wouldn't have believed, when this day started, that he would be praying for it *not* to rain before the day ended. But that's exactly what he was praying as he and Karola continued their search.

"Bernard!"

"Bernard!"

Clad in rain slickers, they rode through fields on opposite sides of the road, each of them carrying a lantern.

"Bernard!"

"Bernard!"

God, he's so little. Keep him safe. Make him answer us if he's within hearing. Don't let him be too afraid of his own father to answer.

"Bernard!"

"Bernard!"

Show me where he is, Lord. I don't know how far he could've gotten by now. He could be anywhere. O Father, keep my son safe.

What if they were looking in the wrong place? What if Bernard had gone to the irrigation canal? What if he'd fallen in? He couldn't swim, and although the water wasn't running at full capacity, it was still too deep—and too swift—for a little boy to stand up in. What if—

"Bernard!" Karola called, her voice muffled by the rain.

Jakob glanced in her direction. He saw the glow of her lantern, bobbing in the darkness like a firefly on a summer's night.

A light in the darkness. Like Christ is a light unto my path.

He felt the encroaching fear retreat. "Bernard! We're here. Answer us, buddy."

As if finishing his thought, he heard Karola call, "Bernard, we love you. Bernard!"

Jakob felt the strongest urge to abandon the road and ride south. It seemed a thought without reason. There was nothing in that direction. No farmhouses. No shelter. No tree-lined creeks. Just barren, rolling, unplowed land. Surely, if Bernard was running away, he would follow the main road.

But the feeling wouldn't leave him. Well, he'd asked God to guide him, hadn't he? He heeded the impulse.

"Karola! This way." He waited until he saw her lantern coming toward him, then he turned south.

Jakob rode slowly, holding his lantern high, switching it from his right arm to left and back again. Twice more, he felt something—or Someone—sending them in a new direction, and both times he obeyed.

Jakob and Karola called Bernard's name over and over, and he prayed their voices wouldn't go hoarse before their son was found. His bones ached, and his skin was cold and damp. He knew Karola must feel the same. But they pressed on, because Bernard would be just as tired, cold, and damp as they were. And he would be frightened, too.

Karola's horse stumbled. She pitched forward, and the saddle pommel gouged her in the belly. She let out a tiny gasp of pain, nearly dropping her lantern as she tried to steady herself. It was almost more than she could do to maintain her grip on the lantern's handle.

"Karola?" Jakob's call came from off to her right. "You all right?"

"I am fine, Jakob, but I must dismount. Do not wait for me. I will find you."

Even as she spoke, she saw his light coming toward her. Shortly, he and his horse became a darker shadow against the black of night until at last she could see him in the glow of his own lantern.

Karola half slid, half dropped to the ground. Only her hold on the saddle kept her legs from buckling beneath her.

"I'm sorry," Jakob said as he drew to a halt nearby. "I should have had us rest."

"There is no time to rest." Despite herself, a sob escaped her throat. "Oh, Jakob. I should have known where he was. If I had been watching him—"

"Don't." He was beside her in an instant, taking her into his arms. "Don't blame yourself. You can't watch a child every moment of every hour. It isn't possible."

Karola pressed her face against the wet slicker that covered Jakob's chest. "Where is he? O God, where is he? How shall we find him? Help us. Please help us."

As Karola lifted her head to look into Jakob's face, the rain stopped. It was as if someone simply turned off a spigot. With the cessation of rain came silence—and the strength to go on. They had to keep searching. She was about to say so to Jakob when she heard something—a soft sound that didn't quite belong in the quiet of the night.

"What was that?" She turned her head, listening. "Did you hear it?"

"Yes." Jakob released her, then lifted his lantern high as he stepped away from her. "Bernard!"

Karola held her breath.

"Bernard!" Jakob called again.

And then came the sweetest sound Karola had ever heard. "Da?"

"It's us, buddy. Your ma and me. Talk to us. Can you see the lights? We've got lanterns. Can you see them?"

"No." The reply was more sob than word. "I . . . I fell in a . . . in a hole. I can't . . . I can't . . . see nothin'."

"We're coming, son. Don't be scared. We're real close now. Just keep talking."

Karola followed Jakob, although his longer strides were quickly outdistancing her. "Are you hurt, Bernard?"

"I–I'm cold, Mama."

Karola saw Jakob's lantern swing wildly, stop, and then drop right out of view. "Jakob!"

"I've got him, Karola. I've got him. He's all right. Thank God, he's all right."

It was three in the morning, and there they stood, the two of them, in Bernard's bedroom doorway, watching him sleep. The search parties had been notified; their friends and neighbors had returned to their own beds, happy that all had turned out well.

"He's something, isn't he?" Jakob stared, wondering, as he wrapped his arm around his wife's shoulders.

"*Ja.*"

"Imagine, thinking he could help me pay for a new barn."

It was a story the people in this valley would tell for years.

Do you remember, folks would say, *when Bernard Hirsch was five and he burned down the barn because he was playing with matches? Well, after his da got all upset and punished him, he heard his folks arguing about what it was going to cost to put up a new one. That was the year of the bad drought, remember? And every farmer hereabouts was afraid their crops were gonna fail.*

Bernard, he figured he'd better do something, being it was his fault about the barn and all, so he took his favorite toys, some wooden soldiers, and started off for town to sell them to his uncle Tulley. You see, Tulley Gaffney had once said to Bernard how great those toy soldiers were and would Bernard like to sell them to him. Tulley was joshing, of course, the way grown-ups sometimes do with kids. Those toys really weren't worth anything much. But Bernard didn't understand that, as young as he was.

So off he went to raise money for his father. And what should happen next? It started raining cats and dogs, like it hadn't rained most of the summer. Torrents of water. Bernard, he tried to head for cover under some trees. But then he saw what he thought was a wolf or a bear—who knows what it really was?—and he got scared and ran in the opposite direction. Straight away from the road, wouldn't you know. And then he fell into some old hole. Nobody knew who dug it or why it was there, but it was deep enough to trap the kid, especially with everything turning to mud from the downpour.

People say it was a miracle anybody found him before he plum died of exposure. Yep, sure enough. A miracle, pure and simple.

Yes, Jakob thought. A miracle, pure and simple.

He glanced toward Karola, standing within the circle of his arm. She continued to watch Bernard, her gaze tender and full of love.

Here was another miracle. God, in his mercy, had reached across an ocean to bring Karola—who had been promised to Jakob so long ago—back into his life, a life that had been lived without hope.

Later he would tell her all the Lord had revealed after stopping him on the way to town. He would share how he'd surrendered the last of himself to God, and then the Lord had filled him to the brim with hope.

He tightened his arm around her shoulders. She lifted her gaze to meet his, and he accepted the invitation in those beautiful eyes, leaning down to kiss her.

Yes, later they would have many things to tell one another. But for now, it was enough they were exactly where God wanted them to be.

Together—and trusting in him.

Chapter Thirty-Six

20 October 1908
Shadow Creek, Idaho

Dear Father and Mother,
   I find it hard to believe October is more than half gone.
I have neglected writing to you, and my only excuse is
how busy a place a farm is in autumn. I thought I had
grown accustomed to being a farmer's wife and to all the
work that goes with it, but I had not experienced threshing season before.
   The harvesting of the wheat is a community event. The
farmers move from one farm to another with their plow
horses and equipment, working from dawn unto dusk. The
air thrums with the low, rhythmic sounds of the engines,
the hiss of steam, the clanking of chains and wheels.
There is a beautiful sense of completion when one sees
the ripe wheat flowing out of the threshing machine.
   Not that I had many opportunities to stand and
watch. When the threshers are present, a farm wife does
little but cook and serve meals to hungry men. Hot cakes
and sausages, sandwiches, cookies and cakes, chops
and steaks, boiled potatoes and fried potatoes.

I had help from one unexpected source. Charlotte White came every day while the men were threshing our fields. I know she did it mostly so she could see Lance Bishop, but I appreciated it all the same. I must admit, I had a great deal of doubt about this young woman. I did not think her worthy of Lance's affections. But I believe God may be working a miracle in her young heart. There may even be hope that she will become a capable farmer's wife, given a little time and some instruction. After all, he was able to work the same miracle in me, so anything is possible.

Our new barn is up, and it is the pride and joy of the Hirsch family, from youngest to oldest. Lucky, our orphaned kitten, who is not so small as she once was, has decided it is a marvelous place to play, although she is unwilling to remain out there at night. She insists on sleeping on the foot of our bed. Jakob still protests that cats do not belong in the house, but I think he would miss her if she was not there. He tries to pretend he does not have a soft spot in his heart for Lucky. He does not fool me.

The nights have grown cold now. There is frost on the ground in the mornings. Jakob predicts we will see the first snow flurries before the month is out. With the harvest over, he is able to spend more time with me and the children. We all love that. I am especially blessed when he sits with me each evening to read God's Word aloud and to share those things God is teaching him. I am humbled as I watch my husband growing strong in his faith.

What a wondrous thing it is to know God loves us as he finds us, but that he is changing us, from glory to glory, to be more like his Son!

Father and Mother, I know there were times you despaired for me. But for some reason, despite all my faults, God chose to bless me with a husband I both love and respect and with three beautiful children whom I adore.

Now I must tell you something wonderful. God has granted me another blessing. In the spring, as the new seedlings burst from the tilled soil of our fields, there will be new life in the Hirsch home as well.

I was unsure how Jakob would take the news of another baby, knowing that it was in childbirth he lost Siobhan. But when I told him, he smiled and repeated something Laura Gaffney told me some time back, a verse of Scripture I did not expect Jakob to know. "As arrows are in the hand of a mighty man; so are children of the youth. Happy is the man that hath his quiver full of them."

I believe Jakob will have a new daughter, and when she is born, we will name her Hope.

> *With all my love,*
> *Karola*

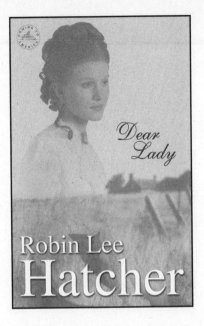

Book One of the Coming to America Series!

Dear Lady

Robin Lee Hatcher

Lady Elizabeth Wellington travels from England to Montana to take a job as a rural schoolteacher, fleeing an engagement to a brutal man—and finds herself falling in love with a rancher who doesn't seem to be able to escape the memory of his first wife.

In the big-sky country of Montana, the past doesn't always stay buried. Circumstances have a way of forcing secrets into the open, sometimes bringing hearts together in unlikely ways, and sometimes tearing them apart.

Softcover: 0-310-23083-7

Pick up a copy at your favorite bookstore!

ZONDERVAN™

GRAND RAPIDS, MICHIGAN 49530 USA

WWW.ZONDERVAN.COM

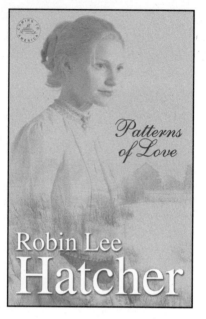

Book Two of the Coming to America Series!

Patterns of Love

Robin Lee Hatcher

Inga Linberg fully expects to spend her life assisting her minister father in his pastoral duties and creating her uniquely beautiful story quilts. Inga has a good heart and is a hard worker, and she is happy to volunteer to help when a beleaguered dairy farmer, Dirk Bridger, enters her life. Dirk is a man whose dreams and faith have dried up. Dirk proposes marriage. But this, he carefully explains, is merely a marriage of convenience. Can Inga accept this kind of arrangement with a man she loves? And if so, how will she be able to live with him without being able to express that love?

Softcover: 0-310-23105-1

Pick up a copy at your favorite bookstore!

GRAND RAPIDS, MICHIGAN 49530 USA

WWW.ZONDERVAN.COM

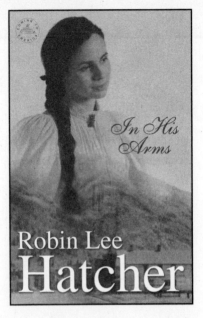

Book Three of the Coming to America Series!

In His Arms

Robin Lee Hatcher

Mary Malone comes to America to join the father of the child she's carrying. Instead she has to flee New York when she thinks she has killed a man. So she escapes to Idaho where men go to find their fortunes and lose their pasts in the silver mines. But as Mary Malone discovers, sometimes the past is not so easily shaken. It will take a good man's strong, persistent love to penetrate the young immigrant's defenses and disarm the secret that makes a hostage of her heart. Mary eventually finds love, family, and faith.

Softcover: 0-310-23120-5

Pick up a copy at your favorite bookstore!

GRAND RAPIDS, MICHIGAN 49530 USA

WWW.ZONDERVAN.COM

We want to hear from you. Please send your comments about this book to us in care of zreview@zondervan.com. Thank you.

ZONDERVAN™

GRAND RAPIDS, MICHIGAN 49530 USA

WWW.ZONDERVAN.COM